No Way to Say Goodbye

No Way to Say Goodbye

Ted Darling Crime Series

'heart-wrenching, compelling crime drama'

L M Krier

LIVRES
LEMAS

Published by LIVRES LEMAS
www.teddarlingcrimeseries.uk

Cover photo
Neil Smith

Contents

Author's Note

Thank you for reading the Ted Darling Crime Series. The books are set in Stockport, and Greater Manchester in general, and the characters use local dialect and sayings.

Seemingly incorrect grammar within quotes reflects common speech patterns. For example, 'I'll do it if I get chance', without an article, or determiner, is common parlance, as is 'should of' instead of 'should have'.

Ted and Trev also have an in joke between them - 'billirant' - which is a deliberate 'typo'.

If you have any queries about words or phrases used, do please feel free to get in touch, using the contact details in the book. I always try to reply promptly to any emails or Facebook messages.

Thank you.

L M Krier

To Bren

*Thank you for your kind help
and valued friendship*

Chapter One

'Yes, sitting on the same bench, under the same tree, and as usual, Evie's out like a light. You could set your clocks by us.'

The young woman was talking on a mobile phone, held in one hand and pressed to her ear. Her other hand was on the handle of a large pram. An old-fashioned style, known as a landau, long out of trend because of its size and bulk. Far too big to slot into the back of the average modern car.

The pram's brakes were firmly engaged, even though the path on which it rested was as flat as a bowling green, but the hand holding it was gently bouncing it on the suspension. The slight rocking movement was clearly doing its job. There was not a sound from the sleeping baby inside the pram.

'I shouldn't grumble because she is such a good baby, but she's a right little grizzle if I try to put her down in the afternoon in the house. She really loves this big old pram, though. I thought my mam was kidding when she dug it out of her shed. It was hers, then mine, and it works wonders with Evie, like it did for both of us. And as soon as we get here and she can see her favourite tree, she's fine. She seems to love trees and I don't even know what type it is. I'm going to have to learn.'

11

Her friend at the other end of the phone laughed at that.

'You getting into nature and stuff? I'd pay to see that! I bet you were thinking more about taking her shopping for shoes and fashions. Are you sure they didn't give you someone else's baby at the hospital by mistake?'

'I did wonder! But I really shouldn't complain. There's a woman who always comes here around this time every day. She's expecting and she's huge. She's got a little lad already, a toddler. Around two. And he's a complete monster. I think there might be something up with him. I feel so sorry for her. He screams and shouts, spits, throws things, bites her if she tries to calm him down. Makes me realise just how lucky I am with Evie, even if she does grow up to be a hippy tree-hugger or something.'

She turned her head to smile at the baby sleeping soundly in her big pram, the fingers of one tiny hand opening and closing occasionally as she lay there.

The woman looked back along the path as she heard a voice calling, 'Finley? Fin, darling? Don't run so far ahead, there's a good boy, mummy can't keep up with you. Fin, be careful, you're going to fall.'

'She's coming now,' the first woman said into her phone. 'The little devil-child is already running off ahead and she can barely waddle these days, poor love.'

Then she shot to her feet as the small, curly-haired boy, legs going like pistons, far too fast for him to keep his balance, lost his footing and fell smack on his face on the hard ground, as his mother struggled to go to him.

Evie's mother was already rushing forward, instinct drawing her to help a small child in pain, pulled by the banshee wails he was now emitting at the full power of his lungs. His own mother reached him first and pulled him gently into her arms, one hand instinctively reaching for the ever-present wipes to deal with the blood coming from his nose and mouth from the impact.

Evie's mother hesitated, calling out, 'Is he all right? Do you need a hand? How bad is it? Shall I call an ambulance?'

Finley's wails were so loud his mother was having difficulty making herself heard over them.

'Thank you, no, not that serious, I don't think. I'll manage. Thanks ever so much for caring.'

Evie's mother gave her a friendly wave, then turned back to walk the few steps to the pram. Her mobile phone in one hand was still connected to her friend so both she and Finley's mother heard her piercing screams as she looked into the landau and saw it empty.

Her baby was gone.

* * *

Detective Chief Inspector Ted Darling was driving back from yet another meeting for senior ranks at the headquarters building in Central Park. Or rather, he was sitting, trying to curb his mounting impatience, in a long tail-back of traffic, with no immediately visible explanation.

His mobile phone rang, and the display showed him it was his colleague and friend, Inspector Kevin Turner, from Uniform, calling him. Ted picked up the call, grateful for any diversion from sitting singing along to Kenny Rogers to while away the time until he could get moving again.

'Ted, it's Kev,' Inspector Turner began, in case Ted hadn't been in a position to see the caller details on his screen. 'Are you still in your meeting, or can you talk?'

'Stuck in stationary traffic on the motorway on my way

back. Do you know the cause?'

'Oh, you'll be there for the duration, unless you can find a way round. A lorry's crashed and jack-knifed across most of the width so everything's on stop. You might just get down the hard shoulder on blues. It's right by a slip road, luckily, so the emergency vehicles have got straight to it that way.'

'Casualties?'

'Driver in the car behind is trapped and badly injured but no reported fatalities. Yet. There are reports of fuel spillage, so an increased fire risk, but it's under control for now.

'I was calling to keep you in the loop on an incident here just now. Looks like a child snatch. Uniform are attending, Mike's sending Maurice and Jezza from your team in case it is that. Can't get much more serious than that sort of a crime. Oh, and the dog section are on their way as soon as they can, as there's no sign of the baby anywhere. And it is a baby, just three months old, so we're not talking a toddler who could have scampered off by themselves. Mother is beyond distraught, as you can imagine. Of course, the press are all over it already, as luck would have it, so perhaps it needs the presence of a senior officer, d'you think? If you're stuck, I could call Jo?'

'If I can get off the motorway, I'll go myself. I'll keep you posted, and in the meantime, can you let Roads know it's me trying to get down the hard shoulder with the blues on, not some joker trying it on. I know Maurice and Jezza will be on top of it but you're right. If the press see a senior rank on the ground right from the start, that can only help our image.'

Ted put the blue lights on and edged cautiously onto the hard shoulder, hoping no impatient members of the public had had the same idea and blocked that, too. Kev was right. The apparent snatching of a small baby was potentially one for his Serious Crime team, however it panned out.

From experience, Ted knew that there had been cases of a tragic accident or a cot death where a mother, consumed by feelings of guilt and grief, had hidden the body and staged a disappearance. Whichever way the one on their patch developed, it was always likely to be a disturbing case.

He was pleased to hear that his sergeant, DS Mike Hallam, was sending DCs Maurice Brown and Jezza Vine to the scene. Maurice was the team's Daddy Hen. There was no one kinder nor more compassionate when dealing with a grief-stricken mother, whatever the circumstances might turn out to be. And despite her own protestations to the contrary, Jezza, legal guardian to her challenging younger brother, Tommy, could empathise with the distress of others in a way not suggested by her hard exterior shell.

There was already more traffic near the park than would be normal at that time of day. Word had clearly spread fast on the grapevine, only to be expected if the press were already onto a potentially big story. A section of the park had been cordoned off to preserve, as far as possible, all traces of whatever had happened there.

Ted signed himself in with the young uniformed constable controlling access, then followed her directions to where the centre of the action was.

As many officers as could be spared were already working methodically over the ground, fanning out from where Ted could see a large pram, standing forlornly next to a park bench. An old-fashioned pram. Ted half smiled to himself, knowing that his mother kept a treasured photo of him as a small child, sitting in one similar, on her living room wall.

He quickly spotted the woman who was clearly the mother of the missing child. She was striding up and down in apparent anguish, flanked on either side by Maurice and Jezza, both clearly trying to persuade her to sit down with them. They would be aware of how much her understandable pacing could potentially make the work of detection dogs more difficult when they arrived. There was no sign of any yet and Ted was hoping that every available canine nose wasn't already tied up on cases equally as urgent elsewhere.

Ted was pleased Maurice was remembering his training and not putting his arms round the woman. He was always so anxious to help and comfort anyone, he could sometimes forget his boundaries.

Ted was just about to go and make his presence known when he was accosted by the local reporter, Penny Hunter. Timid as a mouse but with the tenacity of a Jack Russell terrier, she often got the scoops the more hard-bitten newshounds missed because she was less threatening in her approach. Sometimes people spoke to her because they clearly felt sorry for her. She addressed him in her usual hesitant fashion.

'Erm, hello, chief inspector,' she began, before drying up again.

Ted always suspected this was nothing but a clever ploy on her part. It put the person she was addressing into the position of feeling obliged to respond, if only for the sake of good manners.

'Hello, Penny, and before you ask me, I'm sorry, I know as much as you do for now so I'm not taking any questions, nor making any official statements yet. But I hope you know me well enough by now to believe me when I say that as

NO WAY TO SAY GOODBYE

soon as I have anything useful I can tell you, I will brief you, in person. For now, though, you'll have to excuse me, please.'

There was no mistaking the look of relief on Jezza's face when she saw him approaching. He could imagine the difficulties she and Maurice had been having in getting the mother to sit down and let the police get on with their jobs. That's what needed to happen. Her aimless pacing was helping no one.

'Boss, this is Carrie Fisher, Evie's mum. Carrie, this is Detective Chief Inspector Darling. Head of Serious Crime.'

The woman stopped moving to and fro and turned to look at him. Her expression was somewhere between hope and horror.

'Serious Crime? So that means you believe me? You think someone took Evie? Not just that I've done something stupid and left her somewhere? But if you're Serious Crime, that must mean you think something terrible has happened. You think someone's killed her? You think my baby is dead?'

She reached out to grab his arm, fingers clutching with surprising strength, biting into the flesh of his forearm. Her face crumpled as the tears started to fall.

As gently as he could, Ted put out a hand to extricate himself from her grip. Always softly-spoken, he made more of an effort than usual to keep his voice calm, quiet, and as reassuring as he could.

'Ms Fisher, we are here to do everything we possibly can to find out what has happened to Evie. Everything. For now, the most useful thing you can do to help us is to sit down over there with my officers and tell them absolutely everything you can. Any detail, no matter how trivial it might seem.

'We have trained dogs on their way to help with the search but, of course, the more people walking about where they need to work, the more difficult their task will be.'

Her hand flew up to her face at his words and she looked anguished. Somehow the arrival of a senior officer had got through to her about the potential seriousness of the situation and how she really wasn't helping.

'I'm so sorry. How stupid. I'm just so scared. Please get Evie back for me, inspector. Please.'

Now the situation was a bit more manageable, Ted could deploy his officers to make best use of resources.

'It's fine, Ms Fisher, perfectly understandable. Look, why don't you go back and sit on the bench with DC Brown and talk to him. Tell him anything you can think of. Let the rest of the officers get on with searching.'

As the woman went off with Maurice, Ted turned to Jezza.

'The woman over there with the toddler. Is she a material witness or just a gawker?'

'That's Denise Doyle, with her little boy, Finley. Fin is, in part, why Carrie had her eyes off the pram at the moment Evie disappeared. Fin was acting up, running away from his mother, and fell on his face. Carrie jumped up to make sure he was all right. Even took a few steps towards him, away from the pram. As soon as she saw his mother was looking after him and didn't need her help, she went back to the pram and that's when she found that Evie had gone.'

'A genuine distraction, do you think? Or a staged incident to make sure the mother's back was turned to give someone the chance to snatch the baby?'

'Boss, you know my kid brother Tommy is on the

spectrum, don't you? It's possible that Fin is just an odious little brat, but I'd bet on him being similar to Tom. Apart from anything, he's given his face a nasty bash when he fell, although he seems to have forgotten about that. He's too busy looking at all the police officers now, which is another possible indicator. So yes, I'd say very definitely a genuine distraction.'

Ted was now looking towards where the mother was sitting on the bench next to Maurice, the empty pram a stark reminder of why they were all there. There were shrubs and bushes growing in a clump quite close to the seat.

'So we're left with the strong possibility that someone was quite close by, hoping for such an incident to occur to give them the time to do what they'd come for. And that would suggest some degree of pre-planning, at least. Someone watching and waiting.'

Chapter Two

Ted's next move was to go with Jezza to talk in person to Denise Doyle, the mother of the toddler, who was now sitting on a nearby bench, trying to keep the little boy's interest. All he clearly wanted to do was to run over to see what the police were up to.

Ted had his warrant card in his hand to show to the witness as he introduced himself. The little boy immediately started bouncing up and down on the bench, clawing the air with his hands, reaching towards it, repeating a mantra without intonation.

'Me see, me see, me see.'

Ted crouched down and held up his ID so the boy could see, but not reach it.

'This is to show your mother that I'm Detective Chief Inspector Ted Darling,' he explained.

Finley gave a cackle of evident delight, slapping his small palms against his own chest as he chortled, 'Fin Darling, Fin Darling, Fin Darling.'

Jezza was reading the scene correctly, knowing how difficult things could be with her brother. Tommy was now a lot older than Finley was. But she remembered all too well how stressful it could sometimes be to have a conversation in front of him when he was much smaller and struggling to learn the social niceties.

She got her own card out, held it out of his reach then put

out a hand to Finley.

'Do you want to see my card, Finley? Shall we move over here a bit then you can do that while your mummy speaks to the detective?'

Without so much as a glance towards his mother, the toddler went with Jezza. His mother watched in surprise at how at ease her son immediately seemed to be in her presence.

'That's incredible! Fin can be difficult with strangers. Does the officer have children of her own?'

Ted wouldn't normally talk about his officers' private lives but he knew Jezza wouldn't mind in this instance, if it helped to reassure an anxious witness.

'She's used to small boys. She has a younger brother who lives with her.

'Now, about the disappearance of Ms Fisher's baby. Is there anything at all you can tell us? Did you see anyone in the area at the time?'

She shook her head, looking stricken.

'I really wish there was something I could do or say to help. I feel partly to blame, because if Carrie hadn't been looking to see if Fin was all right, it might not have happened. It was all so quick. She only had her eyes off the pram for a few moments, and I was looking at Fin so I didn't see anything, or anybody.'

'Please don't blame yourself. You had your own child to deal with, and I'm sure Ms Fisher understands that. Even if you saw nothing today, you might perhaps have seen something of some relevance previously, perhaps without actually registering it. Can you start by telling me how often you meet Ms Fisher and her baby in the park?'

'Oh, almost every day, barring really bad weather. And

always at the same time. Fin's too young to tell the time, of course, but his internal clock is incredible. He likes a very set routine. And Carrie is always here at this sort of time as it's when Evie has her nap, so we meet a lot.'

'So you've seen baby Evie a few times?'

'Oh yes, she's absolutely gorgeous! Such a pretty baby.'

She put a hand over her own bulge as she said, 'I'll feel really lucky if this little one is as stunning, although she's bound to be, to me. And I already know I'm having a girl this time. I wanted to wait and see with Finley'

'And did you see Evie today?'

Ted asked it in as casual a tone as he could, but the woman still frowned at his question.

'Today? Well, no. I was distracted by Fin falling over and hurting himself. We both were. Carrie too. Are you thinking perhaps the baby was never in the pram today? That something happened earlier on, perhaps somewhere else?'

Ted gave her his most disarming smile as he said, 'Just routine questions. I'm simply trying to establish all the facts to give us the best possible chance of finding Evie.'

Both of them could hear now that the novelty of having Jezza's undivided attention was starting to wear thin with Finley and he was getting noisy and fractious once more. Denise Doyle looked in his direction, then back at Ted.

'Look, I'm sorry I can't be of any more help today, but I really do need to think about getting Fin back home soon. The wounds on his face need properly seeing to, for one thing, and he'll be wanting something to eat before much longer. He can get very vocal when he wants something and doesn't get it quickly enough.'

'Just one more quick question, please, and then of course you can take him home, if we have your contact details. Can you think of anyone else you see regularly when you're here with Carrie Fisher? Someone else you often see round about the same time?'

'There's an older couple we sometimes see, with a dog that looks much too big for them to manage. What do you call them, those big hound things? You know, like Scooby-Doo.'

Ted didn't know. He wasn't into dogs or cartoons, although he vaguely knew that Scooby-Doo was a dog in a cartoon, and a very big one. He hazarded a guess.

'A Great Dane, is it?'

She beamed at him, clearly relieved to have been able to add something which might be of some use, finally.

'Yes! That's it. A Great Dane. That should make them easy to find, hopefully, shouldn't it, because you don't see them very often. Especially not with older people like that.'

She frowned again, looking round.

'Speaking of them, they would normally be here by now. I hope nothing's happened to them.'

Ted was quick to reassure her.

'I imagine the officers will have closed all entry to the park by now, so they can carry out a thorough search without interruption or hindrance. Can you give me any further details about the couple with the large dog? Do you know their names, for instance?'

'Oh no, nothing like that. We just nod and say hello. I know the dog is called Sidney, though, I've heard them calling it that. It seems quite gentle, although it can be a bit slobbery. Even Finley doesn't start screaming at the sight of it, which he can do sometimes with dogs.

'I don't really know any other details about the couple, though. They're both really old. Seventy, at least. And they both look quite small and frail, but that might just be because the dog is so big, of course. I don't know where they live or anything like that. But they always come from that direction.'

She pointed back the way she had come from earlier, where the path started to climb slightly. The slope had exacerbated her son's fall as his increasing speed had been too much for his legs to cope with.

Ted was reaching for one of his cards as Jezza headed back in his direction, Finley marching determinedly in front of her. He handed the card to the boy's mother, saying, 'If you think of any other details, anything at all, please don't hesitate to get in touch. Thank you for your time.'

'I'd forgotten what Tommy could be like at that age,' Jezza told him as they walked down towards where Maurice was sitting with Carrie Fisher. Ted noticed he was now holding one of her hands in both of his but he wasn't about to pull him up for inappropriate behaviour for that small gesture of kindness and compassion. The missing baby's mother looked as if she needed all the comfort and support she could get right now.

She looked up hopefully at the sight of them returning, as if they would somehow have discovered a way to end her torment. Ted wished he did have something positive to tell her.

'Why has no one seen her?' Her first question showed the anguish she was going through. 'She needs feeding and changing by now. She'll be hungry. Frightened, too. Where is she? A little baby can't just disappear like that in broad daylight.'

Ted was saved from having to mumble platitudes, the only thing he could currently do for her, by his mobile phone ringing. He excused himself and moved a short distance away to take the call. The screen showed him it was Detective Superintendent Sammy Sampson, one of his two senior officers at Stockport. He'd been half expecting the call since he'd heard of the incident and had a pretty good idea of what it would be about.

'Any news, Ted? Tell me there is and that it's good.'

'I wish I could,' Ted told her candidly. 'Nothing at all so far. It's looking more and more likely that someone simply snatched the baby from her pram and went off with her. We're waiting on a dog and handler to see if we can get any indication at all of which direction they could have gone in, at least.'

Ted was looking towards one of the entrance gates as he was speaking so was able to add at that point, 'And it looks like the dog has just arrived, so I should have more to report a bit later, with any luck.'

'You won't,' she told him firmly. 'Not personally. I'm sending Mike Hallam out to take over from you as senior officer on the ground. The team back here are perfectly capable of wrapping up the current case. You have two DSs, after all and DS O'Connell seems well up to the task of holding the fort.

'I need you back here, and sharpish, for a press conference, late afternoon, just in time for the early evening news. Assuming the little one hasn't turned up by then, which we all hope will be the outcome. If not, you need to come and get briefed on how to handle what we tell the press and public at this stage, what to say and what not to say. It's good that you showed your face at the scene, but now you need to get back here to reassure the public we know what we're doing.'

It wasn't quite a rebuke, more of a tug on the lead, which Ted acknowledged with a curt, 'Ma'am'. Something he hardly ever said to Sammy. But he then followed it up with, 'I'd like to stay a bit longer, at least, to see if the dog gives us any indication at all. If the baby's been abducted on foot, that's one thing. It's bad, but at least it could indicate she's not far away and might well be safe.

'If the abductor had an accomplice who's whisked them both away in a vehicle, then that potentially puts a far more serious slant on the whole thing. That would suggest some degree of pre-planning. Possibly professionals at work, rather than a random snatcher.'

'That's an update you could easily get by phone. But I'll give you half an hour. No longer. Then hand over to Mike Hallam and get back here for the briefing.'

Ted was trusting his experience and his hunch as to which direction the kidnapper had probably struck from. If he'd got it wrong, he'd potentially allowed the contamination of a crime scene beyond the skills of the best nose in the dog section.

Even though the baby's mother had her back turned and was even moving away from the pram at the likely moment of an abduction, Ted couldn't believe anyone would have walked boldly up the path to snatch the baby. If he was right, that meant that any traces of whoever it was would be found to the side, where the bushes were, or to the end of the pram opposite the handle. The mother had told them she'd run down the path to look for her child, but there was a good chance nobody had been in and around the nearby bushes, other than the abductor.

The dog handler had stopped a good distance back from where the crime scene tapes were in place. He'd clearly been told who to look out for as SIO and to await further instructions from them. His dog was a German Shepherd, already looking round in eager anticipation of what, for it, was another fun game, but could yet turn out to be a lifesaver.

Ted nodded to the officer and indicated where he'd like them to meet up for a briefing. As ever, he was wary of the big dog, despite knowing full well it would be trained not to react to anyone, not even a DCI eyeing it more than a little suspiciously.

The dog handler listened to what Ted had to say, then nodded.

'That all sounds logical, sir. And I hope your child snatcher didn't walk up a tarmac path where lots of other people have been walking. That would be a worst-case scenario for us. But we'll see what we can do for you. Max is good at his job. It wouldn't be the first time he's been successful, if we can find this baby for you.'

'I need to get back to the nick at Stockport for a press conference in half an hour, so if you have anything at all for me before then, can you call me direct, please.'

The officer's eyebrows went right up as he took the card Ted was holding out to him while stretching his arm right out so he didn't have to get nearer to the big dog.

'Well, Max is good, sir, one of the best. But I think that's optimistic, at best,' he started to say then, seeing the look on the SIO's face, he went on hurriedly, 'but we'll make a start straight away and I'll let you know the minute we find anything of any potential use.'

While he waited, Ted again went over to where Maurice was sitting with Carrie Fisher, now joined by Jezza.

'Is there somebody we should call to come and be with

you, Ms Fisher?' he asked her. He was sure Maurice or Jezza would already have asked, but he wanted to cover all bases.

'I just want my baby back,' she told him, lifting her face to look at him.

He could see straight away that she was already starting to lose her optimism. He couldn't begin to imagine her feelings, but he didn't want to say the wrong thing and give her false hopes.

Maurice spoke for her, standing up to move closer to the boss, speaking quietly.

'Carrie's husband is abroad. He's a long-distance lorry driver. She doesn't want to try contacting him until there's some news. It will be hard for him to get back, especially fast, so we're hanging fire on that just for now. Last thing she needs now is for him to have a road accident driving like a mad thing trying to get back quickly.'

Ted found himself pacing up and down, constantly checking the time on his mobile phone. With a three-line whip summons from Sammy, he couldn't take the risk of being later than ordered in arriving back at the nick for the press conference.

He was starting back towards the gate when he saw the handler and dog coming towards him from the direction of the road. He was trying to read the man's body language, looking out for something, anything, to give them a glimmer of hope.

When they drew level, all his hopes were dashed as the dog handler told him, 'Sorry, sir. Max tracked right to the kerbside outside the gate but no further at all in either direction. The most logical explanation for him behaving the way he did is that the person he was tracking was picked up there by a vehicle and driven away.

'We'll try in different directions, but that was definitely a fresh trail he was following. I really wish I had something more positive to report, but I don't think any dog can get you any further on this one, if that's the case.'

Chapter Three

In the car driving back to the nick, Ted thought he'd better phone Trev to warn him that he was likely to be late home, with the case looking more serious by the minute.

'Hey, you,' Trev greeted him when he answered the call.

'I was just phoning to say I'm going to be late home tonight, almost certainly very late. We've just this minute got a big case on. I've got to do a press conference later, for one thing.'

There was a pause then Trev said, 'Ted, you've forgotten, haven't you? And I only told you last night.'

Ted wasn't going to risk asking 'Forgotten what?', so was desperately trying to recall whatever it was Trev had mentioned to him.

'I'm going to be charitable and assume the latest case is a tough one that's made you forget,' Trev went on. 'Because you do usually remember things. I'm going to be late too. I told you I've been thinking of going back to doing some more formal English teaching again. Classroom stuff, back in the old venue. I'm hoping that kidnapping is like lightning and never strikes twice in the same place. Although that isn't even true, of course.'

Trev had previously been snatched from outside the centre where he'd been teaching English as a Foreign Language. The intention had been to intimidate Ted into not giving a vital witness testimony in a murder trial. Trev had managed to escape so Ted had never had to answer his question of whether or not he would have risked his partner's life by testifying.

'This is a kidnapping,' Ted told him. 'Don't say anything until after the press conference, please, but a little baby of three months has been snatched from a pram in a park. A dog was deployed but tracked to roadside and lost the trace. The handler reckons the kidnapper was driven away with the baby. So at the moment, it's not looking good.'

'Oh, Ted, that's awful! The poor parents, they must be frantic. In those circumstances, I'll forgive the lapse of memory. I'll see you later, and hope for a miracle with the case.'

Ted would have preferred a quick catch-up with those of his team working in the main office before going to find Sammy Sampson, but he didn't risk it. She'd sounded unusually tetchy on the phone so was probably under pressure from higher up the chain of command to wind this one up as fast as possible. It was likely to make the national headlines, as well as local, something as unusual and audacious as a baby snatch in a park in broad daylight.

He found her in the company of his other immediate boss, Superintendent Debra Caldwell. Both were mothers. Sammy had a small grandchild. Both turned hopeful eyes towards him as soon as he entered the office, after a brief courtesy knock.

'Any news, Ted?' Sammy asked him.

He shook his head then sat down as she indicated.

'Nothing concrete. The only positive thing I can think of to say is that we've not found a body. At least not yet. But the dog indicated that whoever took the baby might have been picked up at the gates by someone in a car, so we've more or less come up against a brick wall for now.

'I've arranged as many available officers as possible to go door-to-door round the area, looking for witnesses. We're calling up all available CCTV anywhere near to go through, but other than that, nothing.'

'I can't begin to imagine how the mother feels,' Debra Caldwell put in. 'Does she have someone with her?'

'Her husband's away and she has no family of her own. Jezza's arranged a Family Liaison Officer for her, but at the moment, they can't get her to agree to leave the park, which is understandable.'

'I can certainly relate to that,' Sammy told him. 'And to cover all bases, you are arranging a search of the house, aren't you? In case the little one was never at the park today.'

'I spoke to Mike Hallam on the phone as I was driving back. He's arranging for that to be done. He'll probably get an idea of whether or not the mother is somehow involved by how she responds to a request to hand the keys over for a house search.'

'I know we work with facts, but what's your feeling, Ted?' Sammy pursued. 'Is this genuine?'

'Unless she's a BAFTA winning actor then yes, I would say definitely genuine. From talking to the dog handler before I left, I don't see how she could have staged the convenient fresh trail that ended at the kerbside, for one thing. Unless she had accomplices, but to what end? It's unlikely to be about a ransom, from the information to date. They don't appear to have a huge amount of money, although the address suggests they live comfortably.'

'Right, well, let's hope we get a breakthrough before the press descend, but in case we don't, we now need to go over how the conference is going to pan out. You'll clearly need to lead, Ted, as SIO, but Debs should be there in full uniform so we're presenting a united front and the press can see a bit of impressive hardware on the epaulettes. That always goes down well.

'We need to keep the park shut down tight for now, just in case there's a body to be found and the trail was simply someone making off. We don't want that appearing in the press or even on social media if we can avoid it. Especially with the mother there, and I understand why she won't leave until she knows something, one way or another.

'Right, here's the official spiel, then we need to anticipate lines of questioning and how best to respond to them.'

* * *

Ted was never comfortable in front of the press and media. Especially when he had nothing of any use to say to them. All he could do was to read the prepared statement then field questions as best he could. The bottom line, though, was that they were no further forward than they had been when they'd first received the call that baby Evie had disappeared.

Officers from Uniform had been round to check the house, having asked for and been given the keys by Carrie Fisher. Her willingness to cooperate was a good indicator that she knew of nothing incriminating they were likely to find there, which was the case. No signs of anything out of the ordinary. A neat and tidy home, with everything necessary put ready in anticipation of returning with a small baby who would be ready for feeding and changing.

As soon as he could decently get away, Ted sprinted up the stairs for a catch-up with his team once most of them were back in. DS Mike Hallam would stay on to oversee operations in the park until they were suspended for whatever reason, but he'd sent Jezza and Maurice back as they both looked wrung out.

They reported that Carrie Fisher was still refusing to budge. Uniform had brought back warmer clothes for her from the house as she looked perished. From anguish as much as from the warmth of the day diminishing. Someone had also brought her a takeaway hot drink.

'Has anyone yet checked that the husband is in fact out of the country?' Ted began by asking. 'This is not some custody dispute between the parents, is it? We need to eliminate all possibilities, of course.'

'Nothing to indicate that, boss,' Jezza replied. 'It's certainly not crossed Carrie's mind, I would say. The only reason she didn't want her husband to be informed was she seemed genuinely worried he'd drive like a lunatic trying to get back quickly. We have his work contact details and I did phone earlier to check, without wanting to give too much away. They confirmed he does work for them and said he's currently halfway across Poland on a delivery then a pick-up. So that's a pretty sound alibi and hard to see how it could be contrived.'

'Uniform also reported the house was a real haven of domestic bliss. I know you can never tell, but all the signs are of a happy and loving couple enjoying their first baby. Lots of photos everywhere of them together with little Evie. And no signs they have the sort of money which might warrant an extortion attempt.'

'Similar cases anywhere?' Ted asked. 'How common is the kidnap of a child of this age?'

'I'm on that, sir,' DC Steve Ellis told him. 'More common than I would have thought, certainly, and some of it is organised crime. There are traffickers who snatch to order. Some of the stuff I've been reading is very dark. And there's also a trade in babies to send abroad for adoption where there's a shortage of the kind of baby that's snapped up by childless couples and not always readily available. So largely based on looks and ethnicity.

'Pretty widespread countrywide, less common in rural areas. I suppose possibly people watch out for one another more there, so tend to notice things, perhaps. There's been a few in the bigger cities. London, of course, with two there. Nothing similar round here so far.'

'Right. Can you liaise with any forces who have had something similar and get files for us so we can see if there's any pattern. All of this is, of course, in case of a worst possible outcome with no sign anywhere of Evie.'

Jezza was frowning to herself. She waited for Ted to finish speaking then said, 'Boss, why didn't the dog bark?'

It was Ted's turn to look confused as he asked, 'What dog?'

'It's a metaphor that occurred to me. The "fact absent from record" theory. From a Sherlock Holmes, I think. A dog, on guard, which didn't bark at a murderer when it should have done. It wasn't noted at the time as it was considered insignificant, but it was a material clue. The dog didn't bark because it turned out the killer was known to it.'

'So you think Evie was snatched by someone known to her? Would that work, with a baby as young as that? I confess to knowing very little about babies.'

'Do we know for certain the baby didn't cry? Perhaps it did but couldn't be heard above other sounds,' DC Gina Shaw asked. 'Though surely the mother would be finely tuned to her baby making any noise and would have immediately turned back to her if she did, even if she was moving away?'

'We know that the toddler, Finley, was screaming his head off at this point and both Maurice and I can confirm that that little boy has quite considerable lung power,' Jezza told her.

All the parents on the team were showing disagreement at this point.

'Parents would hear their own child, for sure. And it's not just mothers who can hear their own children in distress above most other noise,' Maurice told her. 'I'll often hear the twins at the same time as Megan does, sometimes even a bit before if she's tired out. Even when we have the telly on, for instance.'

'And when Daisy was very small, if anyone, even me or the wife, went to pick her up while she was asleep, she'd start to grizzle,' DC Virgil Tibbs put in.

'We still don't know for sure if the baby was in that pram, let's not forget,' Ted told them.

'We need to check the mother's mobile, boss,' Jezza responded quickly. 'With a father working away from home, there's a good chance the mother will be sending him frequent photos of her. And "happy sleeping baby under the trees in the park" would be a nice snap to send, and would hopefully be datestamped.'

'Another thing about dogs, boss,' Rob O'Connell put in. 'If the baby wasn't in the pram in the park, then who was the dog tracking from there back to the roadside, on what the handler told you was a very fresh trail?'

Mike Hallam came in to join them at that point, looking weary and dispirited.

'Nothing new to report. We finally convinced Carrie to

go back to her home with the liaison officer, who found one of Carrie's friends from her mobile, and she's also gone round to be with her. Uniform are going to keep on searching until the daylight goes, possibly even after that if they can rig up enough lighting. The dog and handler made a few more passes but found nothing. The dog just kept indicating back to the road, and the handler says it's an experienced and reliable dog, not likely to make such a big mistake, if it is wrong.

'There was no sight or sound of a baby anywhere, and the poor little one would surely be crying by now, so it's not looking very hopeful. Either she's long gone from the park, with whoever took her, or …'

He let his voice trail off, not wanting to be the one to pronounce what everyone was thinking by now. If little Evie was somewhere in the park and making no sound, it was a worrying sign.

'Right, we need a rota to answer the phones, through the night, if necessary,' Ted told them. 'We're bound to get calls following the press conference going out. Mike, can you sort that, please. Everyone needs the time for a proper break, and from the look of you, Maurice, you need to go and get your head down as soon as you can.

'Put me down for an early shift, Mike. I'll come in whenever and work on through. But call me at the first sign of anything, at any time.'

He'd at least have a bit of time with Trev and would make a point of asking him about his English teaching plans, to make up in some small measure for having forgotten all about them earlier on.

* * *

'What are we doing about food? Shall I order something in?' Ted asked his partner when he got home and had greeted all the cats.

'Ted, you really are losing the plot at the moment. I told you I'd leave something plated up in the fridge for both of us, so you could eat when you were ready and I could have mine when I got back. As it happens, my meeting was shorter than I thought. They practically bit my hand off when I said I wanted to start teaching again, so that's all settled, as long as you're sure you don't mind?'

Trev had his head in the fridge for part of the conversation, bringing out the meals he'd mentioned. Ted was concerned that he really had forgotten most of what Trev had clearly told him. He hoped it was just the latest case taking mental priority and he wasn't coming down with some strange illness.

'Of course I don't mind. They're lucky to have someone of your ability and I know you enjoy it. It helps me feel less guilty for the amount of times work gets in the way of us doing things together. And speaking of which, I've volunteered to do an early shift on the phones in case the press conference produces any leads, even far-fetched ones. They'll all need checking. So that means I'll be up and out at sparrows' fart. I'll try not to wake you.'

He said the last part with a broad grin as they both knew how much it took to wake Trev when he was fast asleep. Ted didn't even need to creep about quietly when he had to do an early stint. He could have put the television and radio both on at full volume and left them on when he set out. Trev still wouldn't have stirred until his usual time for getting up.

There had certainly been plenty of calls from members of

the public throughout the night when Ted went back in early on. Nothing of any remote use to the case, as far as Ted could see at a quick glance through the list. At least sightings of Elvis Presley or Michael Jackson in a takeaway in town were getting to be a thing of the past.

It was still early when Ted took a call.

'Sir, I have an update on an earlier call-out for the fire service, a car on fire on wasteland. The fire is now extinguished and officers on site have confirmed that there is at least one body in the vehicle.'

Chapter Four

'Show me as attending, please,' Ted replied, standing up and putting his jacket on.

It would be quicker and simpler to go in person to the location, which wasn't far away, rather than trying to phone and speak to the right Fire Officer, who would probably have more than enough to do without taking his call.

Going himself would also give Ted the chance to get an early look at the scene to form his own deductions, rather than having to rely on photos and videos, if it was one for them.

The coroner's office would almost certainly have been informed of the death, with initial details indicating something out of the ordinary. A death in a burning car, if that was what they were looking at, would be treated as suspicious initially which meant that the Home Office pathologist, Professor Bizzie Nelson, would be likely to be summoned to attend, in case of an unlawful killing.

Ted had no information on the body. He was hoping that it wasn't that of the missing baby.

He was driving his service vehicle and gave a brief flash of the blue lights as he approached the scene, to make it obvious that he was neither press nor public, coming for a ghoulish look at human tragedy. The area was taped off and officers in uniform were there to stop any unauthorised entry, until it was known whether or not it was a crime scene.

Ted parked well away from where all the activity was, reached for his warrant card, then went in search of the senior Fire Officer present. He was pleased to see a Watch Commander he'd liaised with on a previous serial arson case. A man called George. He went over to greet him.

'Hello, Ted. A DCI already on this one? I was expecting a lowly foot soldier at best, and not for some time yet. Couldn't you sleep?'

'We've got a nasty case on and I'm hoping it's not connected. What can you tell me about the body, please, George?'

Ted had previously experienced the distinctive sickly-sweet smell of burning human flesh and had prepared himself for the ordeal by popping one of his ever-present Fisherman's Friend lozenges into his mouth before approaching. He was glad of it. The stench was pungent, especially mixed with the sharper smell of petrol.

'Oh yes, the little baby. I saw that on the telly last night. Well, we've only found one body here so far and all I can tell you is that it's the size of an average adult. But whether or not there is any connection to your kidnapping is beyond my meagre skills to judge.'

'For a start, can we still ID the vehicle or is it too far gone?'

'Plates are still fairly legible. We got here reasonably fast. I'll be able to tell you about the VIN and anything else later on, when I can give the all clear to look at the finer detail, but again we might be in with a chance there.'

An early trace on the car from its Vehicle Identification Number would be a help, although it might turn out to be stolen, or on false plates.

'Is it at all possible, hypothetically speaking, that there

41

would be anything left of a small baby after a fire like this?' Ted asked.

'You think this might be connected to your kidnap case and the baby might have been in the vehicle?' George asked him.

'Considering all possibilities, rather than thinking anything specific,' Ted told him.

'So that would be presuming that our body is the abductor. The thing with that hypothesis is that a considerable amount of accelerant was used in this fire. We brought a fire dog in, which is fairly routine these days, and it's given strong indications on that.

'All the early signs suggest that this is a fire which would have gone up very quickly. There's also clear evidence that more accelerant was sloshed on – using a technical term there – from the front of the vehicle after the initial fire had started.'

Ted was quick to catch on.

'So that indicates that the person inside the vehicle couldn't have got out to do more sloshing then got back into the vehicle to die? That they were a victim of a deliberate arson?'

'I would say them getting out at any point was unlikely in the extreme, given the probable intensity of the fire from the outset.'

'Then either they were already dead and this was a body disposal, or they were somehow incapacitated and burned to death?' Ted posed it as a question. 'While someone on the outside of the car was nearby to make sure it went up as fast as possible and burned away to as little as possible.'

'That's a pretty sharp summarised version of what is likely to be my final report. Good detective work, in other words. That's what all the early signs indicate. So as it's a suspicious death for more than one reason, we informed the coroner's office. And, if I'm not very much mistaken, this looks like our friendly local Home Office pathologist coming to join us now.'

Ted could also see Professor Bizzie Nelson's car making its way towards them, then coming to a halt next to his service vehicle. Ted walked across to greet her. She was one of the few people to even know his full name and to use it. She usually remembered not to in public, but he wanted to be sure. He'd never liked it, much preferring Ted.

'Good morning, Edwin,' she greeted him in her usual breezy fashion. 'I wasn't expecting to see you here, especially at this ungodly hour. I came early myself as I tend to like to get the burners out of the way early on. They do tend to smell rather revolting.'

However dire the circumstances of their meeting, she never failed to make Ted smile with her no-nonsense approach to even the most stomach-churning crime scenes she attended.

'We have a missing baby who was in all probability abducted in a vehicle, so we're checking out any and all incidents involving one.'

'Ah yes, I saw your piece to camera on a late news bulletin last night. Still no sign?'

'None. Nothing, despite the appeals. I was just asking the Watch Commander if there would be anything left of a little baby if it had been in a blaze like this one. Apparently accelerant was used and more was added after the fire had started, so probably not by the victim.'

Bizzie was round by the boot of her car now, pulling on her full suit and green Wellingtons, with covers on, before approaching the vehicle.

'So possibly an execution of sorts,' she commented, hefting out her bag. 'In which case I assume that even with no connection to your missing child, it would be one for your team.'

She closed the boot lid with a hearty thump as she said, 'There might not be a lot left of a tiny baby after an intense fire, but rest assured, I will go through every bit of ash to see what it can tell me. Accelerant, of course, makes this a suspicious death with at least a possibility of other crime, so I will be certainly overseeing the post-mortem examination myself, if not carrying it out. I promise to let you know personally when it will be, and also of my initial findings. But it cannot possibly be before tomorrow, probably quite late on, I'm afraid. We have our hands full already.

'If I find anything at all which could in any way relate to the missing baby, I will definitely phone you, straight away.'

Ted knew he could trust her word. There was no point at all in him hanging about; he might as well head back to the station and direct operations from there. He stopped to buy a hot bacon barm and a cup of tea in a takeaway paper cup on his way. It was likely to be a day when it was best to grab whatever food and drink he could, whenever there was a gap.

Ted was the first one in but Mike Hallam wasn't far behind him. Mike found the boss sitting in the main office bringing himself up to date with all the calls from the night before, and any other development.

Mike wrinkled his nose as he walked across to greet him.

'Sorry to sound personal, boss, but what's that strange smell?'

Ted lifted his arm and sniffed at his jacket sleeve.

'Sorry, yes, a burner in a car, first thing this morning, and you know how that smell clings. I keep some emergency aftershave in my office, so I'll try and do some damage limitation before the rest of the team come in.'

'Is it one for us?'

'I'm trying not to jump to conclusions. The Fire Officer in charge says that someone threw more accelerant onto the blaze after it was lit, from the driver's side, and that it can't have been done by the victim found inside the car. It's possibly a murder, so it may well be for us.'

'So because we had a baby probably driven away in a car, and we later have a dead person in a burned-out car a few hours later, you're thinking there may be a link?'

'I'm saying we would do well to at least consider there's a connection. Right, I better go and clean myself up a bit before the rest of the team come in. Give me a shout when you're ready to brief. The professor has promised to let me know if she finds anything at all of relevance to us.'

'It's probably a terrible thing to say, boss, but if the person in the car turns out to have been the baby-snatcher, I won't shed a tear. I just hope to heaven little Evie wasn't in the vehicle when it went up, if that was the case.'

Ted hung his suit jacket out of his office window for a bit, hoping to at least dampen down the smell which was clinging to it. Some of the aftershave he kept in his drawer would help a bit too, hopefully.

He wrote up his own brief notes from the morning visit, then heaved a sigh and made a start on the day's admin tasks. It was never his favourite part of the job, although he handled it efficiently. He'd always been a hands-on copper, even as a boss, and despite being reminded that was not his current role, he found it hard to let go.

When he heard the team starting to arrive he went out to

join them, leaving his jacket behind as that probably had the strongest lingering smell. He quickly filled everyone in on the morning's development. If any of them noticed the aftershave overdose, no one said a word.

He set out the little he knew to date about the incident, telling them that whether it was connected or not, it looked likely to be one for them, as a death by arson.

DC Steve Ellis was listening even more attentively than usual. He waited until Ted had finished then said hesitantly, 'Sir ...'

He was much more confident than he had been when he'd first joined the team. For some reason, he always seemed in awe of the boss, despite all of Ted's best efforts to be encouraging.

'Yes, Steve?'

'The two abduction cases in the Met area. They were both followed by a death in a burning car. It's noted as an item of interest, but no connection has yet been established. Both those kidnaps and the subsequent arson cases are still unsolved.'

'Good work, Steve, thank you. Can you get all details of those cases and let me have contacts for the SIO on them both. It sounds as if we should, at the very least, be in dialogue to see if there really are similarities with our scenario, as would seem to be the case.

'How are we doing with feedback from the press conference? Anything at all worth following up? And what news of the baby's mother today? Anyone had contact with her FLO yet to check?'

'I have, boss, I called her first thing,' Mike told him. 'Pretty much as you would expect. Carrie hasn't slept at all, nor eaten anything. She keeps pacing up and down to the baby's room and picking up all her stuff. Paula, who's with her, is going to try to get her GP to come round. She thinks she's going to need something to help her get through this. The longer it goes on with no word either way, good or bad, the harder it's going to be.

'Carrie's also adamant she wants to go back to the park. She wants to be there, whatever they find, and it's getting harder to dissuade her.'

Ted looked round at his team. He couldn't begin to imagine the anguish of the young mother. All he could do to relate was to remember how he'd felt when Trev had gone missing and he was trying to hold himself together and carry on doing his job.

'Those of you who are parents, which would be best? Let her be there at the risk of her seeing her baby found dead? Or keep her out of the way and tell her the bad news if we have to?'

The verdict was unanimous. From Mike, from Maurice, from Virgil and Rob, from all those present.

'Be there, boss, whatever the outcome,' they all said. 'She'd never forgive us if she wasn't.'

'All right, let's do that, then. Maurice and Jezza, I know she has a liaison officer now, but you two clearly have a good rapport with her, so I think you should both be there too. One of you perhaps can stay with her, try to get her to recall anything at all that might help us that's not come up so far. This must have been pre-planned, because of the probable getaway car. I can't believe something this slick was done without a thorough recce, so somebody must have been watching, probably for some time before it happened.'

'Carrie did tell us she follows a very regular pattern, boss, and Denise Doyle confirmed that,' Jezza put in. 'She's almost always there at the same time, sits in the same place. It settles the baby to do that. So someone might well have seen someone, perhaps watching her.'

'We need to find this couple with the Great Dane, too. The one Finley's mother said they often see in the park. How are we getting on with that? Mike?'

'I've passed it over to Uniform and PCSOs in particular, boss. Needs local knowledge. An older couple like that with such a big dog can't be that common a sight, so it will ring bells with someone.'

'CCTV? Rob?'

'No cameras anywhere very near the entrances, boss, and none at all in the park. We're looking at all the footage from the nearest ones to see if we can see the same car passing more than once as if it's looking out for someone, but that's about the best we can do with that for now. I'll widen the search if there's nothing locally.'

Gina Shaw had gone very quiet. As Ted was about to get up and go back to his own office, she spoke up. So softly some of the others had to lean forward in their seats to hear her.

'It's always best to know, no matter how bad something is. Always. I had an older sister. Jenny. When she was fifteen, she went off to school as normal one day. We never saw her again. She simply disappeared without trace. No message. No body to mourn. Nothing. None of us even got to say a proper goodbye to her. It totally destroyed my parents. They never got over it. The whole not having any sort of closure thing. Anything would have been better for them than that. Carrie needs to be there, whatever the outcome.'

Jezza was sitting near enough to Gina to lean over and

take hold of one of her hands. Big soft Maurice, as spontaneously politically incorrect as ever, got up, went across to her, and pulled her into a comforting hug.

For a moment, Ted was disconcerted, not knowing what to do or say. All he could think of was all the years he'd thought his mother had simply abandoned him without trace, with no word. Not until he was an adult had he found out the truth about her. It was getting intensely personal and he needed to find a way to get it back onto a professional footing, without sounding heartless.

'Right, then, everyone. You all know what needs doing. Let's do our very best today to find out something definitive. Whichever way it goes.'

Then he went back to his office and did something he so seldom did, and never during work hours. He phoned his mother. Just to hear her voice.

Chapter Five

Calls were still coming in following the press appeal the previous evening. So far, nothing of any use to them, but they would all have to be gone through and followed up so that no possible lead slipped through the net.

Ted was trying to keep eyes on everything. As SIO, it was his head on the block if anything was missed, especially something significant which could have an impact on the outcome of the case.

He was on his second mug of green tea of the morning when, after a brief knock on the frame of the open office door, Mike Hallam came in as invited.

'Boss, one of the PCSOs knows the couple with the big dog, so Rob's going round there with her to get a statement about anything they might have seen at any time which could be of some help.

'It may be something and nothing, but I know how much you distrust coincidences and there is one which may or may not be significant. I checked the logs for anyone turning up at the park yesterday and none of the officers there saw a couple with a Great Dane at all, either already inside when they attended, or trying to get in when it was closed off. Is that a change from their usual pattern, I wonder?'

Ted frowned at that.

'Denise Doyle, the mother of the toddler, said they sometimes see the couple and their dog. She didn't give me the impression that it was a regular set-your-watch by them type of thing, like Carrie's visits with the baby. But we definitely need to talk to them. It's possible they've seen something, perhaps without even registering that they did. Rob's a good choice. If they know anything, he'll find out, for sure.

'What's the situation with Carrie now?'

'She's gone back to the park, with her liaison officer, and I've sent Jezza with them, to see if she can tease any more useful details out of her. I took the decision to put Maurice onto other things today. I thought he risked getting too emotionally involved. We all know what he's like.'

'Good idea, Mike. I was going to suggest the same thing. Try putting him on door knocking round and about, near to the park. We know people will talk to him where they wouldn't talk to an officer in uniform, nor even to most other officers.'

Mike chuckled at that.

'If we could find his secret and bottle it, we'd have the best clear-up results of anyone.'

He turned to go but Ted stopped him with a question.

'The husband, Mike. I know his employers told Jezza he was halfway across Poland, but have we actually checked that it is him driving the vehicle? Not simply someone doing the run for him so he has a solid alibi? Because it's not unheard of for a parent to snatch their own child, if there's family conflict we don't yet know about.'

'Good point, boss. I'll check for his passport being used on dates which coincide.'

'Let's check the couple's families, too, please. We've been told Carrie has none, but is that true?'

'You don't think she staged her own baby's

disappearance?' Mike sounded surprised at the suggestion.

'I don't think anything yet,' Ted told him. 'But I don't want this case to finish badly because we failed to do the basic checks from the start. It's an emotive one. Our sympathies are bound to be with the mother and she certainly seems genuine.

'Jezza had a very valid point with her "the dog that didn't bark" reference, though. You know a lot more about babies than I do, but if the baby didn't cry, then surely the two most likely explanations are that either she wasn't in the pram to begin with, or that she was picked up out of it by someone she knew.

'At least tell me we got an early alert out to all ports and airports, asking for checks on all babies of the right sort of age leaving the country yesterday. And that's something else I know nothing about. Does a baby that small need its own passport?'

'Yes, I put out a bulletin as soon as the dog lost the trail, just in case. And yes, babies need their own passport from birth these days. But some babies might not wake up and start crying when someone picks them up. I suppose it all depends.'

'So an abductor would need paperwork in place in advance if they were going to whisk a child out of the country fast. How feasible is that?'

Mike's smile at that was sheepish.

'Boss, I'll never recover from the shame of the time when my wife was sorting through some old photos to make into albums. She was showing them to me and I commented how pretty our daughter looked in one of them, when she was quite a tiny baby. If looks could kill! My wife informed me, more than a little frostily, that the one I was looking at was my niece, not my daughter. The wife and her sister had their babies very close together and to me they did look alike. So if a dad can mistake their own child in a photo, I doubt someone at a busy port would do much more than glance at the passport of a small baby.'

'And presumably if the baby is still alive and someone has her in the country, the question of false papers isn't going to arise for some time. What would you need any form of ID for with a very little one?'

'Healthcare, boss. Babies tend to get put on the system from very early on and they normally get all sorts of health checks and tests as they develop. Although if she turned up somewhere and there was a plausible explanation about parents recently moving, or perhaps losing all their possessions in a house fire, that might work, at least temporarily.'

'Of course, all of this is pre-supposing that little Evie is still alive and that whoever has her has her best interests at heart. Because the other reasons for a tiny child to be snatched are really not good to be thinking about.'

Once Mike had left the office, Ted made a quick call to Trev. There was no way he was going to get away early enough to attend the self-defence class he and his partner ran for local young people. Not even his own judo session afterwards, the way things were going. Not unless they had a much-needed breakthrough. He seemed to have less and less time to do the things he enjoyed, and often felt he wasn't spending nearly enough time with his partner.

'Hey, you, are you all right?' Trev asked him as soon as he picked up the call. He sounded concerned. 'Only Annie told me you'd phoned her, from work, and you've never done that before.'

Ted smiled to himself. He should have known she would. She and Trev were thick as thieves and spent hours on the phone to one another. He was pleased they got on so well. It eased his conscience slightly about how little time he spent talking to her, and sometimes to Trev.

'We were discussing family disappearances. It made me realise I'm not immune to needing to talk to my mam now and again. Anyway, I was just calling to say …'

'… you won't make it to the dojo this evening. I guessed as much, unless you got a breakthrough on the case. Terry's coming to help me with the kids and I'll give judo a swerve then I can get back and cook something nice for you for whenever you do get back.'

'Flip will be more disappointed than usual. He sent me a text to say he has exciting news he wants to share with you.'

'He has your phone number?'

'Don't sound so shocked, Ted. Most of the kids do, so they can let me know if they're coming or not. Anyway, thanks for letting me know. I'll see you whenever you get back, and good luck with the case.'

* * *

'It's this one, sarge, this little bungalow at the end of the cul-de-sac,' the Community Support Officer, Nora O'Grady, told Rob O'Connell, who was driving. 'Bob and Beryl Norris. Like the Heaton, as he always says. I wonder if he ever gets tired of introducing himself with a place name. I can see it working round here but further afield have people even heard of Heaton Norris?'

'Is he retired? And do they have any family?'

'He is, yes, from some fairly lowly clerical post, in local

government, I think. She was a shorthand typist, back in the day. No family, though. I don't know all the details but I think she might have lost her only child. There's just one old photo of a very small baby, on the mantelshelf.

'They live very modestly, and I've no idea how they feed that big mutt on what their combined pensions probably bring in, let alone afford to eat themselves or keep up the utility bills. Nice enough people, but keep pretty much to themselves. He will phone me though, sometimes, with reports of anti-social behaviour.'

Rob parked his car close to the house. Nora put her hat on and straightened it, as Rob held open the front gate for her and the two of them walked up the short path to the front door. The garden was tidy but devoid of much in the way of colour.

The minute Nora rang the doorbell, there was a deep, baying woofing from within, and the sound of a dogs' claws slipping and slithering on a hard surface.

'That's Scooby-Doo,' Nora told Rob with a broad grin. 'Sidney, he's actually called, but he's just as goofy and clumsy as the dog in the cartoon. Harmless enough, but watch out for being covered in drool and dog hair.'

The door opened a scant crack, just enough for an older man's head to appear, his eyes peering from one to another.

'Oh, hello, Nora, love – Sidney, get down! Nice to see you. Sidney, get back. Have you time for a cuppa? Hang on, let me just shut Sid in the kitchen so you won't get covered in slobber, then you can come in. I'll put the kettle on.'

Rob watched warily from the doorstep as the older man took hold of the big hound's collar and did his best to manhandle the dissenting brute down the hallway and through a door at the end, shutting the door quickly and firmly behind it. He wondered what, if anything, the owner would be capable of doing if the dog ever decided to pull away from him. The man can't have weighed much more than his pet, possibly even less.

The two officers stepped into the house as he instructed them to. They exchanged a glance, nostrils wrinkling, at the smell which assailed them as he showed them into a front room where the gas fire was on. Although it was on a low setting, the room was as stifling as an oven.

'Look, Beryl, love, Nora's come to visit us and she's brought her friend …'

'DC Rob O'Connell,' Rob told him, holding up his ID.

'Oh, hello, Nora, love, how nice to see you. Come in and sit down, both of you. Would you like a brew? Bob, put the kettle on, love.'

'No tea, thank you,' Rob told him quickly.

He didn't much fancy the dog escaping from the kitchen if the man went to put the kettle on. Not to mention the fact that the smell was putting him off all thought of consuming anything.

The couple sat next to each other on the sofa, both looking from one officer to the other in almost perfect sync.

'Nora tells me you often walk your dog in the park near here. I wonder if you happened to go there yesterday?'

Bob Norris spoke for both of them.

'We do usually go, most days, but not yesterday. Sidney's been quite poorly and we had to take him to the vet's yesterday so he didn't get his usual walk. More big bills, and that's not the end of it. He needs to have a lot more tests to find out what's going on. But he's worth it to us, of course.

'What's this about, officer?'

'You probably saw on the news last night that a child

disappeared from the park yesterday, so we're anxious to talk to anyone who was there at the time.'

The woman's hand flew up to her face as her mouth made an O of surprise. Once again, it was the man who answered.

'We don't currently have a telly,' he said, nodding towards a corner where there was an empty unit standing forlornly. 'We … we had to get rid of it and we've not yet replaced it.'

Rob had his pocket book out and was making notes. Even when he didn't need to do so, he found it a good tactic. Innocent people thought carefully before giving their answers, seeing their words being noted down. The guilty tended to clam up, unless they were frequent offenders and used to the routine.

'So when you do go to the park, are there any people you regularly see there? Anyone you might perhaps stop and talk to?'

The two of them exchanged a look. As if by silent agreement, it was the man who answered again.

'There are two nice young women, with their children. One who's expecting and has a little boy.' He looked to his wife for confirmation as he said, 'Finley, is it, she calls him? He's a proper little tinker. He must be a real handful for her. Then there's another woman with a little baby. A girl. Ever so pretty, she is.'

His wife spoke then, her voice wavering.

'Is it one of those two little children who's disappeared? Like Bob said, the little lad is always running off, always getting into mischief. Is it him?'

There was no point in Rob not answering. It had been on the TV and radio, so even if they hadn't the means to have watched it, it would be in the papers and there would probably be posters going up all round the neighbourhood if there was still no sign of baby Evie for much longer.

'It was the little girl. She's been reported as missing. So, even if you weren't there yesterday, can you think of anyone else you've seen recently? Especially anyone you've not seen before.'

There was no mistaking the anguish on the woman's face at the news, nor the evident shock on that of the husband.

'Oh, that poor, poor mother,' she said, in a trembling voice. 'I can't imagine anything worse than losing a child. But to have one taken like that …'

She broke off with a catch in her voice.

Nora O'Grady joined in at that point.

'You can both see now why we're desperate for any help at all you might be able to give us. Anything out of the ordinary you might have seen. Especially any new faces in the park. Have you still got my card?'

She was reaching in her pocket as she spoke, handing the card she withdrew to the two people sitting watching her.

'Here's another one, just in case. Please call me at any time if you can think of anything.'

She exchanged a look with Rob and he gave an almost imperceptible nod. It was clear they weren't going to get much more from either of them. He also took out one of his cards to give to them saying, 'These are my contact details, in case for any reason you can't get hold of Nora. Again, please feel free to call me at any time if you think of anything which might be relevant.'

The husband spoke again, shifting in his seat and looking uncomfortable.

'We've got a bit of a problem with the phone at the moment, but if we do think of something, I'll go next door and ask to use theirs so I can call you. I promise.'

The couple both stood up to show the officers out. As they stood side by side on the doorstep to wave them goodbye, the woman turned to her husband, her whole body now trembling, eyes wet with tears.

'Oh Bob, what have we done?'

Chapter Six

They'd hit the critical twenty-four-hour marker. The first worrying milestone in any missing person case. Of even greater concern when the person they were hunting for was so young and vulnerable. The only positive factor they had to cling onto for the moment was that they hadn't found a body. Yet. And that was scant comfort to the increasingly distraught young mother.

The only place she would settle was in the park. Her liaison officer was having a hard job getting her to stay out of the way of the search, which was still ongoing, although with less optimism the more time went by with no sightings and no trace.

More dogs had been brought in to quarter every inch of the area. The mother hadn't been told that one of them was a specialist cadaver dog, trained to sniff out any trace of a body which might have been hastily concealed somewhere.

Ted wasn't surprised to get another summons from Sammy Sampson, even less so to find Superintendent Caldwell, the formidable Ice Queen, once again in attendance.

'Anything, Ted?' Sammy asked, as soon as he walked into her office.

He shook his head.

'I wish there was but nothing so far. No eye witnesses to anything useful at all, although we are still getting calls.'

'Which is why you and Debs are going to do another televised appeal later today. Somebody must have seen something, surely to goodness. A small baby can't simply have vanished into thin air in a park where there are presumably people coming and going quite often. It's not even one with any wild areas, like your last case, unless I'm mistaken.'

'A much more traditional sort of park. All mown grass, benches and level, well-surfaced paths. Not the typical sort of hang-out for drug dealers, or even youngsters nicking off school or anything like that.

'And if someone simply scooped the baby up and made off with her, wouldn't she have been crying? Surely someone would have noticed that and made a mental note. But we've had nothing like that mentioned in any of the calls.'

'Depends, Ted. All babies are different. My daughter would scream the place down if anyone other than me picked her up when she was sleeping, but they aren't all like that,' Sammy told him. 'My grandson is much more placid.'

'Exactly so. With my two boys, the older one was a bit like that but the younger one? Anyone could have gone off with him at any time and he would have slept right through it, he was such a quiet baby,' Debra Caldwell put in.

'Right, well as you can imagine, Ted, I've had the ACC on, asking what's going on,' Sammy went on. 'I've done all the usual platitudes but the pressure is clearly on for some sort of a result, even if it's not the one we're hoping for.'

Ted's mobile was going off in his pocket. He reached for it, then said, 'I'd better take this, it's Mike Hallam. Let's hope it's some news.'

He listened to what the DS had to tell him, then rang off.

'A glimmer of hope, finally. A phone call from someone who says they saw a woman getting into a car near the park at about the right time. Mike's sending someone round to get a statement.'

'Excellent. Even better if they say it was definitely someone carrying a small baby. It would help us so much if we had even a crumb to throw to the baying press pack this evening.'

'No mention of a baby being seen, but apparently the caller did say the woman was wearing a thick, padded coat. And we know that the weather yesterday when Evie disappeared didn't really warrant wearing something like that. I'm imagining that if a baby was inside a coat like that, it might possibly muffle any sounds it was making, especially if there was traffic noise around as well.'

'This is hopeful, Ted. Best lead yet,' Sammy told him. 'We need a miracle. But I don't think even the heaviest padded coat would have kept my daughter quiet at that age, although I suppose at least it wouldn't have been quite as loud. But then some babies cry, sometimes a lot, so I don't know that anyone would give any particular attention to that.'

'What about this body in the burning car this morning?' Debra Caldwell asked him. 'I see you attended yourself. Do you think there's a connection to the kidnap?'

'It's a possibility,' Ted's response was guarded. 'After all, we know that people who do the snatching are often considered expendable and are disposed of as soon as possible afterwards, so as to break any trail back to whoever is the organiser behind it all. And Steve's found out that two similar cases in the Met area both had as yet unsolved deaths in burning cars shortly after the kidnappings on their patch.

That really is a bit too much of a coincidence to be discounted. I'm waiting on a call from the SIO on those cases, a DI Smith. Steve's passed a message to him asking him to contact me, which he hasn't done as yet.'

'Professor Nelson is doing the PM herself and has promised to let me know when it will be. But not before late tomorrow at the earliest, she did warn me.'

'We'll need a full round-up of everything we have before this afternoon's press conference, and we'll need to get together a good half hour before so we can spin what we have to sound as positive as it can. I just hope to god we find her before then, or at least have some sort of a solid lead to throw at them or we're going to get a mauling.'

Ted was interrupted by his phone ringing again before he could reply to her. He checked the screen then said, 'I'd better take this one, too. It's the professor's assistant, so it might hopefully be news of the PM.'

'It's James, Ted. The Professor asked me to tender her fulsome apologies but your body in the car is going to have to wait until Friday early doors. That means her early doors, of course, when most normal people are still in their beds. She did ask me to tell you, however, that on a detailed initial examination, there were no signs of anything to indicate the presence of a baby's body in the car, although that's subject to confirmation after more detailed analysis.

'She's also waiting on toxicology tests, and DNA. She said to tell you the victim had some interesting dental work, not typically British, so she wants to know more about that to give you the best information available. So Friday morning, then.'

Ted relayed the information to his senior officers, then Sammy asked what more he needed.

'More officers,' Ted told them both without hesitation. 'Everyone is flat out on the kidnap, and if this body in the car does turn out to be a linked case, and a murder at that, that's going to stretch us too thin. In the absence of much else, finding out what that's all about might just give us a lead to little Evie.'

'Debra and I were talking about that before you joined us, Ted. That's going to be essential, and you can leave the two of us to worry about the budget. We need a result. If ever the public got the idea we didn't get one simply because of insufficient officer numbers ... Well, you can imagine what the media would make of that.

'One thing we both thought of is why don't you find out if Jo Rodriguez can temporarily come back from Ashton, if everything is under control there. Then he could run much of the enquiry here, freeing up Mike Hallam, and allowing you to stick more within your designated role. And certainly let's draft in as many extra bodies as we can find. Keep us both posted, well before the next trial by media.'

Ted's phone was ringing again as he went back upstairs to his own office. An unknown number so he answered with a neutral, 'DCI Darling.'

'DI Smith. Oscar. From the Met. One of your DCs has flagged up similarities between your case and two of ours. I was going to liaise by conference call but for some reason, my guv'nor has the strange, old-fashioned notion that I should come up to your neck of the woods to compare notes. Travel and accommodation are being sorted as we speak, so with luck I should be turning up on your doorstep – or that of your nick – first thing tomorrow morning, if that suits you?'

Ted didn't like the sound of that. Didn't like it one bit.

He was trying not to prejudge, but the only reason he could think of why a senior officer would want to send his SIO halfway across the country in the middle of two serious and as yet unsolved cases was if he felt the team was better off without him on site.

If that turned out to be the case, Ted was fairly sure that DI Oscar Smith was not going to turn out to be the answer to anything much, certainly nobody's prayers.

His feeling was about to be confirmed. He was halfway up the stairs when his phone rang again, with another unknown number.

'DCI Darling? This is Superintendent Murray Aird, from the Met. I'm sending you up one of my DIs to liaise on these child kidnappings with possibly related arsons.'

'Yes, sir, DI Smith has just phoned me.'

'Good, good. Look, this is a bit awkward, and it's definitely off the record. Just between the two of us, please.'

Ted replied with a guarded, 'Sir,' in anticipation of what was coming next.

Aird seemed to go off at a tangent.

'Have you ever watched Life on Mars, chief inspector?'

Now Ted was getting worried, wondering where this conversation was heading.

'I have, sir.'

'It's perhaps not by the book, nor very professional of me, but I often spend a lot of my time phoning people after a case to apologise for some of Oscar's unorthodox little ways. So this time I thought I'd try a bit of an advance warning.

'He's a good copper, don't get me wrong. A very good one. Former Military Police, so he knows a lot of tricks our lot have never heard of. But he's about as unorthodox as you can get. Almost as if he models himself on Gene Hunt, from that series.

'You may have seen or heard about our recent serial killer case. I'd unofficially suspended Oscar, but he only went and solved the whole thing by himself, off the radar, whilst on enforced leave. That's why we put up with him.

'What I'm trying to say is that I've been reading up on you and I think you should be able to manage him. But I just wanted you to know that if you feel the need to send him packing, you wouldn't be the first, and I'm certain you won't be the last.'

'Thank you for the heads up, sir,' Ted told him, then risked asking, 'Would I be right in thinking this character trait is the reason you're opting to send DI Smith here in person rather than us doing everything by conference call?'

Aird chuckled down the phone.

'I heard you were sharp. I have a feeling you might be able to manage Oscar effectively. Just remember, if you can't, you won't be the first.'

* * *

Jezza had been sent to talk to the person who had reported seeing a woman in a padded coat getting into a car near the park at about the right time on the right day.

She found the address easily enough and saw a woman on her knees in the front garden, battling with weeds in a small border which surrounded a pocket-handkerchief-sized lawn. A small fluffy kitten with tufted ears and a face like a lynx was busily stalking then pouncing on her feet every time they moved.

Jezza paused at the gate, holding out her ID.

'Mrs Wood? I'm DC Vine, Greater Manchester Police. You kindly phoned us about someone you saw near the park yesterday?'

'Oh yes, come in, please. Do you want to go in the house, or are you all right out here? Only I'm fighting a losing battle with the weeds.'

'Inside might be easier, because I'll need to take notes.'

The woman got to her feet, brushing soil from the jeans she was wearing, then headed for the door.

'No problem, come with me. You too, Bobby, come on.'

'Bobby?' Jezza couldn't resist asking, as the little cat trotted behind his owner like a dog.

The woman laughed.

'I know, it's a bit naff, isn't it? I couldn't think what to call him and he really does have a face like a little bobcat, doesn't he?'

The house was compact, tidy, with a definite no-frills style. Jezza could imagine that was the safest option with the young cat, who began busily racing round the room jumping on each chair in turn as soon as she and his owner sat down.

'Let me know if he's too much for you and I'll shut him in the kitchen.'

Jezza wasn't about to comment that compared to her younger brother, Tommy, in one of his frequent hyper modes, Bobby the kitten was no problem.

'He's fine, honestly. Now, you kindly phoned in after the press appeal to say you'd seen something of possible significance near the park. Could you tell me, please, in your own words, what you saw.'

'I was walking back from visiting a friend. As I got near the park, two things happened almost at the same time. Almost as if they had been synchronised, if you know what

I mean. A woman came hurrying out of the park just as a car was coming along, quite fast. It pulled into the kerb, the woman grabbed the door and opened it, then the car sped off, almost before she'd shut the door and got her seat belt on.'

'Did you notice anything at all, about either the woman or about the car? Colour, make, model? Anything at all. And did you get a glimpse of the driver at all?'

She shook her head.

'I'm hopeless with cars, I'm afraid. I don't have one. Haven't had for years. I prefer to use public transport, or to walk. All I can say is it wasn't a make I immediately recognised, although that doesn't help much as I only really know classics like a Mini or a Beetle. And it was a silvery grey colour, but when I looked online I read that that's the most popular colour, so I don't suppose that helps much.'

'What about the woman?'

Again, the shake of her head.

'The only thing I really noticed was the heavy padded coat she was wearing. It was quite a warm day really. It didn't warrant it. It made her look quite stout, so I couldn't really tell her build. Not very tall, though. She had very black hair, tied back. I suppose that could have been dyed, although it looked natural. And trying not to sound racist here but she wasn't white. Not black, either, nor brown, really. I'm not being very helpful, am I?'

'You are, yes, very. It's the first concrete lead we have to date. What about the driver? Did you see them at all?'

'Not really. A very quick glimpse to register that it was a man. He spoke English, though. He didn't say much, just "get in quick", or something like that.'

'Is there any chance you might recognise the voice if you heard it again?'

The woman looked doubtful.

'It was very brief, and I didn't pick up on any strong accent. I'd be willing to try though, of course, if it might help in any way.

'That's all very helpful, thank you. Do you think, if you came into the station and worked with a specialist, that you could help to produce a likeness of the woman, and perhaps of the car? They would show you different pictures, according to what you describe, to build up a composite, which could prove crucial.'

'I will certainly try my best about the woman, but I'm not optimistic about the car. I do want to help, though, if I can. I can't imagine what that poor young mother must be going through, so I would be happy to offer any help I can. Shall I come with you now? I'll just feed Bobby first and get my coat.'

* * *

'Rob? Bill Baxter.'

Retired sergeant Bill Baxter now worked on the front desk at the station, a role normally done by a civilian. But nobody knew the ins and outs of the job better than Bill, and since he'd replaced the person who had done the job before him, things were much more efficient. Priority cases were sent on as quickly as they needed to be, while timewasters were thoroughly screened and sent politely but firmly on their way.

'I have a chap down here who says he spoke to you earlier today,' Bill told Rob O'Connell over the phone. 'Says his name is Bob-Norris-like-the-Heaton, he will only speak to you, and that he's come in to make a confession. Are you available?'

Rob had already jumped to his feet and was grabbing his pocket book and phone, telling Bill he was on his way.

'Mike, Great Dane man from this morning is downstairs. He's told Bill he has a confession to make,' he called across to Mike Hallam as he made for the door.

'I'll let the boss know. It could be just the breakthrough he's hoping for before the next press conference. Even if we only get as far as " a person is helping police with their enquiries", it's a lot better than we've had up to now.'

Rob went down to the front desk and spoke to Bill first. He could see Bob Norris sitting alone on a chair in the waiting area. No wife, no big dog. He looked calm and serene, not the usual body language for someone who was preparing to make a confession about something serious. Rob's optimism was starting to evaporate as his mind filled with minor offences to which Norris might be about to confess. Not cleaning up after his dog fouled the pavement. Not having a dog licence, although they hadn't been required since the 1980s.

He went across to speak to the man, inviting him to accompany him to the interview room which Bill had told him was free.

Once they were both seated, Rob put his book ready to take notes. Only when he heard what the man wanted to say to him would he put things onto a more formal footing, cautioning him, advising him of his right to silence and to be legally represented, recording what was said.

'So, Mr Norris, what was it you wanted to say to me?'

'I'm an accessory to the kidnap of that little baby. I told the kidnappers where to find her. Me. Acting alone. My wife wasn't there. She knows nothing of this.'

He put his hands together and held them out to Rob, clearly anticipating handcuffs being applied.

'I'll tell you everything you want to know, but it was me who did it.'

Chapter Seven

'Mr Norris, I'm going to have to ask you to stop there, please,' Rob O'Connell told him firmly. 'It's important that I'm certain you understand your rights before we go any further, and for that reason, I would really suggest you speak to a solicitor before you say anything more to me.'

The man frowned. He looked almost disappointed.

'But I did it! I'm confessing. You need to arrest me. And I can't possibly afford a solicitor.'

'This is potentially a serious offence. So, depending on your means, you might be entitled to legal aid. But I really do suggest you let us call a solicitor for you. A duty solicitor, if you don't have your own, before you say anything further.'

'You've no idea how much financial difficulty I've got myself into. Even the wife doesn't know. But I can't go on like this. The guilt is killing me.'

'Please don't say anything more at this stage, Mr Norris. I need to go and talk to my senior officer before we continue. So is there someone you need us to contact for you? And would you like me to arrange a drink for you while you're waiting? A cup of tea? Or some water?'

The man's eyes filled with tears and there was a catch in his voice as he replied.

'You're very kind, and I don't deserve it. I did a truly dreadful thing, and I did it for the money.'

'I'm going to get someone to sit with you now while I

consult my chief inspector, Mr Norris. I'll try not to keep you waiting too long.'

The man worried him. Too much for him to take the risk of leaving him alone for even a short time. His mental state seemed fragile. Rob went outside into the corridor and left the door open so he could see Norris at all times, not taking his eyes off him until an officer from Uniform came to keep an eye on him in response to Rob's phone call.

Rob hurried upstairs to find the boss. He was in his office, the door open, in discussion with DI Jo Rodriguez, who had come over from Ashton as soon as he got the summons. Both looked hopefully towards him as he stepped into the room.

'How's it going, Rob?' Ted asked him.

'I've paused it for now, boss. I've left him with someone to keep a close eye on him, in case he might think of harming himself. He's admitted tipping off the kidnappers for the money, and he's said he's in all sorts of financial difficulties. He's also told me, twice, that his wife wasn't with him, and knows nothing about what he did.'

'So you don't believe him?'

'Not on that, boss, no, he's protesting too much. But my instincts tell me the rest of what he's saying is likely to be true. I think this is going to be a delicate one. I know everyone's busy, but I feel I'd like someone else sitting in, to make sure I'm not missing anything.'

Jo Rodriguez stood up from his seat.

'Well, if you can fill me in on everything in the time it takes us to walk downstairs, I'm all yours.'

Rob asked the Uniform officer to leave when he and Jo arrived to take over. He began by introducing himself and the DI then started the recording, after first cautioning Norris.

He went on: 'Mr Norris, this is a voluntary interview, at your request, under caution, and it will be recorded and filmed. You are not under arrest at this stage and you are free to stop answering questions at any time and to request legal representation. Are you happy to proceed on that basis?'

'Yes, more than happy. I did a dreadful thing and I'm prepared to face the consequences.'

'Then would you like to tell us in your own words what exactly it is that you've done?'

Norris paused and looked up at the ceiling, clearly seeking inspiration about how best to start.

'I would never, ever knowingly bring harm to any child. The wife and I had a little daughter ourselves once. Flora, we called her. A long time ago. She didn't get to her second birthday. Meningitis, they said, although at the beginning they kept telling us it was just a harmless childhood virus. Lots of babies got it, they said, and she'd recover. We should of insisted. Got a second opinion from a specialist, but there was no time. She died very quickly. We couldn't have another, although we tried, so we had dogs instead. To help fill the gap.

'Great Danes, we've always had. The wife loves them. Her family used to breed them when she was a child. They can have a lot of health problems, though. Heart, digestive, that sort of thing. Not to mention how much they cost to feed. Of course it gets harder to manage now we're both retired and our pensions don't seem to go as far as they used to.

'The latest one, Sidney, he's been the worst of all for vet bills. I try not to worry the wife with the finances. But things have got a lot worse than she realises. I told her the telly broke down, but I sold it. I cancelled the phone contract, too.'

He looked directly at the two officers sitting opposite him as he said, 'I hope you don't think this is me trying to make excuses. I'm just trying to give you all of the detail.'

'Please go on, Mr Norris.'

'We take Sidney to the park almost every day, when he's not too poorly. He enjoys it and my wife loves to see children out and about enjoying themselves. It makes her sad, thinking of our little Flora, but then she loves to watch them, too, if that makes sense.

'One day, about two weeks ago, as we were walking into the park, I saw a photographer taking pictures of some of the trees. When he saw me with Sidney, he said he was a beautiful dog and would I like him to take his photo. The wife wasn't with me, but I knew she'd be thrilled at the idea. But I also knew I couldn't afford what he was likely to charge.'

He paused to take a sip of the water Rob had arranged to be brought to him. His voice, all the time he spoke, was monotone, showing no emotion.

'I started to say no thank you, but he must have realised I was worried about the cost because he said he was working on a commission for someone and he needed to find a certain number of photos of various subjects by the end of the day so he'd do it for free. So I let him take some. They were very good. He showed me on his camera.

'I haven't got a phone he could send them to, of course, so I gave him my address and he promised to post them. Then he said he needed to get some shots of babies and small children, for a children's clothing catalogue. He said he hadn't found any pretty enough so far, but that if he did, their parents would be well paid, and if I suggested anyone, I'd get a fifty-pound finders' fee.'

Jo Rodriguez couldn't stop himself looking sideways at Rob, trying not to make his expression judgemental. He was the father of six children and a practising Catholic. Rob was neither but even with his scant knowledge of the scriptures, he caught the look and could guess that Jo's thoughts were turning to the thirty pieces of silver, the symbol of betrayal.

'It sounds dreadful. Stupid. Who could possibly be that gullible? But I was desperate for money. We had more vets' bills coming up. Fifty pounds would help. A fiver would have helped. So I told him about the little baby. Little Evie. I said how pretty she was. I told him her mother brought her to the park almost every day, at round about the same time. I even told him where they liked to sit, and what a lovely baby she was. And he gave me the money as soon as I told him the details. I thought that was honest of him. I really was that naive and stupid.'

He dropped his head into his hands and made an anguished noise like a stifled sob.

'But I swear I had no idea what was going to happen. You won't believe me, but I really did think I was doing something nice for the mother, thinking that she'd get a few quid and it might give her a start in some modelling work for her little baby. I honestly did think that. '

'And you say your wife wasn't with you that day, Mr Norris? Why was that?'

'No, she wasn't.'

His reply was quick, emphatic.

'She had a bad headache,' he went on. 'A migraine, so she'd gone for a lie down. And I didn't tell her anything about what I'd done. I couldn't, really, because I've not told her how serious our financial situation is, so she wouldn't have understood how important that fifty pounds was to us.

'Yet you said just now "as we were walking into the park". We. Not I. Why did you say we if your wife wasn't there?' Rob asked him.

Norris's eyes widened slightly at the question, but he recovered his stride.

'I meant me and Sidney. We, as in me and the dog. My wife wasn't there.

'I'm so sorry. So very sorry. You'll have to arrest me now, I suppose. Please can someone let my wife know? But ask them to do it gently. It's all going to come as a dreadful shock to her.'

'We're not quite at that stage yet, Mr Norris,' Rob told him. 'This is a complex issue. It will need the advice of the Crown Prosecution Service, before we could proceed to a charge.'

Norris frowned and looked from one to the other.

'I don't understand. I've confessed to a crime.'

Jo addressed him next.

'DS O'Connell is quite right, Mr Norris. Before we go any further there would be the question of what charge would be appropriate in a case like this, for instance.

'What I would suggest is that I'll now go and discuss what you've told us with the Senior Investigating Officer on the case, who will in turn report to CPS to establish the next step.

'In the meantime, the most useful thing you can do is to tell DS O'Connell everything you can remember about this man, the supposed photographer. Every detail. Then you'll be asked to work with someone else to see if you can produce a composite of what the person looked like. And that will need to happen as quickly as possible so that we can release the details and picture to the press and public.'

A faint flicker of hope crossed Norris's face as he looked from one to the other.

'You mean there's still a chance I can do something to put right my stupidity?'

Jo was already on his feet and heading for the door so Rob answered, trying to stay non-committal.

'Well, let's see how you get on helping us build up a picture of the man. I'll send someone to come and work with you on that.'

* * *

'This is a complex one, certainly,' Ted said, once Rob and Jo had told him about the interview with Norris. 'If he genuinely had no knowledge of the intentions of this photographer – always assuming he is the link to the crime, although that seems likely – then has Mr Norris actually committed any crime for which a charge would stick? It's certainly one for CPS input from the beginning. I'm not even a hundred per cent sure what we should charge him with, without consulting, to be honest.'

'I keep saying stupidity should be a criminal offence,' Jo said drily. 'I can't believe he fell for that trick and has potentially put a baby's life at risk by being so gullible. And greedy. I think the wife was there, too. I agree with Rob. I don't think he was telling the truth about her being at home with a migraine. His whole body language changed when he was telling us that bit. And she of all people, having lost a baby herself, should understand the grief their actions were going to cause.'

'Could they reasonably have been expected to know,

though? That's the first thing CPS are going to ask me. Could "the man on the Clapham omnibus" be expected to anticipate a serious crime would result from their giving information to someone who seemed to them to be genuine in what he was asking?'

Jo chuckled at the old legal reference as he said, 'I hate it when you quote relevant case law at us, boss. Especially when it's so ancient and obscure. Because any halfway decent defence counsel would be all over that one. How could the average man in the street be expected to know the sort of thing it could lead to? Rob can confirm there was no sign of a telly in the house, so they clearly don't watch the news. Or even any crime dramas. Given their financial state, I'd say it's a racing certainty they don't take a newspaper. I imagine there are genuine photo touts out and about with their cameras, and to some people these days, fifty quid isn't a huge amount to receive. Not enough to rouse suspicions.

'I hate what he did, but I do concede he might have done it in exactly the innocent circumstances he outlined to us. Let's hope he comes up with something of use by way of an ID for the photographer.'

Ted went down to report to Sammy in person about the latest development.

'So there's a chance we might possibly have something solid to wave at the press mob later today? Can we at least lead with 'a person is helping police with their enquiries?'

Ted shook his head.

'I'd rather not, at this stage. I don't see how we can remotely charge Mr Norris and keep him in police custody yet and I think we'd potentially be putting his life at risk if we mentioned anything, then let him go. Whoever the kidnappers are, they've already shown us that they're both clever and ruthless. They might suspect who the person was and go after him to ensure his silence.

'It looks likely that they killed the probable snatcher on at least two previous occasions, shortly after the babies were taken. Neither Evie's mother nor Denise Doyle mentioned this photographer type at all. I'm betting that the camera disappeared out of sight before he went anywhere near them, because otherwise at least one of them would have commented about him.

'My best guess is that he would simply have done a walk past, quick glance at the pram and the baby, but no other contact, and then put the snatcher onto the job of watching and waiting. And we know how she finished up, in all likelihood.'

'I shouldn't say it, but the mother and grandmother in me is struggling to feel a lot of sympathy for Mr Norris at the moment. I might do if and when any information he gives us leads to us finding little Evie alive and safe. In the meantime, I suppose we better put a watch on his house for now, and on him whenever he leaves it. That way, at least, we should be able to make sure no harm comes to him should he turn out to be a useful witness.

'So no one officially helping with our enquiries, but hopefully, two mugshots, of the snatcher and the phony photographer to get the press to put out there.

'It would have been perfect if we could have put up the mother to make an appeal direct to the cameras. But clearly she's not going to do that until the husband knows what's happened. My personal view is that she should have told him. Straight away. Got his employers to inform him, and to arrange to get him home as quickly and safely as possible. I think that whatever the outcome, he's going to have a hard time accepting that she didn't.'

The press conference started out slightly better than Ted dared hope. The ID composites produced by both Norris and Mrs Wood, the woman who had called in to report seeing someone get into a car outside the park and depart at speed, were detailed. There was no way of knowing how accurate they were, but they were at least something to go on and might bring in some useful leads.

Even though Ted and his team had reason to believe that the woman who took the baby was already dead, someone might still recognise her from the picture and be able to supply some details about her.

Ted's personal belief was that the photographer, phony or otherwise, would be long gone. If their job was simply to spot suitable children and pass those details on to someone, they were likely to be close to the operation and would in all probability melt away and start again. Either that or become a passenger in another burned out car.

As predetermined, Ted was fielding most of the questions. Debra Caldwell stepped in at any mention of anything touching on budgetary matters, staffing levels, or other areas more under her direct control.

Then, just as Ted thought he might be off the hook and able to get away, one television journalist posed the question he'd been dreading most of all, and he felt all the camera lenses zoom in on him at once. His answer, which they'd discussed in advance, depending on his credibility in delivering it, could be a career maker. Or a breaker.

'Are you still hoping to find baby Evie alive, chief inspector?'

Chapter Eight

'Well, I think that went well, all things considered,' Sammy Sampson, who had been watching the press conference from a safe distance, told Ted and Debra Caldwell when they regrouped to debrief in her office, once the press and media had departed.

'Coffee, everyone?'

'Tea, for me, please. Too late in the day for coffee,' Ted told her. Then he noticed an involuntary wince as she made to get up and went on, 'Shall I be mother?'

He knew Sammy still had some problems from the surgery she'd had some time ago. He didn't like to pry but he could tell she was sometimes in a considerable degree of pain. He suspected, too, that she must be worried at the slowness of her recovery and how it might affect her career.

'Bless you, Ted, that would be good. And congratulations on how you fielded that last question, too. I think you struck exactly the right balance between confident optimism and unrealistic expectations.'

'My thoughts exactly. Very well done.'

Ted had his back turned to the two of them as he made the drinks. Probably as well because he couldn't contain the look of surprise which appeared on his face at Debra Caldwell's words. Such fulsome praise from the Ice Queen was almost as rare as the twenty-yearly Preston Guild.

'Realistically, though, what are baby Evie's chances like

after this much time?' Ted asked, as he put drinks down in front of his two senior officers then sat down with his own. 'Bearing in mind how little I know about babies and their needs.'

'As long as she's fed appropriately and kept hydrated, she should have come to no harm within this amount of time,' Sammy told him. 'It all hangs on who's taken her and for what purpose. If it's a straightforward kidnap for a cash ransom we would surely have heard by now, with a demand being made.

'Best case scenario in terms of the baby's welfare, although not remotely for the poor parents, is that someone is snatching babies to be adopted by childless couples in countries where that's hard to do. Or where the children available might be not what they have in mind, for reasons like age, potential behavioural issues, ethnicity. They'd be wanted, loved and well taken care of, at least,' Sammy replied.

'The worst case – I'm sure we've all been round the block enough times to know, but I'll spell it out anyway – would be a snatch for something like the porn trade. Snuff films, at the very worst. We all know it happens. You better than most, Ted, after your trip to Spain for something similar. And with the likely link of bodies in burned out cars, whoever is behind it is certainly ruthless enough. They're covering their tracks well.'

'And, excuse me for asking, chief inspector,' the Ice Queen, staying as formal as always, began. 'I know you are experienced and unlikely to overlook anything, but are you one hundred percent certain that there was no family involvement? Not something staged because of a bitter dispute somewhere?'

Ted shook his head.

'We've checked and double-checked. Nothing at all to suggest any such involvement. DC Shaw has spoken to the friend Carrie Fisher was on the phone to from the park. Nothing there that's suspicious. The call stayed connected the whole time and she confirms everything. She was so worried she actually called 999 to report the incident as soon as she heard the mother's screams.

'And it's not simply a case of someone so wrapped up on their mobile they're not paying attention. Denise Doyle, the little boy's mother, confirms Carrie only rushed away from the pram because her son fell on his face. I saw the fresh signs of an injury on him myself, so it wasn't likely to have been a deliberate or staged distraction. All the signs to date suggest it was a pre-planned kidnap by a person or persons as yet unknown to us who knew exactly what they were doing.'

'And when is the husband back?' Sammy asked him.

'Some time tomorrow morning. Carrie Fisher has stayed adamant all along that he shouldn't be told before he gets back because he might put himself at risk, trying to drive home like a maniac. She has been advised that it would probably be better to tell him but she's refused. She's clearly hoping beyond reasonable hope that little Evie will somehow be found safe before he gets back.'

'And this is definitely not some attention-seeking thing the wife has come up with? She doesn't like the husband being away so much, she's struggling with a new baby, she wants things to change and she doesn't know how to make it happen?' Sammy asked.

Ted shook his head.

'We've so far found nothing at all to indicate that. Mike

Hallam is trying to arrange access to her medical records to see if there could be any indication of something like that, but you know how hard that can be.

'The Met officer, DI Smith, is arriving tomorrow morning, first thing, so we might get some useful information based on the two similar cases he's been dealing with.'

'I hope he will be of some help,' Sammy said, a note of doubt in her voice. 'I have to say the only reasons I can think of for physically sending an SIO to the other end of the country during an open case are not good ones.'

Ted's phone pinged with an incoming message. He checked the screen in case it was a relevant development. An SMS.

'Ted. Give me 5 mins before you leave. Kev.'

'A lead?'

Sammy Sampson looked and sounded hopeful. It was too soon to get much back after the press conference so they were definitely at the stage of clutching at straws.

'Kevin Turner, wants a word.'

'I think we're probably done here, unless you have anything else, Debs? Keep us posted of any new developments, Ted, whatever the time.'

Inspector Kevin Turner had been one of Ted's friends since he'd first started at the Stockport station. Ted was usually the one who drove Kev home if he'd had a bad day, ended it in the pub, and drunk too much to be left safely to drive himself home.

Kevin was at his desk, elbow deep in paperwork. He looked up as Ted came in.

'Any news on the baby? And not the version you gave the press just now. How's it really going?'

Ted shook his head as he sat down.

'That really was the truth I told them, not a line I was spinning. We've no real leads but we're still hopeful she's out there somewhere, alive and well, and eventually we'll find her.'

'So what did you want with me?'

Kev looked up and held up his hands in mock surrender.

'First of all, don't shoot the messenger. I know you're flat out. I know it's the last thing you need, but I'd welcome your input, if nothing else. It's another missing person case ...'

Ted started to speak but Kevin cut across him.

'I know, I know, you've got enough on your plate and this should be one for us. But it doesn't seem to be cut and dried. Can I at least tell you what's sounding wrong to me, see if you think I'm just being melodramatic?'

'Fair enough. Give me the broad outline.'

Kev presented him with the basic facts, briefly and succinctly. The woman who'd come into the station to report her elderly father, John Berry, as missing. Well spoken, articulate, in her forties. A doctor, she told the officer who had taken her statement.

She'd explained that her late husband had been a medical research scientist who had spent time in Africa, researching and treating one of the diseases which cost the lives of many young children, if not caught early enough.

Ironically, he'd caught and succumbed to another, lesser disease. Lesser but, in his case, still capable of proving fatal. She'd opted to stay on after his death to try to bring his work to a point where it could be managed by local medical staff and she could return home to the UK.

She'd had to leave her elderly father behind while she was away. He was in good health and still sharp in his mind, but as a precaution she'd arranged for a daily carer to go in, at her own expense, to check up on him, and to be a bit of company.

It had been working well and she'd had regular contact and positive feedback both from the care company and from her father. But then she needed to tour some more out of the way places, where telephone reception could often be problematic. When she was finally able to get back in contact, she failed to get hold of her father at all, either on his mobile or on the landline. She was due some leave anyway so she flew home at the earliest opportunity, thinking it would be a nice surprise for him.

'You can imagine her surprise when she managed to get back, went round to the house and found a young family living there and no sign of her dad. Shocked, later, when they told her they'd bought the house very recently and showed her the legal paperwork to prove it.

'All they were able to tell her was that her father had said he was selling up quickly to go on an extended holiday with a friend while he still could. They said he seemed to be perfectly lucid and in his right mind. Excited at the prospect of the big adventure. And that he was in the company of a young man who, from the description they gave, she was able to identify as the person the company she'd engaged had sent as the main carer to her father. He'd helped her father to send her a selfie of the two of them together, cooking supper.

'She contacted the care company who confirmed that that particular young man hadn't worked for them for some time, although they'd been sending someone else. Then they said that her father himself had contacted them and said he had no further need of them. They couldn't get hold of her so they simply suspended their services and paused the billing until they could get in contact with her and get it all sorted out.

'So what d'you think, Miss Marple? Does it sound dodgy to you?'

'What I think is if anyone wrote that as a storyline for a book or a TV drama, no one would believe it.'

'So you'll put one of your team, at least, into taking a look at it? Because after all, an elderly and possibly vulnerable person could conceivably be at risk here. The house didn't sell for peanuts, for one thing, even at a bargain price. His daughter is worried that someone – perhaps the young man – has coerced him into selling the house and using his money to go swanning off round the world. Whilst, of course, paying all the expenses for his devoted young companion and carer.'

'We're at full stretch, as you know. But I'm already thinking of the negative press if we get this wrong and it's a serious case of elder abuse, extortion, and goodness knows what else. Possibly even something worse, if we don't know for certain where the father is, or even if he's still alive. Or what's happened to the money.

'I'll put one officer on it, for one day initially, until we see if there is a serious crime involved, since that's our remit. Best I can offer you, Kev, and it is a take it or leave it offer.'

'I'll take it, Ted, and thanks. All my instincts say there's something not right about this one.'

Yet another ping on Ted's phone as he headed back upstairs, this time an SMS, from Trev. Ted was surprised to see how late it was. He'd lost all track of time.

Trev was at the dojo, about to start the session for the youngsters. He'd attached a photo of young Flip, the boy Ted had met through one of his toughest cases, and who had come to idolise him.

Flip was looking straight at the camera, beaming with a big smile. He was wearing a new police cadet beret.

Trev had typed simply, 'This was Flip's news. He's so proud. Say something nice.'

Ted stopped where he was on the stairs. Despite everything he had going on, he had to smile. Flip was so determined he was going to follow in his hero Ted's footsteps by joining the police, and here he was, on his first step of the journey.

'Well done, Cadet Atkinson. Welcome to the family.'

* * *

The front door to the house burst open with such force that it flew back on its hinges and hit a wall, the extra sound reverberating throughout the quiet of early morning.

Heavy footsteps headed straight for the living room.

A voice bellowed, loud enough to be heard, no doubt, through the thin party walls to the next door semi.

'What the bloody hell have you done with my daughter, you stupid bitch?'

Carrie Fisher cringed back into the armchair where she'd once again spent a night of little sleep, just the occasional micro-nap from which she always snapped awake, heart thudding, swamped with yet more feelings of guilt and panic, listening out for the cry of a baby in the silent house.

Her liaison officer was still with her, because of serious concerns for her welfare if she was left alone. She'd also been catching what sleep she could, stretched out on the sofa with a blanket thrown over her. The instant she heard the door crash, she was on her feet and putting herself in front of the baby's mother to protect her.

'And why the fuck didn't you tell me? Why did I have to find out for myself seeing the news on the ferry? How could you lose her? How?'

'Mr Fisher, this isn't helping anyone ...' the officer began.

He swatted her out of his way with a vicious backhander which saw her trip and fall, banging her head on a low table. Despite it, she was instantly back on her feet, radio now in hand, calling for urgent assistance.

She wasn't in uniform. Didn't have any of the equipment she would have had. But she did have the training. In no time, she had the man immobilised, despite the blood now running down from a cut above one eye.

Carrie Fisher was shaking, crying, and whispering, 'I'm sorry, I'm sorry,' over and over.

She pulled her knees up to her chest, making herself as small as she could, wrapping her arms round them in defensive posture.

Fisher may have been physically restrained, but he wasn't done yet.

'I bet you were on the bloody phone, weren't you? Talking to one of your stupid bitch friends and not taking care of Evie? And then not telling me. Not even telling me she'd gone. Where is she? Where's my little girl?'

Then, as quickly as it had erupted, his anger evaporated and he started to sob. He visibly crumpled, only the officer's hold keeping him on his feet.

'I'm sorry, love, I'm so sorry. I know it wasn't your fault. Whatever happened, I know you would never have put our Evie at risk. I was just so bloody scared when I saw it on the telly on the boat. I couldn't believe it. I couldn't believe you hadn't told me.'

'I'm sorry, too. I should have told you. I just didn't want you driving back too fast, taking risks, if you were worried. I knew you wouldn't hear it on the radio. You never listen to the news. And I kept hoping against hope she'd turn up safe before you got back.'

'I'm sorry, officer, I should never have hit you. That's not me. I'm not a violent man. Especially not to women. The wife will tell you. I was just so scared. Am I going to be arrested?'

The officer was back on her radio, cancelling the back-up, assuring the call handler that the situation was now under control and assistance was no longer required. She let go of the man as she did so, keeping a careful eye on him.

As soon as he was released he dropped on his knees in front of his wife, holding out his arms to her. She moved into them without hesitation.

'I will have to report exactly what happened, Mr Fisher,' the officer told him. 'Any decision about prosecution will be up to someone more senior than me. The most important thing now is for you and your wife to support one another, while you leave the police to get on with the job of finding your daughter.'

Chapter Nine

Ted had asked the visiting Metropolitan Police officer, DI Oscar Smith, to arrive half an hour before morning briefing so they could have an exchange of ideas and information first. He was expecting an ex-military type to be prompt. Ted was, by his own admission, a bit obsessive about punctuality.

He was pleasantly surprised to find, when he arrived five minutes before the appointed time, a tall, bulky figure, dressed in a suit and sporting what looked like a regimental tie, waiting for him.

The man was finishing off a phone conversation in a foreign language, sounding impatient. Even without knowledge of the language, Ted could tell he was trying to end the call which he did, abruptly, seeing Ted approaching.

'Ted Darling, is it?' the man asked, stepping forward and holding a hand out for a shake in greeting. 'Oscar Smith.'

Ted immediately noticed two things about the man. Firstly that the back of the outstretched hand was covered in fine lacerations which could only have been inflicted by an angry cat, as Ted knew to his cost. The second thing was the unmistakable strong odour of TCP hovering round him.

'It is, yes, but I'm the old-fashioned sort who likes to keep things formal in the workplace, please.'

He shook the hand which was offered, somehow not surprised to find something of an Alpha male-establishing grip going on. Ted hoped DI Smith was going to be professional and that he wouldn't have to waste time asserting himself in the pecking order.

He handed the man his security pass then led the way upstairs to his own small office. A few of the team were in early, already at their desks. Ted didn't bother with introductions. He'd save that for when everyone arrived for morning briefing, which they'd need to hold in a larger room downstairs. With more officers being drafted in from other stations all the time to help, it would be too crowded now in the main office. It would also mean some faces Ted didn't yet know himself.

'There's going to have to be a fair bit of hot desking now our numbers are going up, so I can't for the moment say where you'll be installed. You're welcome to share a corner of my desk for now, as I'm currently in and out of meetings rather a lot.

'I'm particularly interested in the details surrounding your two bodies found in cars and what, if any, definite connections you've been able to establish between them and the missing children.'

'What were the PM results of yours?' Smith asked him.

'It's not yet been done. It's tomorrow morning, break of dawn, which is when our Home Office pathologist likes to begin complicated cases.'

'D'you want me to attend? Having been to both of ours, I might perhaps have some useful input for him.'

Ted hoped the gender assumption was not indicative of any lurking misogyny in Smith. He also smiled to himself at the mere thought of this somewhat brash incomer telling Professor Nelson anything.

'It might well be useful for you to be there. Our pathologist is Professor Elizabeth Nelson. Where are you staying? D'you want picking up?'

'They've put me in a budget B&B,' Smith told him with a grimace. 'I need to walk a lot at the moment. I'm trying to get back into better shape. So if you tell me where to go, I'll head straight there on foot and maybe catch a lift back here from you afterwards, if that suits?'

'That's fine. So, what about your victims in the cars?'

'Probably not entirely innocent victims,' Smith told him. 'We have strong reason to believe in both cases that they were the people who did the actual baby-snatching, then handed the child on to someone else, presumably for delivery.

'PM results showed that both were heavily drugged shortly before they died, spiked with a rape drug variant, so they were unconscious but still alive when the fire was started. It was the fire which actually killed them.

'The other significant factor was that both the women had given birth themselves not all that long ago. Two months, in one case, three and a half for the other. Our working hypothesis on that was that their own kids were being held hostage to force them to comply in snatching others. And neither was of British origin. One was from the Philippines, the other from Sudan. Not on any records anywhere that we've found to date, so probably illegals.'

'In other words, almost certainly victims themselves,' Ted told him, with a note of mild rebuke. 'Possibly trafficked into the country, and their own babies used to coerce them into snatching others. In those circumstances, they would probably do anything. They were then clearly murdered when their services were no longer needed, and presumably no trace of their own children?'

'We've not even looked for them. They may not even be

in the country, and we haven't the manpower to go chasing about looking for them.

'What about your torched car? Any ID on that which leads anywhere? Ours were on false plates and the VINs were unreadable.'

'We're waiting on the details for ours but we might be luckier as our fire was extinguished reasonably quickly. So where are you up to with tracing the babies you're looking for? Any solid thoughts or leads on that?'

'I'd say it's unlikely in the extreme that they're staying in the country, although I'm still keeping an open mind to that possibility. Again, we're working on the probability that they're being taken abroad, as soon as possible. Major airports are unlikely. All that hanging around with a possibly screaming kid could attract attention, and we know that airport security has never been tighter. With so much press and media coverage of the kidnaps, on the law of averages, we'd be getting swamped with reports on any baby that stood out in any way.

'The same goes for the major Channel ports. So much queuing, heightened security. Not the ideal for smuggling babies out of the country. I've read your reports, like you'll have read ours, so we know the initial snatch appears to have been done by stuffing the kid inside a bulky coat. Do that for any prolonged period and the thing would likely suffocate or die of dehydration. Even if the mules have not a shred of compassion, it's a valuable commodity they don't want to lose.'

Ted leaned back in his chair and looked at the officer sitting opposite him. He didn't want to start their working relationship appearing to nitpick, but he believed that correct personal pronouns were important, always, to show respect.

He strongly disliked the use of the word "thing" or the pronoun "it" in the context. He'd better lay a few ground rules before he let Smith talk to the rest of the team. Ted would never allow any of them to get away with referring to any crime victim in such a disrespectful way.

'A word about personal pronouns, DI Smith. We try to stay respectful in the team, which means using appropriate ones. And "it" is never appropriate when speaking of any person. "They", please, especially in regard to missing babies, or where you don't know a person's pronoun of choice.

'I have a bit of a thing about respect, and that includes a strong no swearing rule in the workplace.'

He didn't miss the eye roll his comments produced but didn't pursue it. The man was here to liaise, nothing more, and his enquiries were further on, so he might well have valuable input.

'Noted,' was Smith's only comment, then he went on, 'We've been favouring the idea that the kids have been taken out of the country either by private plane or possibly even on a yacht. That's what my team are working on at the moment, and obviously they'll keep me posted.'

'Thank you. We'd better go and join the others now. Before we do, though, who won?'

Smith frowned.

Ted nodded towards the injured hand and smiled as he asked, 'You or the cat?'

Smith laughed at that then replied, 'Me, just, on points. I wasn't sure how long I'd be up here so I thought it best to shove my moggy into the cattery. He was not impressed.

'You know about cats then, if you recognised cat scratches. It could have been from gardening. Roses fighting back.'

Ted smiled back at him, glad of some connection to be made, at least.

'I have seven of them at home. Do you have children of your own? I'm not prying. I feel it's valuable knowledge from a welfare point of view on a case like this.'

'One, somewhere, allegedly, although I don't know if it's ...' he corrected himself quickly, 'they're a boy or a child. But seven cats? That's something.'

Smith was still shaking his head and repeating 'Seven' in a disbelieving tone as he followed Ted out of the main office and down the stairs.

The room was filling up. Anyone with any involvement in the case was there, already including some officers drafted in from other stations.

Mike Hallam walked up to the boss with an officer Ted didn't know.

'Boss, this is DC Whittaker, he's joining us from Bolton. Chris, this is DCI Darling, who's SIO on this case.'

'Good to have you with us, DC Whittaker. We need every available officer on this one. We're up against the clock.'

'Happy to help in any way I can, sir,' the DC told him. 'More than happy going round on the knock. I like walking, and people will generally talk to me. It's the Mel Gibson looks that does it.'

He said it with a straight face but Ted took it for what it was. Copper's humour. The thing which got them through the worst cases that faced them. Ironic, irreverent, but never disrespectful.

'Boss, I have an update,' Mike Hallam told him. 'Well, something to flag up, really, but it could be significant. Can I start with that?'

Ted first introduced DI Oscar Smith to those present and explained his liaison role, then Mike Hallam began.

'The missing baby's father arrived home in the early hours. The mother, Carrie Fisher, had consistently refused to let him know what had happened. Probably hoping baby Evie would be found before he got back. But he'd seen the news on TV on the ferry, while he was having a drink and a meal, so he must have tripped every speed camera on the return route because he arrived back much earlier than expected. Dropped his rig off at his workplace, jumped into his car, raced round to the house and burst in, shouting the odds and demanding to know what was going on. When the liaison officer tried to intervene to calm things down, he backhanded her, knocked her to the ground. She cut her head on a table, but luckily nothing serious.

'She reported that the angry outburst was over as soon as he did that, and he did seem genuinely remorseful. She also said the wife hadn't shown any sign of being afraid of him or fearful of his return, until that happened. But it does now raise the question of was the relationship quite as harmonious as we've thought up to now or are we back to the possibility of something going on behind the scenes?'

'What's the family situation behind your two cases, DI Smith? Any signs of friction in the family there?' Ted asked him.

'None at all,' Smith told him. 'And we did dig, very deep, on the basis that it wouldn't be the first time someone had come up with such a scheme for some reason.'

'DS Hallam, can you put someone onto checking with the neighbours, especially next door both sides, to find out how harmonious the family home really is. DC Whittaker, that might be one for you, given your attributes. And where are we up to with the mother's medical records? Any sign there of domestic abuse or anything out of the ordinary?'

'Still chasing those, boss, for both the parents, just in case, but you know how long these things can take. And then there's the PR nightmare,' Mike Hallam went on. 'Are we going to charge him with assaulting a police officer? The liaison officer is very experienced. She's convinced it was a one-off. Would a charge be in the public interest? I suppose the same goes for any speeding fines he might get. The newspaper headlines for that wouldn't be ideal, from a PR point of view.'

'Same rules as for any other case. Get a report put together and we'll see whether further action would be the right way to go, or not.'

'Why didn't he just phone?' DI Oscar Smith asked. 'As soon as he saw on the telly that his kid had disappeared, why didn't he just phone his wife to find out what was going on? He'd be looking at driving time of, what, six hours, from the Channel ports? More if there were hold-ups, like getting off the ferry and clearing customs, for one thing. So why the f ...'

He caught himself just in time, remembering the DCI's little pep talk earlier on. Switched horses in midstream with a barely perceptible break.

' ...flippin' heck didn't he just phone her? To ask for an update, at least, and to offer her some words of comfort? So maybe yours really is different to ours in that in this case, the husband knows a lot more than you think he does at the moment.'

Jo Rodriguez answered that.

'I doubt any of us know how we would react in circumstances like that. Not rationally, for sure. I have six kids to keep an eye on and I know the wife and I have snapped at one another on occasion if one of them has wandered out of sight for even a minute. It's a reflex thing, sometimes. People can often turn on the one they're closest to first.'

Ted asked DI Smith to fill everyone in on the theories his team were working on about getting a missing child out of the country, adding a note of caution.

'Baby Evie might, of course, already be long gone. If these people are as slick as they appear to be, she could be abroad by now.'

Smith gave all the details he had, adding in turn, 'If they're taking them abroad, they will have had a forged passport sorted for them from the moment they were told about the next target. And they'll have got that from whoever their eyes on the ground was. You're lucky that you got the lead about the so-called photographer. We've had less luck in finding who their scout was for ours. The cover stories were different, for a start. But you might get somewhere with that one.

'The thing working in our favour is that these are very young babies, so statistically, there won't be that many of them passing through any exit points. Hopefully. So there is a chance, staying on the optimistic side, that even if they have left the country, we could still trace where they went to and try to follow up from there.

'The other point we considered is one of, er, ethnicity.'

Oscar Smith was surprising himself by his efforts to try to stay politically correct. It was alien to him, but having had one jerk on his chain already by the diminutive DCI, he was trying to stay the right side of the line.

'The two women who died in our car fires, who we

presume to be the snatchers, weren't IC1. One possible reason for them to be disposed of, apart from risking revealing the identity of the people behind all this, is that they might well draw more attention to themselves from Border Control simply through travelling with a baby of, for want of a different expression, a different colour to themselves. For this to work, they'd need to be as anonymous as possible.

'I'm betting that the PM on your fire victim tomorrow will also reveal something other than Northern European ethnicity.'

'So we need to be looking at private travel out of the country as well as commercial,' Ted told them. 'That does make sense, if the children are being taken abroad for whatever reason. Who's on passenger manifest checks?'

Steve Ellis spoke up, less hesitant than he used to be in front of strangers.

'I am, sir, and I've already made a start on private aircraft passengers. Some fly from Manchester Airport, but also from Manchester Barton, so I'm checking both for any sign of a young baby listed. Nothing so far'

'Good work, Steve, thank you. Right, everyone, let's get back to it. I'm open to any suggestions anyone has to make, but let's aim to get at least one solid lead today. Remember, the more time goes by with no news, the less hopeful the outcome is.

'Virgil, I've got something new I want you to take time today to look into, as a priority. It's another Misper report, but an older adult this time. Inspector Turner asked me to at least do a bit of digging as something is certainly a bit odd about the sound of it. If you go and find him, he'll fill you in with all the details. Spend some time on it today, see what you think, then report back to me, please.'

Smith couldn't disguise his look of surprise at the pleases and thank yous. He couldn't remember any occasion when he'd used either to any of his team.

Once the briefing wound up, some of the team headed back to their desks, others going straight out on the actions already allocated to them by Mike Hallam. When Ted and Oscar Smith went back up to the main office together, Steve was already back at his computer, head down, absorbed.

'I could murder a coffee by now,' Smith said, looking hopefully round the room.

Ted said nothing, interested to see how the man operated.

'Steve, is it?' DI Smith asked, immediately picking the person who seemed to be the youngest on the team, as well as the one who probably wouldn't say boo to the proverbial goose. 'Any chance of a coffee? Strong, black, no sugar.'

The Steve Ellis of old would have turned bright red, jumped to his feet and complied with the request of a visiting ranking officer from the Met. But the old Steve had disappeared. Ever since he'd arrested his own abusive, bullying, police sergeant father, Steve had found an assertiveness he never knew he possessed.

His expression was pleasant, his tone perfectly polite as he replied, 'Every chance, sir. You'll find everything you need on the table in the corner there. There's an honesty jar to put your subs in, and there's a list there of what everyone else drinks.'

Jezza Vine had come up to her desk to collect her things before going out. She couldn't contain a loud snort of laughter at Steve's response. Ted stayed silent, interested once more in how Smith would react.

After a long pause, the Met officer said, 'Fair enough,

then, but I'll have to put a note in the honesty jar for now. I don't carry cash these days. Not after my pocket got picked one time.'

Chapter Ten

'DC Whittaker, Greater Manchester Police. Do you have a few minutes to answer a couple of questions, please?'

The newcomer to the enquiry team held up his ID to the woman who had just opened the door to him. It was the semi-detached house adjoining where Carrie Fisher and her husband lived. If anyone might be aware of a lack of harmony within that household, it would be the resident sharing the partition wall.

It was all quiet there at the moment. No sign of anyone, inside or outside. So far, the press and media didn't seem to have got hold of the address. All to the good. If the husband was indeed violent, nothing would be more likely to provoke an outburst than finding the press pack camped on his doorstep.

The woman who had opened up in response to the ring on the doorbell looked to be in her sixties. She held the door open and indicated for him to enter.

'This is my daughter's house, not mine,' she began by explaining. 'I'm just round here minding my little grandson while she's gone to the dentist. She's got to have a big root canal job, poor thing. Come in, if you can cope with a very inquisitive little boy.'

He might be wasting his time here, if the woman didn't live in the house, Chris thought to himself, but it was always worth a shot.

As if reading his thoughts, the woman showed him into a bright and pleasant front room, where a small boy was happily spreading toys in all directions over the carpet, then asked, 'Is it about the poor little missing baby from next door?

'My daughter and I saw it on the news and knew who she was, straight away. Such a terrible thing. I spend a lot of time here looking after Samuel so my daughter can go out and do things. I also prefer it to being in my flat by myself. Is there any news of little Evie yet?

'Oh, sorry, excuse me, please sit down, officer. I'll just move some of Samuel's things. Do you want a cup of tea?'

'No tea, thank you, Mrs …?'

'Ardern. Pamela. This is my daughter's house. Julia Ardern. She kept her maiden name. This is her son, Samuel, and I'm afraid he might start climbing all over you shortly. He's very inquisitive. What can I help you with?'

'Evie is still missing so we're trying to build up as complete a picture as possible of the background to this case. Do you know the parents at all?'

'Yes, a lovely young couple. They were so pleased to show Evie to us when she was born. We see them all quite often. Such a happy little new family.'

Her expression turned shrewd as she asked, 'I suppose this is about early this morning? When Dave got back from his latest run? The shouting?'

The little boy was trying to climb onto the sofa next to Chris, eyes fixed on the pen with which he was taking notes. The woman stood up to scoop him out of the way and plonk him back amidst his toys.

'He'll be back in a minute, I'm afraid. I'll have to keep distracting him.'

'Did you see Dave Fisher arrive back?'

The toddler was already on the move again, heading straight for the visitor. Pamela Ardern took a moment to distract him by pulling a little wooden train around whilst making appropriate noises.

She looked up and went on, 'Sorry. I don't even know why we make that choo-choo sound these days. It's only the old steam trains that sounded like that. Anyway, see Dave get home, no. But I certainly heard him. My bedroom is against the dividing wall, at the front of the house, and I woke with a start because there was such a crash.'

'D'you often stay over, Mrs Ardern?'

'Pam, please. If you're allowed to be informal. I've never been interviewed by the police before. And yes, quite often. My daughter gets home late quite a lot of the time when she has me babysitting, and she knows I don't like going back to the flat alone at night, so I stay here.'

'What does your daughter do for a living, Pam? Just for the record.'

'Something clever with computers, but no matter how often she tells me, I still don't fully understand. The simplified version is that for any workplace that's having problems with its systems, she goes in and makes everything work again.'

'So you heard a crash, which woke you up. Anything after that?'

'A lot of angry shouting. I think someone must have left the front door open because I didn't hear it close and I could hear the voices clearly enough, even though I couldn't make out what they were saying. Then there was a bit of a thump, which sounded like some furniture falling over, and then it all went quiet again.

'The poor man, though, it must have been terrible, being out of the country and hearing his baby had disappeared. I can understand why it might have got a bit heated to start with, in the circumstances. Everyone's nerves must be frayed by now.'

'Have you heard raised voices next door before now?'

She shook her head emphatically, once again using distraction techniques on the toddler.

'Oh, no, far from it. They always seem like such a lovely couple. Supportive of one another and so proud and loving with little Evie. We go round there most days, just to say hello. Samuel's unusual for such a little boy in that he loves to go and see the baby. He's very gentle and loving. Moves his little head in so carefully sideways so he can give her a kiss. He'll make a lovely dad one day when he grows up, I'm sure.

'Whenever we see the mum and dad together they look so happy, wrapped up in the new baby. I can't imagine how they must be feeling now. And him being away when it happened. He must have been beside himself by the time he got back. I think a bit of shouting might be normal in such circumstances. All that pent-up anxiety. Carrie never seems to be worried by Dave at all. I do hope you can find the little one, soon.'

'Just one more thing, Pam. I know a new baby can be a big expense. Do they seem to be managing?'

'Well, we're not the sort of neighbours who ask one another about their financial affairs. But I get the impression that Dave is quite well paid for his lorry driving. He would need to be, I would say, to voluntarily be going away for days at a time with a new baby he clearly dotes on. And they do seem to have all the very latest and best things for her.

107

That's why I was surprised to see the hand-me-down pram. It is a beauty, though, and I can understand the advantages of it if you have nice places to go for walks with a new baby. Without having to get the car out.'

Then she frowned as she went on, 'Except of course, it wasn't a safe place. But it should have been. A mother would expect to be able to take her baby to a local park and for both of them to come home safely.

'I hope you find that poor little child soon, and catch the people behind such a wicked crime.'

Wherever he went and whoever he asked, Chris Whittaker received the same response. The new parents seemed happy and both besotted with their baby daughter. No one had anything bad to say about either of them. Not even the sort of snide sideways digs people liked to trot out at such moments. 'No smoke without fire'. 'I always thought there was something not quite right about him/her'. 'They were splashing the cash on all the best clothes and things for her. How were they paying for that?' No matter how much walking and turning on the charm he employed, the answer was always the same. A loving, devoted couple, enjoying their first baby together.

* * *

'Mrs Berry? Detective Constable Tibbs, Greater Manchester Police. I'm here about your report of your father going missing.'

Virgil had phoned ahead to ask to see the woman. She met him in the bar area of the hotel where she was staying, near to the station.

She looked pleasantly surprised.

'A detective? I wasn't sure this would be taken seriously, but I'm pleased that it is. I thought the police would simply write it off as an old man splurging all his money on one last big adventure while he can. And probably thinking I was the jealous, money-grabbing daughter not wanting to see him spending my inheritance.

'It's Doctor Berry, to be picky, but I'm not, so please call me Alison. There's the makings of tea and coffee available here, if you'd like something? It's drinkable, but that's all I can say for it.'

Virgil shook his head in response, then asked if she minded him recording their conversation.

'No problem, and I am very grateful you've at least come to see me. I've seen on the news how busy you are with this little baby who's been kidnapped. I can't imagine how that must be for the parents. Is there any news?'

'Nothing yet. So, your father. John Berry, I see from your initial report.'

'I use my maiden name. Not to blow my own trumpet, but my late husband and I were both fairly well known in our individual specialities, which complement one another, so it made sense for me to do that, to avoid confusion.

'As for my father, my concern isn't about his money, except in the sense that I don't like to think that he might have been conned out of it by someone ruthless. I was out of contact with him for a couple of months, which I know can seem like an eternity to a lonely old man, but my dad simply isn't like that. I always joked that he has more of a social life than I have, with my work. And I'd told him I would be unreachable at times, and explained why. He was fully supportive, as ever.

'His mind is still sharp. He plays chess to a high standard, usually twice a week, as well as whist, for amusement and the social contact. He reads avidly. A library member who goes to all the events they put on. Talks, debates, film shows. He has very wide interests.'

'Yet you felt the need to employ a carer for him whilst you were away,' Virgil said, posing it more as a question than a statement.

'It's quite hard to find the right person for what I wanted. Dad still has absolutely all his marbles but he can be a little bit of an absent minded professor type, who can forget to eat if not reminded. He's very gregarious, though, and loves entertaining. So it's a dream job for someone. Go round at midday, watch and pass things while he cooks, enjoy a nice meal and some good conversation. Then help with the washing up, do a bit of tidying around, and generally make sure dad was all right.'

'That sounds like a nice job. I can imagine carers lining up for that. Did you advertise?'

'I did all of this in consultation with my father, although he kept saying it wasn't necessary and he would be fine. In the end I decided to go through an agency, because I imagined they would vet their employees, and if there were any niggles, they would at least be on hand to deal with them.'

'And, forgive the personal questions, but who was paying for this?'

'I was, because it was my idea, but it's true that my dad is more than comfortably off. His late brother was a financial advisor, so he helped make sure dad would be all right after he retired. Dad was also a doctor, a GP, so not exactly rolling in it, but not living in poverty either.'

'I understand the house was worth a fair bit. And

presumably no outstanding mortgage on it?'

'Exactly so. House prices have gone up beyond recognition since dad bought it. Especially a nice property like his. I was shocked to hear what he sold it for, though. He could have got a lot more, but it seems to have been a knockdown price for a quick cash buyer. Very quick indeed. That's one of the things which worries me the most. That and the fact that, when I contacted the agency to find out what they knew, they told me my father had effectively sacked them. That was shortly before I was out of contact with him and he never said a thing about it to me. That was very unusual in itself. He's not like that.'

'Do you have brothers and sisters? And is your mother still around?'

She shook her head.

'Mum died when I was ten. I'm an only child. That's another thing about this carer which worries me. Mum was carrying a child. She was killed in a road accident. A drunken driver, ignoring a red light at a pedestrian crossing. She died instantly. The baby too. She and dad had been trying for ages for a second child. It was a little boy. They were planning to call him Simon.

'Dad has never been the sentimental sort. No room for it in the medical profession. But he was clearly touched by the carer. He said he was called Massimo, because his mother was Italian, but he always called himself Simon. Simon Ropley. I think that struck a chord with possibly the one sentimental fibre my father has in his body.

'Look, officer, I know all of this must sound very trivial in comparison to a tiny baby being kidnapped. But I am genuinely worried about dad. I can't get hold of him. His phone seems to be out of service. He's not contacted me and

I have no idea where he is.'

'I understand that. Based on everything you've told me, subject to me checking a few details for myself, I'm going to go back to the station and tell my senior officer that I think this might well be a case where a serious crime has potentially been committed, so it will need further investigation. If you give me your father's phone number, I might be able to see where and when it was last used, as a starting point.'

* * *

Sharing work space with someone the size of Oscar Smith only served to emphasise how compact Ted's office was. The two of them were going over every detail of their respective cases looking for any similarities, not yet picked up, which could point them in a new direction.

Smith was surprisingly organised and methodical in his work, with an eye for detail and a formidable memory bordering on total recall. Apart from the occasional unfortunate way of phrasing something, readily corrected as soon as he saw Ted's look of disapproval, he was so far not living up to the reputation which had preceded him.

There was a brief tap at the door, which was closed to allow them both to concentrate on the task in hand, followed by Jo Rodriguez stepping inside.

'Boss, a glimmer of something, at last. A very fractious small baby at the airport. Actually in departures. Someone who'd seen the news phoned in to report it. A girl, she said. She was suspicious because the woman holding her didn't seem to be able to do a thing with her. Now, that might not be significant. One of my brood was like that with my wife.

Only dad would do at bedtime, which was tricky, with my job.

'Uniform are on their way to check it out. Mike Hallam's following on, just in case it could be Evie.'

Oscar Smith looked up hopefully as Jo withdrew, shutting the door behind him.

'Are we going? If it's your missing kiddy, there's a chance of a live lead back to the kidnappers, if we can get to the couriers before they start with the 'no comment' stuff.'

'And if it's a genuine family going on holiday with a little one that's, I don't know, teething or something, there's a greater chance of clicking phones spreading our public humiliation all over social media and beyond. It won't help either the case or our image.

'We'll put an alert out for the airport authorities not to allow them to board, pending enquiries, then we'll leave it to Uniform and to Mike for now. It's on me if I've got it wrong. If and when they report back that there's any suggestion of a serious crime connection, we'll pick up from there.'

Chapter Eleven

Ted knew that inevitably, someone with Oscar Smith's reputation and history would start to push boundaries to test them for weaknesses. He hadn't expected the first attempt to come so soon.

Ignoring everything that Ted had just said, Smith got up, went to the door, put his hand on the doorknob and started to open it, saying, 'Can't hurt to have someone senior from Serious Crime on scene. The Woodentops can't always be trusted to ask the right sort of questions.'

He'd barely finished speaking before Ted was out from behind his desk, a foot flying up to slam the door shut from Smith's grip.

Ted regretted his loss of control the minute it happened. He hadn't done that for a long time and had vowed not to do so again. But he'd needed to make the point, as firmly as necessary, that he was the boss and he didn't expect to have his orders challenged. His instinct told him that if he didn't stamp his authority from the start with Smith, their relationship was simply not going to be a workable one.

Ted was nothing if not stubborn. He didn't want to join the ranks of those who'd given in and sent Smith packing. At least not until he'd had a chance to see some of the qualities the man's senior officer said he possessed.

Smith looked down at him from the advantage of his greater height and seemed, if anything, mildly amused as he replied, in a distinctively ironic tone, 'Fair enough ... sir.'

They both retook their seats. Ted paused a moment to regain his composure before he went on.

'Firstly, DI Smith, within this station, we show respect to one another, from all branches. That begins with referring to our colleagues from Uniform as precisely that, and never by any derogatory or inappropriate term.

'Secondly, I'm SIO on this case. That means I make the decisions, and I deal with the consequences if I'm wrong. If you disagree with something, you're welcome to make your case. But don't, please, ignore my instructions and go off on a maverick mission. It's not how we work.

'Are we clear?'

'As crystal, guv,' Smith told him, again with a distinctly sardonic note.

It would have to do for now. Ted had neither the time nor the patience to deal with attitude in an officer who was old enough and senior enough to know better. Especially one from a military background who should be used to accepting orders without question.

Smith's mobile phone had gone off a few times since he'd been in the office. Each time he'd simply glanced at the screen then dismissed the call.

As a bit of a white flag gesture, Ted told him, 'If that's important, DI Smith, feel free to take it.'

'It's personal, though, not work.'

'All the same, if it's something that needs dealing with ... otherwise it will be a preoccupation you could do without.'

Smith surprised him with his question in response.

'D'you speak German, guv?'

Ted shook his head.

'I'm rubbish at languages. Best I can do is count to ten in

115

Welsh.'

'I'll take it then, thanks.'

Smith stood up, stepped away a few feet and turned his back while he made a call. It was as much intimacy as was possible in the confined space.

He seemed to be having trouble getting a word in edgeways with whoever he was speaking to. Ted took the opportunity to fire off a quick text to Trev to tell him he almost certainly wouldn't make karate that evening, to apologise and to make his usual promise to make amends when he could.

Smith finally managed to say something, then ended his call and sat down.

'Sorry about that. My grandmother, in Germany. She's a bit of a character. Doesn't always get on with the carers I find for her. She keeps firing them, then I have to phone them, smooth things over, and ask them to stay on. I think we're sorted now – at least for today.

'By the way, I was going to ask you if there's a decent pub nearby to get lunch. Perhaps I could buy you a pint.'

'There is. The hotpot is very good. But I prefer it if the public don't see local officers boozing it up in a pub while we have such a high profile and sensitive case unsolved.'

Smith spread his hands in mock innocence.

'A pint of lemonade, I was meaning, but fair enough.'

Ted decided he better hold out an olive branch. It might be an idea to at least have a quick one with the Met officer, to see if they could find some common ground. Especially as he'd already let Trev know he'd be late.

'But I'll take a swift one with you in The Grapes when we knock off this evening. The landlord's ex-Army, so you might get on.

'So, now you've had chance to go through our case notes, what's striking you as the main differences and similarities between our cases?'

'You had your dodgy photographer as the scout; in both our cases it was "friends" trying to find someone they were supposed to meet but they couldn't spot them in the places where they'd been looking. A man both times, but nothing in his story to raise red flags. He was perfectly plausible: the people he spoke to all said that. Well turned out, polite, quietly spoken. A doting godfather about to meet his newish baby god-daughter in the flesh for the first time, but he wasn't familiar with his surroundings and had got a bit confused. And of course, he'd forgotten to bring his mobile so he couldn't simply phone his supposed niece, the baby's mother. He said he was looking for a young mother with a very pretty small baby girl, and they were supposed to be meeting up in a park. All seemingly perfectly innocent.'

'Do people still fall for that sort of thing?' Ted asked in surprise. 'We thought our photographer was just about plausible, but that yarn sounds a bit far-fetched, surely?'

'You know how it is with conmen. To be any good at it they need to be able to charm the birds out of the trees. And some of them are very good at it.

'The chance of tracing our look-outs is far lower than yours, I would say. A photographer, flashing the cash, is bound to stick in people's minds a bit more than a doting godfather. If nothing else, people might be keeping an eye out for them in the hopes of getting a bit of that money themselves. And our godfather seems to have been so plausible. We didn't get any decent ID hits at all. What was produced could have been any actor from an older film. Well dressed, neat hair, well spoken, no distinguishing features at all.'

Oscar Smith made sense when he talked about work, Ted thought to himself. He was beginning to get a feel for why his results were so good. His powers of observation and attention to detail were excellent. If he could keep his undesirable traits firmly under control, he was clearly going to be able to add something useful to their investigations. The 'if' remained a big one, though.

'So what else struck you, as the main similarities or differences between the MOs in yours and ours? Anything we've not yet touched on.'

'One thing, for sure. Something which might lead us somewhere. Sorry if I'm teaching granny egg-sucking here, but you may or may not know that in the criminal world, there's a considerable amount of pride amongst the skilled service providers, as you might call them. The forgers, for instance, and there will certainly be some of those involved in both our cases, for the false papers for the sprogs.'

Ted let that one go. He didn't want to spend the whole time pulling the man up on his choice of vocabulary, especially as it was just the two of them in the office.

'There's also the ones supplying false plates for cars, plus doing things like rendering the original vehicle ID number unreadable and supplying a false one. I think we both know it's a racing certainty the car used in your case and later torched will have had the full treatment to anonymize it. And if it's the same slick outfit on your case as on ours, that will have been done by someone skilled at their craft, probably local to you.

'Now, it just so happens that we have probably the best in the country at supplying anonymous vehicles on our manor. Rain Man, we call him. He's what they used to call an idiot savant.'

He made exaggerated quotes in the air with his fingers as he went on.

'On the spectrum, we have to call it now. Rain Man knows more about cars, especially dodgy ones, than anyone you've ever encountered, I can guarantee you that. And people like him take a huge amount of pride in the work they do. So they know who their rivals are, and what their work is like. Countrywide. Especially him, because that's absolutely all he has in his life. It's a total obsession. And the best thing about ours is he tells us things. Anything we ask him. He's pathologically incapable of lying to us, nor even of refusing to answer. We ask, he tells us.'

Ted frowned at that.

'How is he still alive, never mind in business, in that case? Surely everyone who knows him must know he's an informant? So why is he still employed by them? And why hasn't he gone down for doing what he does?'

'We've had endless case conferences with CPS about him. It's always come down to "not in the public interest". He'd admit to anything and everything that was put to him. He's like that. Anything. Seriously. Even cases from before he was born.'

'So what's the relevance to our case? Are you saying that he could identify whoever did the plate and the VIN for the vehicle used here? Has he not done that already for you, and did it not lead you anywhere?'

'He has done, in a sense. He did both the vehicles used in our cases himself. But the trail he set us on, and like I've said, he's pathologically incapable of lying, didn't lead us anywhere we wanted to go. It took us to brokers, you might call them. Middle men. Their job is to source the cleanest cars and sell them on to whoever needs them, with a solid guarantee of silence. Those bastards definitely don't squeal. They know they'd lose their lives, never mind their job, if they did.

'They're paid well enough that they don't mind going down for the odd stretch. They know their family will be taken care of while they're away, and no one will be allowed to muscle in on their territory while they're inside.

'I've been round in person to see most of them at some time, and I can be very persuasive when the occasion calls for it, believe you me. I've hauled every one of them in for interview and had the sum total of jack shit for my pains. Every time.'

'What are you suggesting?'

'If you give the green light, I could send one of my team round to see Rain Man, with photos of your torched car, the false plates, and whatever was done to the VIN to make it untraceable. There's a chance – a slim one, but what else have you got? – that he will recognise the work. It could even be his own. He will tell us what he knows, without fail. Isn't it worth a shot?'

'It's just hearsay, though, surely? I'm assuming we couldn't put him up as a prosecution witness, if we needed to?'

Smith let out a loud snort of derision.

'God, no. I doubt CPS would countenance it. But it might just, in a roundabout way, tell us if our cases are connected by a common supplier of dodgy motors and that might just possibly rattle some skeletons out of cupboards.'

Ted leaned back in his chair while he considered. On the face of it, it was further off piste than he preferred to go. But anything which might lead them closer to baby Evie, while there was still the possibility of finding her alive, couldn't be dismissed.

He nodded his head.

'Do it. We should be getting the photos any time now. They may already be in. So send them to your team, see what your informant can tell you, if anything. We'll keep our fingers crossed.

'Just one more thing, though. Can we please refer to this person by his real name, especially in front of the team. Rain Man has derogatory overtones. Not suitable for briefings, certainly.'

Ted was thinking in particular of Jezza and her younger brother, Tommy. Jezza tended to have a low flashpoint around anything to do with people on the spectrum.

This time Smith's eye roll was unmistakable as he replied, 'Whatever you say, guv. Barry George Stephens it shall be.'

* * *

Two uniformed police officers were walking slowly through the departures lounge at Manchester Airport's Terminal 2. Their eyes were everywhere but their ears had already picked up the likely cause of the reports. A small baby was crying non-stop at the top of clearly considerable lung power.

They made their way over to seats near the window, where a harassed-looking young woman was doing her best to quieten the child, so far with no sign of success.

PC Julie Holt stopped and crouched down in front of the mother and child, smiling pleasantly.

'Oh dear, someone's not looking forward to their trip,'

she said, a note of sympathy in her voice. 'Is everything all right? Teething?'

The woman shook her head, her stress evident in her expression.

'I don't think she can be. She's only three months.'

PC Holt's eyes widened in genuine surprise.

'Three months? Gosh, she's a big baby then. I thought she was at least four.'

The mother's smile was rueful.

'She was always big. I was like an elephant carrying her, and she's always looked older than she is. I've no idea why. As you can see, me and my husband aren't big at all. It must be genes from further back.'

'She's gorgeous. What's her name?'

'Amelia Grace.'

'How lovely! Where are you heading to?'

The officer asked the question, although clearly she and her colleague already knew the flight's destination. She was making seemingly light conversation whilst the other officer was carefully watching the reactions of both the adults with the baby.

'Alicante. My parents live there and they've not yet met their granddaughter. Well, not in the flesh, and they're dying to cuddle her, instead of just looking at her on a phone screen.'

The husband was staring at them, open hostility on his face. Eventually, he spoke.

'You think we kidnapped her, don't you? You think she's the missing baby. The one that was snatched from the park. We've seen all about that, on the telly. You couldn't find her so you're just going round randomly accusing people with young babies of being the kidnappers.'

The male officer spoke to him, keeping his tone polite and calm.

'Just doing our jobs, sir. We had a report of a seemingly distressed baby in the departure lounge, of approximately the right age, so clearly we needed to check. Do you have anything to show that this is your baby?'

The mother looked shocked, but then said, 'I've got her passport, of course.'

Her husband scoffed.

'They won't accept that, they'll say it's a forgery.'

He reached in his pocket for his mobile phone, tapping swiftly and efficiently to find his photos. He flicked through then held it up so the two officers could clearly see the screen as he said, 'Here you go. Just born. Cord still attached. You can see that's my wife. If you look closely, you can see that Amelia has a tiny coffee stain birthmark, on the side of her neck, there.'

He zoomed in on the photo as he went on, 'You can see she still has it. The photo's date stamped too, of course, so you can see when she was born. It said on the TV that the missing baby is three months. Amelia's three months, even though she looks older. You can see that she looks a lot bigger. This is our baby, not the missing one.'

Julie Holt straightened up and smiled at them both, hoping to defuse the rising tension.

'Thank you both very much for your cooperation, and sorry to have troubled you. I hope Amelia settles down soon and hopefully sleeps on the flight. Her grandparents are going to love her. How could they not? Safe journey.'

The two officers moved away to a quiet corner, then Julie radioed in.

'False alarm on the baby at the airport. It's definitely not baby Evie.'

Chapter Twelve

'Thanks for finding the time to talk to me, Mrs Mason,' Virgil Tibbs began, sitting down opposite the manager of the care providers who had previously been looking after the man, John Berry, now reported as missing.

'We were very concerned about Mr Berry when he phoned to cancel the carer we were sending. He's a lovely man. Sharp as anything, but I know his daughter was worried he might forget to eat, left to himself.'

'And the carer you sent round was a Simon Ropley, is that right? Does he still work for you?'

'It was Simon initially, yes, and that was all very strange. He was a nice young man, very good at his job. We had no complaints about him at all, and certainly Mr Berry couldn't praise him highly enough. Then one day, Simon simply handed in a week's notice, which was all he needed, worked that and then we didn't see him again. This was quite some time before Mr Berry told us he didn't need our services at all any more.

'I spoke to Mr Berry myself to explain that we couldn't really cancel the contract without hearing from his daughter, because she'd signed it and she was paying us. He was adamant, though, and said he was going on holiday abroad shortly so he wouldn't be there. In the meantime he agreed to us sending someone, just to check up on him. He sounded as lucid as ever, there was nothing to raise our concerns. We tried to contact his daughter, but couldn't, so in the end we stopped sending anyone and suspended taking payment until it could all be sorted out.'

Virgil was recording what she told him, at the same time scribbling himself notes of the key points.

'First of all, was there anything different about the arrangements with the new person you were sending? And may I have that person's name, please, in case we need to interview them, too, if they're still on your team.'

'That was Emma Forrester and yes, she still works for us. Same thing with her. Nothing at all on the checks we made on her and no complaints. She and Mr Berry also seemed to get on well. He really was a very pleasant and easy-going gentleman.

'But now you come to mention it, there was a change in the arrangements. Mr Berry told us he was lunching with friends more and more often, so asked us to send someone late afternoons instead. Although he did say then that he really didn't need anyone at all, it was just to humour his daughter. Emma went for a short time then he cancelled the cover altogether.'

'What can you tell me about Simon Ropley? Had you had any problems with him? Any dissatisfied clients? Anything at all out of the ordinary.'

'Nothing of the sort. Quite the opposite, in fact. He was good at his job, always smiling and cheerful. Very calm and gentle with those he needed to handle in any way. A very polite young man. All our clients loved him, men and women alike. Lots of them asked for him by name. We had trouble sharing him round with all those who wanted him. He seemed, in particular, to get on like a house on fire with Mr Berry, as he did with Simon.'

'And I presume you do full background checks on all the people you employ, before sending them into the homes of potentially very vulnerable people?'

'We do, yes, and there was absolutely nothing of concern about Simon at all. Massimo. You might not know that his real name is Massimo, which is Italian, but he always called himself Simon, which he said was the closest name in English. He said he got teased a lot at school for having a foreign name. Some of them called him Eskimo. Children can be little monsters like that, can't they?'

Virgil wasn't about to mention some of the names he'd been called at school. Virgil wasn't his real name, which was Dennis. Virgil was a nickname, but one with which he was perfectly happy. He'd started it himself; a reference to a classic Sidney Poitier film.

'Simon came up squeaky clean. Nothing recorded against him. Glowing references, which we checked thoroughly and they were genuine. We thought ourselves lucky to have him, and he never did anything to cause us to regret taking him on.

'Oh, I'm sorry officer, I haven't offered you a drink. Would you like some tea, or coffee?'

'It's fine, thank you. Would it be possible for you to let me have copies of anything you have on Simon Ropley? Background checks, references, that sort of thing? If necessary, I can get a warrant ...'

'No, that's fine, I can quite see why you would need such things, if Mr Berry really has gone missing. And I know his daughter isn't the fanciful type who would make up a story like that for some reason. I'll get copies made for you but it might not be before you leave. I might have to send them on.'

'Thank you. So, what reason did Simon give you for leaving his job?'

'He said he had a new carer's position but that it was abroad. He'd always wanted to travel so he was very excited about it. Again, there was really nothing there to set off any alarm bells. He was a personable young man who would have no difficulty getting a post anywhere. We gave him a glowing reference and a little leaving do to wish him well. That was the last we heard of him.'

'I might need to talk to some of your employees who possibly knew Simon both inside and outside work, if you would be happy to supply contact details?'

'I'm happy to do whatever I can to help with finding Mr Berry. Such a lovely man, and such a worry for his daughter. And for all of us who knew him, of course. But this isn't really the sort of job where our employees have much social time together. The most crossover they get is at things like care plan meetings. Some of them might meet in off duty time, but not all that many, I don't think. It can be a time-consuming and tiring line of work. But I'm happy to do anything at all that might help you.'

Virgil was winding up, getting his things together, ready to leave, when the woman asked him,

'Are you allowed to tell me if there's been any progress in finding that little missing baby, officer? I cannot imagine what those poor parents are going through. She's so young to be out there somewhere, away from her mother.'

'I'm afraid there's nothing I can tell you, Mrs Mason. We're pursuing all lines of enquiry, but she still remains missing.'

It was the official line and it even sounded trite to Virgil's own ears. As soon as he got back to his car, he took out his phone, opened his video folder and spent a few moments looking fondly at images of his own young daughter, Daisy May. Smiling. Always smiling. He could imagine the feeling of having the heart ripped out of his broad chest if ever anything happened to deprive him of being able to see and to hold her.

* * *

Ted was on the phone to the ACC and was getting his ears chewed off, to put it mildly.

The top brass, including Assistant Chief Constable (Crime) Russell Evans, usually thought highly of Ted. He was a good, diligent officer, with an excellent record of success, and ran his team well, with no friction. But the press and media were having a field day with a small baby missing and coming up to the third night away from her mother. Everyone wanted results, and at the moment, Ted wasn't in a position to provide them.

DI Oscar Smith picked exactly the wrong moment to wander in through Ted's open door, without so much as a courtesy knock, not even looking at anything other than the sheet of paper in his hand and announcing without preamble, 'I know this bastard's face ...'

Ted jerked his phone away from his ear and bellowed, 'Out! And shut the door behind you.'

'Who was that?' Russell Evans asked, having heard the exchange.

'Sorry, sir, that was DI Smith, on secondment from the Met. I'll have a word with him.'

'See that you do. He's presumably supposed to be helping. Don't whatever you do let him anywhere near any media cameras, if that's how he normally behaves. Our image is already taking a pounding. He'd be all we need.

'Which takes us back to what this call is about. The chief, as you can imagine, is not happy. Not happy at all. He's meant to be going to a squash tournament this weekend. Clearly he can't do that if the baby is still missing and the press pack are camping out on our doorstep. He wants a result, so he can pack his bags and go, with a clear conscience. We've given you every available spare officer. We need something to show for it, and soon. Surely it's about time you persuaded the parents to appear on camera, now that the husband is home and knows all about what's happened.

'Do something, Ted, and soon. Something to show the public that you really are leaving no stone unturned.'

Ted's 'Sir' in acknowledgement probably went unheard, as the call was ended abruptly from the other end. He knew how the system worked. In circumstances like these, the one at the top kicked the one lower down, and so on. Except with Ted, who never passed it further than himself. He took his responsibility seriously. If the team were getting nowhere, it was up to him to get out there and find a better direction in which to send them.

But first, he needed to mark Smith's card for him. More firmly this time.

He deliberately moved the spare chair before going to find Smith. It might appear a petty gesture to the visiting officer, but Ted needed to set some boundaries before they went any further. The ACC was right. They were under the media microscope and the wrong word in public from the brash Met officer would only succeed in turning the tide against them even more, especially if they couldn't manage a positive outcome on the case.

Ted found Smith in the other partitioned off workspace, with Jo Rodriguez. He deliberately paused in the doorway, hoping to make a subtle point, then asked, 'Do you have a minute now, DI Smith, for whatever it was you wanted to tell me? I'd also like a few words of my own.'

Ted didn't miss the broad grin on Jo's face. He knew what it meant when the boss spoke as quietly and politely as that. Whatever it was that Smith had done, the DCI was not pleased.

It was Smith's turn to grin when he followed the DCI back into his office, shutting the door behind them as instructed. He spotted the obvious absence of anywhere to sit and reacted by giving a parade ground perfect snap to attention. The sound of his big foot crashing to the ground must have scared the wits out of whoever was in the room directly underneath.

Ted didn't even acknowledge the ironic gesture. He didn't have time to waste with games.

'We're quite informal here, within limits,' Ted began. 'But please don't barge into my office without at least a brief knock to check that I'm available. And certainly not when I'm clearly on the phone. That was the ACC I was talking to. He heard what you said and was not impressed.'

Smith's 'Whoops' was not remotely convincing. He clearly didn't much care what people thought of him, whatever their rank was.

'As I mentioned before, we try to keep things respectful, and the language workplace appropriate when on duty. Can you please try to remember that in future?'

He stood up himself to retrieve the spare chair and put it in place for the DI to sit down. The proverbial olive branch.

'Right, you mentioned recognising a face.'

Smith was still clutching the sheet of paper he'd had in his hand earlier. He put it on the desk between them.

'I have many annoying habits, as you're finding out. I do have some attributes, though. Face recognition is one of the most useful in our line of work. I literally never forget a face. I can't always say where I've seen it before. That's beyond my conscious control, it seems. But it's there, logged away in my memory banks, so I will know immediately if I see the same person again.

'This could be someone from my manor, of course. But my gut feeling is it's someone I've seen since I've been up here on yours. I looked at this,' he brandished the composite of the phony photographer which had been released, 'but that didn't fully trigger the memory, although it looked partly familiar. So I went back over all the witness statements that have come in about this bloke.

'Your old boy who sold his soul to the devil was next to useless, bless him, but there was one woman the so-called photographer spoke to in the street who described the eyes differently to anyone else. I looked at the ones she picked out, put them against this one and that's the face I've seen before. This face, but the eyes she described. It's possible that the likeness you've released is not a hundred per cent accurate.'

Ted sat back, considering. Smith sounded sure of himself. Too sure, perhaps? Composites were not always all that accurate, but the person creating them could only go off the information given to them. Where there were differing opinions about a feature, like the eyes, they would go with the majority verdict. It was their job, and they were experienced in it.

DI Smith, on the other hand, had already shown himself to be arrogant and opinionated, and Ted had no way of knowing if his tale about recognising faces was true. If they released a second, slightly different, composite picture it risked causing confusion and getting either fewer phone-ins or a spate of them, none of them leading anywhere. But they needed a breakthrough. So badly.

'Get a second one made up, with the different eyes. I'll go and talk to Superintendent Sampson now about releasing it. The ACC wants the parents put up in front of the media, now the husband's back and in the know, if they'll do it. If we all bash on, there's a chance we can get something, at least, out in time for the early evening news.

'How are you going to pin down when and where you might have seen the face before, assuming you're not mistaken about it?'

'I'm not wrong. I'm never wrong about faces.'

Coming from him, it could so easily have sounded like more of his customary arrogance. On this occasion, from the way he said it, Ted was inclined to trust his judgement.

'I'll get the new one done, then send it straight through to my skipper, Tony Taylor. I need to kick ars … backsides,' he corrected himself automatically now, 'while I'm away, so I'll do that, then get Tony to cross-check it against anything we've had recently. I need to speak to him anyway to get him to go and see Barry George Stephens about your car job. Then after the press conference, we might as well head to your local for a swift one. After all, in a far-fetched TV drama, we'd find our suspect propping up the bar next to us.'

Ted smiled to himself as he got up and went in search of Sammy Sampson. Smith was nothing if not persistent on the subject of going for a drink.

He knocked at the Superintendent's door and waited for her invitation before going in. Her voice sounded slightly muffled, and when he entered, he didn't miss her wiping her eyes quickly with a handkerchief, then blowing her nose with it, before inviting him to sit down. He didn't comment. If it was something she chose to share with him, she no doubt would.

'So what do you think?' he asked her, after relating his phone call. 'We definitely need to put the parents up in front of the camera now, if they will agree. The ACC's right about that one. I can phone their liaison officer first to see if they'd agree, then phone the press office to set it up. There's just about time, if I crack on. And what do you think about releasing the second composite? Too confusing, or worth a shot?'

'Coming up to three days and nights with that little baby missing, I think anything is worth a shot.'

Ted stood up and made for the door, then hesitated, looking back.

'Tell me to mind my own business if you like, but are you all right?'

This time there was no mistaking the tears starting to her eyes as she fished out her handkerchief once more.

'No, I'm not. And this is strictly between us for now. You're the first person I've told, and thanks for asking. You may know I recently had a second follow-up medical, after the surgery I had. The news isn't good. How I am now is the best it's going to get. And that best is not good enough to continue serving. I'm on my way out, Ted. Enforced early retirement on medical grounds. So at least let's find this baby, before I go. Let me have a decent swan song, at least.'

Chapter Thirteen

If Ted had a quid for every time he resorted to 'we're exploring all avenues' or 'we're keeping an open mind' at the press conference, he could have afforded to take Trev on a really nice holiday, to make up for all the extra hours he was putting in on the current case.

'Do you think baby Evie has already been taken out of the country, chief inspector?'

'We're exploring all avenues.'

'It's coming up for the third night missing for a tiny, vulnerable baby. What are the chances of her being found alive after all this time?'

Ted was sitting next to the parents of the baby. The mother closest to him. He couldn't recall ever having been put on the spot so much in his career to date.

The young couple were already in pieces. They'd clearly hardly slept at all since their baby was snatched. They'd shown incredible composure so far in how they were coping. Especially the husband. Once he'd got his initial anger out of his system, their liaison officer had reported he was doing everything he possibly could to make up for his outburst. He was kindness and compassion personified with his wife and constantly apologising to the officer he'd knocked over.

Superintendent Caldwell was also present. So far she had remained quiet. Ted half hoped she would jump in to answer at this point, but she stayed silent. The message was clear.

He was out on a limb by himself on this one. And this really was the question which would come back to bite him if the case ended with the outcome they all dreaded – baby Evie being found dead.

'We are using every available resource to find Evie and to bring her safely back to her family.'

He glanced towards the Super out of the corner of his eye. Saw her barely visible nod, to his relief. The message was clear. That's enough. Wind things up.

'Thank you for attending, ladies and gentlemen, that's all for now. You will be kept informed of any significant developments as they occur, but no more questions at this time. Thank you, and we'd be grateful if you could circulate the second ID composite.'

He and the Super stood up almost in sync, both of them ignoring further shouted questions from the baying media. They shepherded the parents, still with their main liaison officer, out of the glare of publicity and into a designated vulnerable persons' interview room, where they could be sure of not being disturbed.

They sat down together for a debrief. Dave Fisher was staring hard at Ted.

'Why didn't you answer the question about finding our baby alive?' he demanded. 'Is that because you don't think she is?'

'The honest answer is that I simply don't know, Mr Fisher. I hope she is. We all do. We're doing everything we can to find her and bring her back safe. But I can't speculate. That wouldn't help any of us. And I want you to know that you can trust me to be honest with you at all times. That's why platitudes are never helpful in a case like this.'

'Have any of the other babies been found? Found at all,

either alive or ...' he broke off there, seemingly incapable of saying the word he and his wife must dread more than anything. 'You said you were liaising with the Met and other forces about similar cases in their areas. So have any of the other babies been found? Anywhere?'

'I promised always to be honest with you, Mr and Mrs Fisher, and I will. No, to date, none of the missing children that we know of have been found.'

Carrie Fisher gave a small gasp and her hand flew to her mouth. She'd clearly been clinging to a forlorn hope that there might have been a positive outcome in at least one of the other cases. Something which might give her reason to stay optimistic.

'So how are you going to find Evie?' Dave Fisher demanded. 'If no one else has ever found one of the missing babies, why should we trust you to do any better? What real hope can you give us of getting our baby back?'

Ted fervently wished he had the answer to that question. The only things he could offer now would be platitudes and he didn't like doing that.

The Ice Queen picked up on his dilemma, his hesitation, and waded in to say her piece.

'We have finally been able to establish a clear link between the disappearance of Evie and two cases in London, as you heard just now. An officer from the Metropolitan Police has joined us to liaise, enabling the pooling of vital information.

'As soon as your case was reported, DCI Darling alerted all ports and airports with a full description, making it harder for Evie to be taken out of the country. We really are doing everything possible to bring your baby back to you.'

* * *

Ted had managed a quick get together with the team before the press conference, desperately hoping for a crumb he could throw to those assembled. There was precious little. They were all clinging on to the thought that as long as they didn't find a body, there was a chance that baby Evie was alive and possibly safe, somewhere out there. But that was hardly something he could say to the media.

Virgil found time for a quick word with the boss before he hurried off to face the wolf pack, ready and eager to tear him to shreds for the best front page news story.

'Boss, I really do think there's something to this missing retired doctor, John Berry. I've spoken to his daughter and she appears the sort who doesn't go in for drama and fantasy. At the end of the day Mr Berry did sell his house at a knockdown price and has seemingly disappeared without trace. At the same time as this young man, Simon Ropley, has dropped off the radar, saying he was going off to a new job abroad. He and Mr Berry were very close, by all accounts.

'I don't yet know the timings of this, but it could well be a significant factor. Simon's real name is Massimo, but he took to calling himself Simon. I don't know when he did that, but Mr Berry's wife was killed in a road accident when she was carrying their second child. A boy, and they were going to call him Simon.'

Ted frowned at that.

'I could see why that's a bit much of a coincidence. That he might perhaps have changed his name to match, to get even closer to Mr Berry. It's not as if we can really take this on until the baby is found, but if you want to carry on by yourself for the time being, you could do worse.

'Does the daughter have any theories about where he might be?'

'None, boss, and that's what's worrying her.'

'It's not simply an older person with the onset of dementia, acting on a whim, out of character?'

'An expensive whim, though. Even at its lowest price, the house was worth a fair bit. And there's also the question of where the money went, as well as where Mr Berry himself has gone.

'So can I apply for warrants to look at his financial affairs, to see if that tells us anything? After all, it is just possible that this Simon Ropley somehow persuaded Mr Berry to sign the money over to him and that the poor man may have been done away with.'

'Do it. We're going to be hung out to dry and I'll probably be reduced to running road safety courses for schoolchildren if we can't find Evie. So let's not take the risk of having a serious outcome on another Misper case because we had our eye off the ball. I can't spare anyone else, but if you need more help, ask Inspector Turner if he can find anyone. But bear in mind we're already poaching a lot of his officers. At least try to establish if this is in the serious crime remit or not.'

Ted knew Trev would have a meal prepared for the two of them when they got home, later on. For some reason, though, he decided to have a hotpot with Oscar Smith in The Grapes before he went back. If necessary, he could always eat two meals. Ted had a good appetite and knew the coppers' trick of always eating when he could because there was no guarantee of when he'd get the next meal. He'd need to be careful, though. He seemed to be finding less and less time for his usual physical activities – martial arts, hill walking, going riding. The increasing lack of activity risked manifesting itself, despite his normally fast metabolism.

He found Smith in with Jo Rodriguez, who was packing his things together ready for the off. The Met DI was on his phone.

'Did you need me for something, Ted?' Jo asked him, informal now the rest of the team were not there, and only another DI present.

Ted shook his head.

'It's fine, Jo, get off while you can. If you can be in early to man the fort tomorrow, DI Smith and I are going to the PM on the suspected snatcher death early doors.'

'I'll have to go to confession for even thinking it, but I'm struggling to find sympathy for anyone who would snatch someone else's child. And yes, I know, they were probably under duress and possibly trying to protect their own. It's easy for me to stand here and think noble thoughts about how I would do it differently when of course I have no idea how I would react, and would hope never to be in the position of having to find out.'

Ted tried not to lurk too obviously but he'd need to be back in his own office in order not to hear Smith's tirade to his sergeant, although he noticed he tempered it slightly at times.

'Look, Tony, I don't care what else you have on or what Aird's telling you to do. Get someone round to Rain ... to Barry George Stephens' place, tell them to shove the photos of the car and plates I sent you under his nose and don't leave until you have chapter and verse on whose work it is. By whatever means necessary.'

DS Tony Taylor was quiet for a moment, then asked

hesitantly, never sure what sort of a reaction he would get from his gaffer, 'Guv, are you all right? You've not been kidnapped and you're sending me a coded message to let me know something's wrong? Only you called Rain Man by his real name. Are you somewhere you can't speak?'

Tony Taylor could be sharp when he needed to be, Smith gave him that.

'Something like that, yes, but that's fine,' Smith replied, hoping that conveyed the right message. 'Everything's fine. Just get someone round asap and phone me as soon as you have an answer. This is critical. I'll sign off on overtime. Just do it.'

He ended the call and looked at Ted.

'Tony will call me back, night or day, if there's anything to report.'

'Please keep me in the loop if he does. Again, no matter what the time is.'

Smith agreed then asked, 'Pub?'

Ted nodded in agreement and said, 'Pub.'

It might be a good idea to spend a bit of down time with the man. He must have some good features to account for his clear-up rate. Perhaps they might yet reveal themselves.

The bar was quiet when Ted strolled in with Oscar Smith. Dave, the landlord, was behind the bar, busily arranging things in anticipation of a bigger footfall as the evening wore on. He looked up when he saw Ted, greeting him with a warm smile. Then his eyes narrowed as he saw the big stranger alongside him.

'Dave, this is Oscar Smith, from the Met. He's joining us for a while with this kidnap case.'

The smile lost some of its warmth as he greeted Smith.

'Welcome to my humble hostelry. All are welcome here.

141

Even Monkeys.'

The sudden tension between the two men was palpable but Ted had no idea what it was about. Some military reference, he guessed, as Oscar was wearing what looked like a regimental tie, and Dave was ex-Army, though seldom talked about it.

'What are you having, Oscar? My shout,' Ted said, hoping to defuse whatever was going on. 'And do you want to eat? I'll have my usual, please, Dave, and a hotpot, if you have some on the go.'

It was his way of asking about Dave's wife, Susan, without appearing to do so in front of a stranger. Without pre-judging, he strongly suspected that everything about Susan might be a step too far for Smith.

'And can we use the back room, please, so we can talk a bit of shop without being overheard?'

'Hotpot's ready when you are, and as good as ever. And the back room is always available to a good customer like yourself, Ted.'

That was Dave's way of letting Ted know that Susan was well enough to be working in the kitchen as usual, although they both knew she still had a long road to recuperation ahead of her.

'Have you got any decent schnapps?' Smith asked him. 'Not ersatz, I will know the difference. And I might as well try some of this hotpot. When in Rome, and all that.'

'Coming right up, sir.'

Ted couldn't work out if Dave's use of the word to Smith was in mockery or a case of old habits dying hard. He knew that ex-military types could often spot one another without any seemingly visible identification, and he imagined that went for ranks, too.

Ted led the way through to the rear then, once they were both sitting down with their drinks, he asked, 'What was the monkey reference all about?'

Smith took a pull at his schnapps and made an appreciative face.

'Not bad, that. Definitely drinkable. And it's one of the less complimentary names for the Military Police, my old unit. What was he in? Dave?'

'I honestly don't know really, he never talks about it. Although he did once help me out on a case with a Pathfinder who'd gone rogue.'

'Did he now? Interesting. I can find out about him, easily enough.'

He was interrupted by his mobile phone ringing. He grabbed it, looked at the screen, then said, 'Hotpot might be on hold. It's my DS.'

'Guv, I'm sorry, we've looked in all the usual places and Rain Man's not in any of them. We'll keep looking, all night if we have to, and I'll let you know if and when we do find him.'

'Shit,' Oscar said as he ended the call. 'Barry George Stephens has gone to ground. My team will keep looking until they find him but at least for now, we can eat this famous hotpot. Then we can drop everything and go, if we get word on who did the work on your car. Always supposing they're up here rather than down south. If they're there, you can safely leave them to Tony and the others to haul in and start grilling them.'

'I want it done properly. On a warrant. I don't want anything about this case to risk collapsing because correct procedure wasn't followed.'

'That'll slow us right down,' Smith protested. 'This is a

chance to get ahead and get that kiddy found.'

'We want the baby found soon, and safe, of course,' Ted told him. 'But the family are entitled to justice, and they'll get none if the case collapses. Whoever supplied the car is likely to be a middle man. I doubt they will know enough to lead us to Evie. If they do have her and we go steaming in unprepared, we potentially put her at risk.

'Keep me posted, on anything you hear from your DS. At any time of the day or night. No lone maverick stuff. No putting anyone's life at risk. You call me first, before you take any kind of action. Are we clear on that?'

'As crystal, guv,' Smith told him, with not a shred of sincerity about his tone.

Smith was once more interrupted by his phone. Once again he spoke in rapid German, which appeared to get more than a little heated at times.

He made an apologetic face towards Ted as he rang off.

'My Oma, again. My grandmother. Sorry about that. I can't ignore her. She's old, could go at any minute, and I keep imagining how I'd feel if she was calling to say goodbye because she knew she was on her way out, and it was the one time I didn't pick up.'

It made him sound human. He clearly cared for his grandmother.

Ted offered to run him back to his B&B when they'd finished eating but Smith said he needed the walk. Ted hoped he was doing the right thing in trusting him to follow orders about their informer, Barry George Stephens. He wasn't interested in any information obtained under duress.

Trev was back from karate when Ted got home, in the kitchen preparing food, talking on his mobile which was clamped between his shoulder and his ear as he worked.

'Ted's back now, pa, so I'll have to go, but I will try to have another talk with her soon, I promise.'

Ted was surprised to hear he'd been speaking to his father. They did talk occasionally, but after so many years estranged, it was never easy. Their main point in common was Trev's rebellious younger sister, Siobhan Eirian.

'I've eaten already, sorry,' Ted told him, stepping over cats to go and kiss him. 'I was trying to bond with the new DI over a hotpot.'

'How's it going with him? And what about the case? Any news of the poor little baby?'

Ted let out a pent-up sigh of frustration.

'Nothing yet, but it's possible I might have to shoot off out at some point in the night.

'I'm guessing your father was talking about your sister. More problems with her? And despite being supposedly an adult, an ex-Army captain, and a DI to boot, I reckon Oscar Smith could give Eirian a run for her money on the stroppy teenage behaviour stakes.'

He looked round the kitchen hopefully.

'I can't manage another main course after the hotpot, but that's all I had. I wouldn't mind a pudding, if there is one?'

Trev smiled fondly at him.

'Isn't there always pudding?'

Chapter Fourteen

Ted was tired. Feeling the effects of not enough sleep, three days of intense pressure, and the frustration of knowing that he was no further forward on the case than he had been on day one.

Despite the fatigue, or perhaps because of it, he'd found sleep hard to come by. It didn't help that the other occupants of the bed – Trev and all seven cats – were out like lights and not stirring.

Ted knew that only the youngest cat, Adam, in his usual place against Ted's shoulder, would move if he tried to get up and go in search of something to help him to settle. He still didn't want to risk disturbing any of them, so he lay alternately snoozing fitfully and staring at the ceiling, trying to think of something, anything, he should be doing with the case which he wasn't already.

Eventually he gave up the losing battle, got up early, showered, grabbed some tea and toast then spent half an hour at his desk at the station, looking for anything he'd overlooked so far, before heading off to the hospital for the post-mortem on the body in the car.

Once again, DI Oscar Smith was already waiting for him, ahead of the appointed time, leaning casually against the guard rail around the steps leading to the mortuary. At least being late didn't appear to be one of Smith's faults. He looked remarkably chipper, certainly much fresher than Ted felt. If he had been disturbed by a call from his grandmother or his DS, it didn't seem to have affected him.

As if reading his thoughts, Smith began with, 'Morning, guv. Nothing from my DS yet, which is why I didn't disturb you. Once we're done and dusted here, I'll make a start on trying to find that face I've seen before.'

'Steve, DC Ellis, will be ahead of you there. One of his actions for today is to run the second likeness we released through the system to look for likely matches.'

Smith tapped the side of his head as he said, 'But this computer is faster and more accurate.'

Ted said nothing, simply leading the way down the steps. They were well ahead of the scheduled start time. Even allowing for the two of them getting into all the required protective clothing, they would be early.

If Ted was known for his obsession with punctuality, the professor was even worse. Heaven help any poor soul who dared to turn up late for either her PMs or the lectures she delivered to various medical students. There were no second chances for those who broke her rules. She told her students, not entirely in jest, that the only excuse for being absent from or late for one of her teaching post-mortems was if they were laid out on the steel table as the subject of the autopsy.

Ted and Oscar had just finished donning their suits when the professor swept through the entrance, gowned, gloved and ready for action, followed closely behind by her assistant, James.

With most pathologists, there would be a brief informal chat about the case, often over tea or coffee. Bizzie Nelson was not a social chit-chat type. She would tell them everything they needed to know as she worked on the body. The famous 'chat and chop' as she liked to call it.

'Ah, chief inspector, as punctual as ever, I see.'

'Morning, professor. This is DI Smith, from the Met. He's here because he's investigating two seemingly similar deaths on his patch, both also linked to child abductions, so he's liaising with us on our case.'

'Morning, prof. Happy to throw in anything I gleaned from ours, in case that can help advance things with this one.'

Only the twinkle in his eye betrayed Ted's amusement. He'd rather set Smith up for that, knowing how much Bizzie Nelson hated to be addressed as 'prof' by anyone.

One of the skills which had put the professor at the very top of her profession was her ability to spot any and all detail at a glance and make correct deductions from them.

'Please not "prof", DI Smith. Nor yet "m'am" since I am not royalty,' she pronounced it with the short vowel sound, said to be the Queen's preferred mode of address informally, rather than the long one more usually used.

'Professor will suffice. I shall now show off horribly with my own detective powers, before we begin. Ex-military man, I deduce. RMP, from the tie I spotted. Based on age and bearing, I would wager on the rank of captain. Which means I get to choose how you address me, and my choice is professor. Always.'

She must have caught a glimpse of Smith's military tie, hanging with his jacket, and already made her deductions. Ted wasn't surprised she'd instantly picked up the military link. He knew from her Wiki entry that her late father had been a renowned Guards general.

'So now, gentlemen, shall we begin?' she invited, sweeping on into the inner sanctum of her post-mortem suite.

'Oh, and chief inspector, to answer your question from

the scene, I can now confirm that this body was the only one in the burned out car. There was absolutely no trace there of your missing baby's remains amongst the ashes, although I do have more on that score. No infant body is good news in a sense, I imagine, although a death would at least have provided the dreaded closure that everyone seems to set so much store by these days.'

The remains on the table bore little resemblance to most of the bodies on which Ted had watched post-mortem examinations being carried out. They were lucky that the fire brigade had attended early and brought the fire quickly under control, so there was still something resembling a human body on which the professor could work her usual magic.

'I'm sure you gentlemen are familiar with the pugilistic pose, seen in victims of fire, which our guest here is displaying, though not to the full extent sometimes seen, because as I've said, the time of exposure to very high temperature was relatively brief. You can observe here the flexing at fingers, wrists, elbows and knees, caused by muscle shrinkage from extreme heat.'

'That was present on both of the bodies we found, to a greater degree,' Oscar Smith told her.

The professor gave him one of her special looks, usually reserved for a student who was determined to show off to the rest of the group by displaying superior knowledge.

'Thank you, Inspector Smith. I have, of course, read through both of those reports in preparation, as they were sent to me by colleagues in the capital.

'Let's start with the differences, because the main one in your case is something of a godsend, evidentially. The fire here in Stockport was tackled and extinguished far more quickly than either of those in the London cases, perhaps due to a lower volume of call-outs. That meant that I was left with rather more to work with than either of my colleagues in London.

'You'll remember from the scene, chief inspector, that extra accelerant was thrown onto the vehicle after the fire was started, and that was done from the front. That, together with another improbable factor, left us with a small but significant piece of evidence. I've worked on that in advance, so I have some interesting results from it. And also, it might surprise you to hear, a theory of my own on which I would like to hear your views.'

She was working all the time she spoke, James anticipating her every request, the right instrument always in his hand a few seconds before she asked for it. It was seamless team work based on long collaboration, which required little by way of spoken communication.

The idea of the professor making a suggestion, even a hypothetical one, was so far out of the ordinary as to be almost unheard of. She was, on her own admission, a woman of science, of provable fact. Whatever her theory was, Ted would listen to it with interest, knowing how it would have been weighed up before being propounded, especially in the presence of a detective with whom she was not familiar.

'If your rather charming Inspector Rodriguez were here, I'm sure he would be telling us we are looking at the hand of god. I don't believe in any of that sort of stuff, but will gratefully accept anything the fates can throw our way to help in a case like this.'

The professor had promised Ted she would prioritise any and all samples such as DNA recovered from the scene or the remains, to give them as much chance of success as possible. All of that would have been done early on

Wednesday morning, so it was encouraging to hear that there were already some results.

'First of all, from the DNA, our deceased person was female and of Malay origin. And whatever part she played in your case, for our purposes, she is a murder victim, as this fire was clearly started deliberately by a third party or parties. It was undoubtedly the effects of the fire which caused her death and I will be able to confirm that for you once we are finished here.'

'We had a Filipino and a Sudanese. Probably illegals. That's the theory we're going on,' Smith put in.

The professor studiously ignored his input and went on with her discourse.

'The dental work, which I think James has already mentioned to you, might well accord with the Malay connection. There's quite a decent faculty of dentistry at the Universiti Kebangsaan in Kuala Lumpur, apparently. As the work done on our victim here is unusual and distinctive, there is at least a chance that they may be able to identify where and when exactly it was done, and that may in turn eventually provide us with identification details for this person, if there are none on record anywhere. But none of that will happen quickly.

'So in the meantime we are left with the supposed miracle. An against all odds finding.'

For a moment, she turned away from the remains on the table and indicated something in a transparent bag nearby. Charred in the main, but less so at one end, and still identifiable as some sort of fabric.

She looked directly at Oscar Smith as she asked, 'Did any items of clothing survive in your cases, inspector?'

'Not a thing. I'm guessing that, as you said, response

times for emergency services might be better in a small town like this, rather than in the big city. Was there something significant about the clothing?'

'Possibly,' she said, her tone guarded. 'This is the somewhat miraculous part of our findings. This object is a remnant of something resembling a padded coat or long jacket of some sort.'

'We have a witness who saw someone coming out of the park and getting into a car, which left at speed, very shortly after Evie was snatched. She mentioned they were wearing a padded coat, which struck her as unsuitable for the weather at the time,' Ted told her. 'DI Smith can confirm there was mention of similar clothing, too, in both his cases.'

'Does her description of the car match your burned out one?' Smith asked him.

'She admits to being no authority on cars, and she's certainly not yet picked out anything which would tally with the one we found,' Ted told him.

'But has she been shown the right ones?' Smith demanded.

Ted mentally counted to ten. He wasn't about to start spelling out the whys and wherefores of not leading witnesses, and certainly not during a post-mortem examination. Especially as the professor clearly had important details to share with him.

'Neither the time nor the place for this discussion, DI Smith,' he told him, hoping his tone would be sufficient to indicate that the subject was closed, for now.

Then he turned to Bizzie Nelson to say, 'Sorry, professor, you were saying?'

'Your divine intervention/incredible stroke of luck – delete according to your beliefs – means that this piece of the garment survived the flames, for two reasons. Principally because the very bottom of what might well have been a longish coat was caught in the door when it was shut. It then became detached from the rest of it as the fire caught hold, so didn't burn away completely and this surviving portion fell to the ground, effectively extinguishing itself.

'As we know, further petrol to increase the efficacy of the blaze was thrown onto the car from the front, and from the driver's side. So not much, if any of it, would have come in contact with this piece of cloth, as our victim was in the front passenger seat. And in anticipation of your asking, yes, the victim had first been spiked. We found traces of a drug which was injected into her and would have effectively immobilised her totally.

'We've also established that this woman had herself given birth comparatively recently. I may be able to pin down a precise time-frame for you from further analysis. I stress once more, though, that there was no trace of an infant anywhere at the scene.

'The second factor in your favour is that this garment is entirely natural fibres. Cotton, with some sort of very fine wool we've not yet identified as its filling. Nothing like nylon, which would melt and burn readily, so possibly of a lower combustibility.

'What would you deduce from that, chief inspector?'

Ted frowned. He knew so little about babies of any size. Certainly not little ones like Evie. The most experience he'd had came from successfully singing Trev's god-daughter, Aspen Jade, to sleep at her own christening, with the bit of *Suo Gân* he could still remember in Welsh. The best he could do was to try to relate things to cats.

'I imagine that would be cooler against a baby's skin so

they might possibly feel safe and settled, and not make too much noise. Perhaps less likely to trigger any sort of allergic reaction, too. Assuming this person was simply the courier who would be handing the baby over, she wouldn't want to risk her perhaps getting too hot, coming out in a rash, or something like that, and not looking at her best at handover.'

'Exactly my theory, chief inspector,' the professor agreed with him. 'And now the really good bit of news for your enquiry.'

She said it with the air of a magician about to produce something more spectacular than a rabbit from out of a hat.

'As well as the DNA from our victim herself, we also found faint, but undeniable, DNA evidence which matches that of the child, Evie Fisher.

'So at some point, this person here was in very close contact with your missing baby, who was not in the car at the time of the fire.'

* * *

Ted tried another quiet word with Smith after the PM, as the two of them were walking across the car park to where Ted had left his service vehicle. He didn't want to be forever on at him, but he couldn't afford to let things slide to the point where shortcuts or sloppy procedure could cost them a conviction. It could happen so easily when rules were not followed to the letter.

'I'm sure it's not what you meant, DI Smith, when you hinted at coaching a witness about the car model,' Ted began, starting out diplomatically, although he was far from sure about that, in reality. 'But I don't want anything which could be construed in any way as leading witnesses to come back and bite us.

'As I've said, our objective here is two-fold. The absolute priority is to recover Evie, safe and sound. The second thing is to see that whoever's behind this gets to court and we get a safe and solid conviction based on evidence we can prove beyond reasonable doubt. It's not just a case of justice for the family, although that's a priority. But a positive conclusion and a conviction for a case like this, hopefully with a hefty sentence, might hopefully deter someone else from thinking they've found a quick money-making idea.'

'Roger that, guv. Received and understood.'

Ted was quickly learning that it was impossible to tell when Smith was taking the mickey or not. He let it go for now.

They'd reached the car and both got in.

Ted started up, then told his passenger, almost by way of an olive branch, 'You're about to witness my guilty secret. Or rather, one of many. For some reason, PMs always give me a ferocious appetite, so I always stop on the way back to pick up a hot drink and a bacon barm.'

'I don't even know what a bacon barm is. It sounds vaguely medical. Like some strange northern form of a poultice.'

Ted laughed at the imagery then replied, 'Bacon, in a bread roll. With or without brown or tomato sauce, to taste.'

'Aah, right. You mean a bacon banjo. Without the egg. But with a roll rather than flat bread. Gotcha. I could go one of those myself by now, but I am once again without funds.'

Ted was starting to get Smith's measure. He'd clearly push boundaries of any sort until someone said thus far, but no further.

'I'll sub you again for this, Oscar, but only until we pass

the first hole in the wall and you draw out enough to start paying your way. Starting with the honesty jar for the coffee. Are we clear on that?'

'As crystal, guv. As crystal.'

Chapter Fifteen

'Boss, before we begin, I've finally managed to get a sight of medical records for the baby's mother,' Mike Hallam began. 'Took some doing but in light of the seriousness of the case and the fact that it's getting time-critical, I got there in the end. I also had a look at the ones for the father and baby Evie, in case there was anything there of relevance.

'Carrie Fisher had an early miscarriage the year before Evie was born and had a bit of a tough time getting over it, it seems. She was put on mild medication for depression for a time, but apparently with their help she then recovered well. She had a trouble-free pregnancy with Evie.

'The baby has never had an illness. Nothing of any note on her records. She's been doing well all along so far, no cause for any concern.

'The father has only seen their GP once since he's been with that practice, and that was for sciatica. He's a bit young for it to have started but it's apparently not uncommon in long-distance lorry drivers. His was brought under control by medication and some physio.

'Not making excuses for his behaviour, but that might in part explain his outburst when he arrived home. It sounds like he barely stopped on the way back, if at all, so even if he has decent seating in his cab, he could well have been in physical pain, as well as emotional, by the time he got there.'

'So the wife has had mental health issues?' DI Smith

immediately pounced on the information. 'Are we a hundred per cent certain the baby was ever in the pram that day? Is there a witness to that? Do we know when it,' he remembered to correct himself, 'when the baby was last seen?'

'Is victim blaming taken from the Met Manual, sir?' Jezza asked him, a dangerous glint to her eyes. 'Always start by suspecting the victim of a crime? Suffering depression after a miscarriage isn't that unusual. And why on earth would someone who'd suffered the pain of losing one child be involved in any way in losing another?'

Her fury was palpable. Not everyone present knew she'd suffered a miscarriage herself. Ted knew. He'd been in the car with her when it happened. He could understand her anger, but was not about to let morning briefing deteriorate into a slanging match.

Oscar spoke before Ted had time to.

'Rule Number One. First establish whether or not a crime has been committed. Who else saw the baby in the pram that morning? Are we busily chasing our own arses on a crime which didn't happen where we're all assuming it did? Yes, you have a lot of similarities to our cases but have you begun with the fundamental basics? How do we know beyond doubt that the baby was ever in the park that day? Who else saw her there?'

There was silence for a moment. Then Ted spoke first.

'You have a point, DI Smith. From my own contact with the mother, I have no reason to believe she was involved in any way with the disappearance of her own baby. She handed over the keys to her house without protest, for one thing. There has been nothing about her demeanour to date to implicate her. Plus the dog tracked someone from the pram to the road. I'll get someone to check with the handler, but she couldn't surely have staged that, could she? If it was her scent leading to the road, wouldn't the dog have indicated on her?

'And then there was the body in the car. That would be a considerable coincidence if it was unrelated to our baby going missing.'

'It still doesn't get past the point that no one seems to have seen the baby in the park that day so we only have the mother's word that she was there and was snatched from there.

'What about her phone? I presume that's been analysed for any sign of anything dodgy? Any shots of the baby on there for the day in question? And the friend she was talking to at the time. Have they been questioned?'

They were all valid points to raise, Ted conceded. Even if Smith's delivery of them was less than tactful.

'That's another thing about the mother,' Ted put in. 'She was more than happy to hand her phone over to be looked at. So that would suggest that there's nothing incriminating to be found on there, which would implicate her in the case.

'Steve, have you had time to go through the phone yet?'

'I've started, sir, but not yet finished. I have looked at the more recent photos, in case there was anything there which might help us. Perhaps someone in the distance on a shot who might have been watching the pram, and the mother didn't notice.

'And sir, DI Smith might just have a point. It's full of photos of the baby, almost every day, but there were none at all on Tuesday, the day she disappeared.'

Smith was about to respond when his mobile interrupted him. He grabbed it at once, then said, 'My DS. We might finally have a lead on the cars.'

He moved to the far corner of the room to take the call, although his words were still audible to everyone.

'What d'you mean, he's not telling you anything, Tony? Stand on his broken foot until he does. We need that intel from him, and fast, however you get it.'

Ted was trying to keep the team focused on what he'd started to tell them about the results of the post-mortem examination. Even raising his voice above his usual quiet level, everyone could still clearly hear what Smith was bellowing down his phone. Finally he was quiet for a moment, then gave a fist pump of triumph as he exclaimed, 'Yes!', before ending his call.

'Right, my team finally tracked down Rain ...' he interrupted himself with an impatient noise as he again corrected his wording, 'Barry George Stephens. He turned up in A&E to get his foot plastered after he tripped on a kerb and broke something.

'At first he was a bit reluctant to talk, which is unusual, but my skipper said he was in a lot of pain and they'd given him some hefty pills. Once they kicked in, he was back to his usual self and singing like a budgie.

'He gave them a name, Ian Hardy, and a location. At least I assume Chorlton-cum-Hardy is a place name and not some old music hall act? Or some northern joke relating to the suspect's name. Anyway, d'you want me to take that, if I can get a vehicle, with or without a driver? This could be the breakthrough we need to get started from. If the work on the car in your case was done up here and not down south, there's a chance that they used other locals, too, rather than shipping someone in from outside the area.'

It didn't warrant sending a senior officer. It would be

risky sending Smith, even with someone to try to restrain him if necessary. The best person for that task would have been Virgil, who was at least physically strong enough to haul him off a witness if necessary. But Ted had given Virgil a bit longer to look into the apparent disappearance of John Berry, and he didn't want to risk pulling him off that in case it did turn out to involve a crime, potentially a serious one.

He made a split-second decision, and hoped it wouldn't come back to bite him in the future.

'You and I will go together, DI Smith, to at least establish if the person whose details you've been given has anything they can usefully tell us. Jo, can you take over here, please, and I'll keep you posted with any updates.'

* * *

'Hello, I'm DC Tibbs, from Greater Manchester Police. I wonder if you had a moment to answer some questions, please?'

Virgil held up his warrant card to the man who had come to answer the door in response to his ring on the doorbell.

The man looked mildly surprised, nothing more, to find a police officer standing on his doorstep asking to speak to him. Then he clearly had a lightbulb moment as he opened the door wider, saying, 'Oh, I suppose this is about the man we bought the house from? Mr Berry? His daughter came round, of course, as soon as she got back from abroad and she was very surprised to see us here. She had no idea her father had sold the house.

'Come in, please.'

'Thank you. I'm not disturbing you?'

'Well, I work from home and I was about to stop for a

brew, so perhaps you'd like to join me, and I'll tell you anything I can. It won't be much though, I'm afraid.

'My wife and I were looking for our own place, as we've been living with her parents as a temporary measure. We saw this house in the paper and we couldn't believe the price. It was such a bargain we thought there must be something wrong with it. Like a new road going in right by, or a big housing estate being built just behind it or something, but no.'

He'd headed to a bright and pleasant kitchen at the back of the house, Virgil following as instructed. He put the kettle on and started to get out mugs and the makings of a brew from the cupboards.

'We fixed up an appointment as soon as we could, because we couldn't believe it wouldn't be snapped up by someone offering more than we could. Even as cheap as it was, it was still right at our upper limit, but we did at least have the advantage of having no chain, and we had a mortgage offer ready subject to survey and various checks.'

'Did you meet Mr Berry himself when you came for a viewing, or was everything done through an agent? Could you please tell me which agent it was? And may I have your name, please?'

'I'm Mark Scott. And yes, we both met him. A very nice man. The agent sent us round, but they didn't come. Mr Berry showed us round himself,' the man explained, naming the agent.

'He didn't happen to mention why he was selling up at all, did he? Because as his daughter might have mentioned to you, it was a very sudden and unexpected decision on his part.'

Scott's eyes narrowed at that.

'We bought the house legally. We didn't put him under duress or anything.'

'I wasn't suggesting that, Mr Scott. No one is. I simply wondered if Mr Berry had mentioned anything to you about what his plans were, that's all. We're just trying to establish where he might be and to make sure he's safe.'

'I told his daughter all I knew, which was that he said he was going away on a long holiday with a friend – a few months, he said – and when he came back he was going to get a much smaller place. That's why he wanted a quick sale so he was looking for someone with the funds ready.

'My wife wasn't here when the daughter came round. When I told her about the visit, she reminded me of something she'd seen when we were looking round the house. She said it was a brochure for those really expensive luxury round-the-world cruises, on the side table in the bedroom. I was going to phone his daughter to tell her that. She gave me her card for if we thought of anything, but it completely slipped my mind. Sorry.'

'I can pass that information on when I report back to her.

'Did you buy the property furnished or unfurnished?'

'Unfurnished. He had some really nice things. Antiques, that sort of thing. But they weren't really our style at all. He said he was going to put the lot into storage until he got back and found another place. That's clearly going to cost him a bob or two, but we formed the impression he wasn't exactly short of money.

'I'd forgotten all about the cruise thing and I should have remembered because my wife looked up online how much that sort of thing costs. We were both staggered. At least twenty grand a person, depending on what type of cabin you choose. Of course his friend might have been treating him, I suppose, but still. A lot of money.'

Or Mr Berry might possibly be treating the friend, who might quite likely be a certain ex-carer by the name of Massimo, who'd found himself a rich sugar daddy, Virgil thought to himself as he went back to the car.

He'd need to check with the boss about how much more time he wanted him to spend on the case. But the more he found out, the more he was becoming concerned about the whereabouts and welfare of John Berry.

* * *

'More Chorlton itself, than Chorlton-cum-Hardy,' Ted observed as he punched the address Smith gave him into the sat nav. 'Makes sense for something like a garage or a workshop.'

'So do you know him, or of him, this bloke Ian Hardy?' Smith asked him.

'Doesn't ring any bells with me. And you say it's likely to be a reliable tip-off from your man Barry Stephens?'

'No worries there. Pathologically incapable of lying, as I said, and he knows the work of all of the competition anywhere in the country. So are we nicking Hardy or inviting him to accompany us for a friendly chat?'

'I would say that depends pretty much on how he reacts to our polite request to answer a few questions. We've nothing at all to arrest him for at the moment, unless he turns violent on seeing us, for some reason.'

There was nothing about Ted's service vehicle to immediately suggest police. Except, clearly, to someone who knew as much about cars as Ian Hardy did. People seldom took Ted for a copper, but it might have been the sight of Smith's bulk standing up out of the vehicle and straightening his regimental tie which put the wind up the man.

When he'd heard a vehicle pull up outside the workshop, he'd slid himself out from under a vehicle on which he was working, on a creeper. He summed up the scene in an instant, dropped the tool in his hand and sprinted for the rear entrance.

Smith was after him from a standing start, Ted not much behind him. The man burst through a door into a service road. To his right was a dead end, the high brick wall beyond easy reach by jumping. Hardy turned left and set off at full pelt along the couple of hundred yards to a road at the end.

For the size of him, and on his own admission, not at full fitness, Smith could certainly sprint. He set off at a blistering rate, but it quickly became clear he lacked the stamina to maintain it for the full distance.

As he started to fade, Ted comfortably cruised past him, caught up to his quarry, then neatly and carefully grabbed him and swung him towards the nearest convenient wall, putting him in an effective arm lock which would keep him there, immobile, until they needed to move him.

Smith lumbered up then bent forward, hands on his thighs, while he tried to catch his breath.

'Bloody hell, guv, I thought you were a desk-bound pen-pusher. Where did you learn moves like that?'

Ted grinned at him, barely out of breath.

'You're perhaps better off not knowing.'

Chapter Sixteen

'Have you brought cuffs?' Smith asked Ted when he got his breath back.

Ted was enjoying himself. He always liked the odd excuse to get out from under the paperwork and be a proper, hands-on copper again, for a change. It didn't happen often enough.

'Jacket pocket,' Ted told him.

They both sensed that the minute he slackened his firm hold on Ian Hardy, the man would be off again, this time using his local knowledge to find a bolthole, now he knew what he was up against.

'We just wanted a few words with you, Mr Hardy, which we could have done here,' Ted told his prisoner. 'Given how you reacted, I'm now going to have to ask you to come with us to the station at Stockport to answer those questions. You can, of course, call a solicitor. But because you've now shown yourself to be a flight risk, you will be handcuffed for your own safety, and for ours, for the journey.'

'Rear stack in case he tries anything on the way?' Smith asked, once he'd located Ted's cuffs. He was already pulling the man's arms behind him to secure them at the back.

Ted wasn't keen, but it was standard procedure in the circumstances. With his hands restrained in front, the man still presented a significant risk to the officers in the car. Ted wasn't thrilled by the sudden escalation in the situation, but the man clearly had something to hide and they needed to find out what it was.

'I'm not going off with you leaving this place unlocked. The thieving bastards round here will strip it bare if I do,' Hardy told them, in tones of outrage.

'Is there no honour amongst thieves up here in the north?' Smith asked sardonically, clicking his tongue. 'Are you really telling me you'd get robbed of stuff you probably robbed in the first place?'

Hardy was struggling against the cuffs being put on him.

'I'm not a thief! I don't steal anything. All the stuff I use in there on the motors I fix I buy, legal like, with receipts and stuff. For the taxman.'

Ted intervened before Smith got the man to incriminate himself by saying things which would be of absolutely no use to them in a court of law, said by someone who hadn't been cautioned or arrested and who wasn't being recorded.

'Mr Hardy, now we've caught up with you, let me introduce myself and my colleague. I'm Detective Chief Inspector Darling, from Serious Crime, based at Stockport. This is Detective Inspector Smith, from the Metropolitan Police. We're looking into something a lot more serious than a few knocked off car parts. What brought us to you was a seemingly reliable witness statement from someone who tells us that work to disguise the original identity of a vehicle used in a recent serious crime has your distinctive stamp on it.'

There was no mistaking the instant panic on the man's face at his words. He started to struggle in Smith's restraining grip.

'I don't know nothing about no serious crime. All I do is fix up motors for people. That's it. I'm saying nothing. I want a lawyer.'

'Everything will be arranged for you, Mr Hardy, as soon as we get back to Stockport. For now it is not only your right but my strong recommendation that you say nothing at all by which you might potentially incriminate yourself before you've taken legal advice.

'For now, if you tell DI Smith where the keys are, and the code for any alarm you need us to set for you, we'll ensure your workshop is secure before we leave here.'

Hardy looked outraged at the mere suggestion.

'I'm not telling him the code if he's from the Met, like you said! I know how bent that lot from down there are. We all keep seeing on telly how often they fit people up for stuff they haven't done. The filth round here are bad enough, but I wouldn't trust a Met cop further than I could spit.'

Smith made a sudden threatening movement towards the man. Then he saw Ted's warning look and revised his ideas. He'd assumed this small, quiet, desk-driving copper would be soft. A pushover. Ted had already shown he could outrun him easily. Smith had noted that flying kick to the office door and wondered where the man had learned tricks like that. He'd find out more about him in due course. But for now, he wanted to be the one who at least helped to get a result on this complex case. If he could assist in tying things up here in the north, that would in turn hopefully give him and his team the steer they badly needed in their own cases.

Oscar Smith's police career was a never-ending juggling act. For all the good conclusions to cases he achieved, there was almost always some niggle of procedure, yet another bending of the rules. He was, according to his Det Sup, rapidly running out of second chances. This trip to the north could be the opportunity he needed to redeem himself.

Hardy was clearly facing a dilemma. He wanted his workshop locked up securely and the short copper was right. That would involve entering a security code. As much as he ever trusted any police officer, his instincts told him the one who had outrun him probably played things by the book, so he would be the one to give the code to.

The big one, built like a brick shithouse, he didn't trust an inch. If he told Shortarse the code and the man went off to set the alarms, that would leave him alone with the Met bloke. And Hardy didn't like the idea of that. Not one bit. He weighed people up by body size and build, and the sheer bulk of the southerner bothered him.

He came to a reluctant decision.

'I'll give you the code to set the alarm and show you where the keys are to lock up. But he stays here. Out of earshot.'

'Yeah, you'll leg it the moment I let go of you,' Smith scoffed at him.

'No I won't,' the man told him. 'I'm not going to get very far cuffed like this, am I? Besides, I know this bloke here can outrun me but you couldn't outrun my old granny with her Zimmer frame.'

Ted saw the man wince as Smith tightened his already vice-like grip on his arms.

'You can let go of him now, please, DI Smith. It will be fine.'

It was a toss-up, from their expressions, who was more surprised by the DCI's politeness, DI Smith or Ian Hardy.

Hardy shrugged and stretched his shoulders as much as he could once he was released from Smith's hold. He led the way across to the building, muttering as he did so, 'He's a nutter, your mate. Crap runner, though. I'd've left him standing if you hadn't been there.

'Keys are up there on the hook,' he lifted his chin to indicate as he spoke. 'That green fob. Both keys. Lock it from outside then you set the alarm on the key pad.'

Hardy made no attempt to flee as Ted slid the door shut and turned keys in both locks, then the man gave him a four digit code to punch in.

Ted couldn't swear to it but he had a strong feeling that whatever Hardy thought the police had turned up at his place for, he had no inkling that it was about anything as serious as the kidnap of a baby girl. He'd put money on the man suspecting nothing worse than a visit about false number plates. If that was the main part of his livelihood, he would be worried enough about going down for that and losing his trade. But it took a certain type of criminal to be knowingly involved in something like the trafficking of small children.

Unless the full searches which the team were doing on Hardy's background, whilst Ted was out here bringing him in, revealed anything unexpected, he didn't get the feeling they were going to turn up any hint of anything to do with the kidnap, although they were possibly edging closer to some answers. And one of the first things he would need to do would be to get a search warrant for the premises to find out what, if anything, was to be found in there about any activities which were not on the books.

Ted installed Ian Hardy in the back of the car, a hand on his head as he got in to avoid injury, carefully doing up his seat belt for him. He then gave the car keys to Smith. He wanted to make sure the DI's hands were fully occupied at all times, in case Hardy hadn't yet given up all hope of making a break for it, although he seemed compliant for the moment. Ted slid into the front passenger seat as Smith was getting into the driver's place. Or attempting to.

'Bloody hell, guv,' Smith muttered half under his breath, fiddling with the lever to shove the driver's seat right back. 'How can you outrun anyone with legs this short?'

Ian Hardy was still grumbling to himself in the back, ignoring Ted's patient attempts to explain his situation to him.

'You've got no right arresting me. I'm losing money, me. If I don't work, I don't earn. Simple as that.'

Smith opened his mouth to reply but caught Ted's warning look and held his peace. It was a tense drive back to Stockport. Ted wasn't surprised to discover the Met officer was an aggressive driver; his language towards others at the wheel, although mostly under his breath, was colourful.

Safely back at the Stockport station, Ted escorted Ian Hardy inside, instructing Smith to change the handcuffs to the front so he would be in a more comfortable position. He then requested someone from Uniform to babysit him for the time being, arranged for him to summon a solicitor if requested, then nodded for Smith to follow him up to the main office.

Jo Rodriguez was at the helm once more, a thorough and steadying hand at the tiller. He looked up when Ted and DI Smith came in.

'Any luck with Hardy?'

'Total denial, and he wants a solicitor. He ran off pretty much as soon as he saw us, which is not traditionally the action of an innocent person.'

'You caught him all right, though?'

Oscar Smith grinned, half turned towards Ted and pointed both index fingers at him as he said, 'And I thought this DCI was going to be a pen-pusher like most of them. He was after him like a whippet.'

'What have you dug up about Ian Hardy?' Ted asked.

'I haven't had chance to go through his file in detail yet, but there's nothing to suggest he'd knowingly be involved in the sort of gangs who would be behind child trafficking. Not that you can ever tell. A fair bit of petty stuff as a juvenile, mostly thieving. Hub caps, he started with. Couple of Band C fines as an adult but he's clearly been much more careful of late as there's not a lot recently.

'We're looking into his known associates. We've not yet found anything that immediately jumps out, but we're still digging. This could be it, boss, though, eh? This could be the link that's been evading us so far. We might finally be getting closer to a lead to where Evie is.'

'Who's in who can start the initial interview with Hardy?'

Smith looked at him in surprise.

'I thought I'd be doing that, guv. Or at least the two of us in tandem.'

'That would be overkill, DI Smith. Any one of the team members is quite capable of doing the initial interview with someone low level like Hardy seems to be. You, on the other hand, are the only one with the necessary knowledge to liaise with Jo to find out where there's any crossover with any names from your patch linked to Hardy. You can start straight off by reading his file in more detail than Jo's had chance to do yet. We need to be well up to speed on this one.

'Another reason it makes sense to put someone else onto starting off with Hardy. He'll probably want to wait for his brief before he'll talk, anyway, if he has something of a record. Who have you got spare, Jo?'

'Rob O'Connell,' Jo said without hesitation. 'He's already working on Hardy's known associates so he's partly up to speed, and it won't take you long to brief him on what else he needs to know, and to find out. We know he's good in interviews, too. Proven track record.'

Smith was visibly fuming. He'd not only been outrun by the DCI, he was now being outmanoeuvred by him. He'd been looking forward to showing this by-the-book lot how he got the results he did. He was convinced that after a few minutes of his questioning technique, Hardy's tongue would have been well and truly loosened.

He was made even more angry by the knowledge that there was absolutely nothing he could do about it. Ted Darling outranked him, it was his case, his manor, so his rules. Plus Smith was there purely in a liaison role, so he was stuffed and he knew it. He'd simply have to bite his tongue and bide his time, in the hopes he'd get a chance at some point to show what he was capable of. At least Shortarse was including him in the pre-interview briefing, which was probably the best he could hope for, for now.

That took place later in the DCI's office. A bit of a squash with three of them in there, but it gave Smith chance to weigh up the DS who would be doing the interview which he still believed himself to be the best person to tackle.

Ted's briefing was thorough, professional. He left nothing to chance. Smith knew he would have ignored more than half of what the DCI was instructing should happen. He was still convinced he would have got the answers they needed much more quickly using his own, unique, methods. They didn't yet have anything concrete with which to charge Hardy, but in the hopes of finding something before too long, he would be interviewed under caution and it would be recorded.

There was a call to the DCI's phone to let them know that

Hardy's brief had arrived. The fact that he had one to call up at short notice might or might not have been an indicative factor in his guilt or otherwise.

Rob went into the interview room to introduce himself, Ted and Smith went in turn into the room with the monitors in so they could see what was going on for now. Rob had seen the lawyer before and knew she was good, and not cheap. Another possible indicator as, at this stage of the game, there would be no legal aid in play and she would certainly not be working pro bono.

He started out by introducing himself, then cautioning Hardy, at which point the solicitor asked him, 'Before we begin, sergeant, why was my client brought here in handcuffs if he's not been arrested for anything?'.

'Purely for his own safety. Because he'd run off in panic when the officers went to speak to him, they were concerned that in such a state he might be capable of running out into traffic and being seriously injured, at best.'

It was glib, and they both knew it, but she seemed happy to let it go for now.

Rob began again, politely, with an explanation to the man sitting opposite him.

'Thank you for your cooperation, Mr Hardy, we really appreciate it. Now, I'd like you to look at some photos for me, please. As you can see, they show a close-up of car number plates, slightly damaged by fire, but still legible. These plates are false. We've been told by what we consider to be a reliable witness that they were supplied by you.'

Hardy was shaking his head vigorously.

'I told them other cops. I don't do anything dodgy these days. I just fix up motors for people. It's all legit. All on the books. You can ask my accountant, if you don't believe me.'

He sat back in his chair, something of a smirk on his face, clearly convinced they could prove nothing against him.

'The thing is, Mr Hardy, both the plates and the doctored VIN have been identified by our witness as definitely your work. The problem with that is that the car on which the plates were found was burned out. Deliberately. And there was a body discovered inside, killed by the fire. So they are being treated as a murder victim and you are, by implication, suspected of being involved in that incident. We have every reason to believe that the body was that of a woman suspected of snatching a small baby from a park on Tuesday. You may well have seen details on television.

'That baby is still missing, Mr Hardy. And now it would seem that you are connected to the vehicle used to drive her away. The car in which the presumed snatcher was later killed.'

The colour drained from Hardy's face so quickly that for a moment Rob thought he might faint. Then his lawyer jumped in to his rescue.

'That's more than enough for now, sergeant. I need to talk to my client immediately. Alone.'

Chapter Seventeen

'Thank you for agreeing to see me at such short notice, Mr Lloyd-Parry,' Virgil Tibbs told the man into whose office he had been shown by a secretary.

The person behind the desk, late fifties or early sixties, with the look of a man for whom retirement couldn't come soon enough, indicated the chair opposite him, barely glancing at the warrant card Virgil was holding up for him.

'Your phone call was somewhat concerning, officer. John Berry has been with this firm since before I started. I was worried to hear he may have disappeared.

'There may be things I cannot immediately tell you because of confidentiality issues. But I will certainly help you in any way I can, given the circumstances, which sound disturbing.'

'Could you begin by telling me about the house sale, sir? And would you object to me recording your answers? Always more accurate than me trying to read my own scribble back.'

'As long as we are clear that I'm speaking unofficially, off the record, in an attempt to help to locate my client. Well, originally one of my father's clients, that's how long he's been with this firm.

'But if Mr Berry really has gone missing, then of course I will do whatever I can to help to locate him. I imagine his daughter must be frantic, coming back from Africa, finding the house sold and no sign of her father. I rather assumed he would have kept her in the picture all along.

'On the other hand even had he done so, I'm sure I'm right in saying that he was not due back yet. Not for a few days yet, if my memory serves me correctly, so he would presumably have told her that.'

'Back from where, sir?' Virgil asked him.

John Berry's solicitor, the person who had handled the conveyancing for the sale of his house, as Virgil had discovered from the purchasers when they showed him their purchase file, looked at him in surprise.

'Well, from his round the world cruise, of course. Are we talking at cross-purposes here? I assumed all along when his daughter contacted me, and then when you did the same, that Mr Berry had disappeared somewhere on the course of his cruise. Are you saying that's not the case? Did he not go on the cruise? Or did something happen to him whilst on it? Was he lost at sea, or perhaps failed to re-board after a stopover in port somewhere?'

'I think we're all a bit on different wavelengths here, sir. Mr Berry's daughter doesn't appear to be aware of any cruise her father might have gone on. She was out of touch for a time because of poor mobile communications in Africa when she was away from base. As soon as she got back she tried to contact him but couldn't. Then when she flew back she found strangers living in his house saying they'd bought it from him, which was a total surprise to her.

'She's had no contact with him for weeks now. No texts, no letters, not even a postcard, so of course she's very worried. So anything at all you can tell me would be a great help.'

The man stood up and went to a table in the corner of his

office, where a coffee maker was filling the air with the aroma of something strong but of high quality.

'I think this might possibly call for coffee. It's sounding rather complex. Would you like some? I don't have milk or sugar in here because I'm trying to wean myself off both, but I can easily get my secretary to bring some in, should you require either.'

'As it comes is fine, sir, thank you.'

'I have to confess to being a little surprised when John Berry came to see me to say he was selling his house. Not so much that he was selling, because it was a large property, a lot for him to keep up as he got older. I thought he was perhaps thinking of getting a smaller place which would be easier for him to manage. It was what he planned to do with the rest of his money which rather surprised me.'

'That wasn't the case, then? Simply buying a smaller place?' Virgil asked him.

'In part, yes, although he wasn't going to buy again immediately. He told me he intended to spend a good deal of his money first by indulging his love of overseas travel to the maximum.'

'Has he recently made any changes to his will? Are you able to tell me at this stage who the main beneficiary is?'

'Unless he did so elsewhere, his will is the same one that he made here shortly after his wife died. I wouldn't usually discuss a client's personal or financial matters without a court order to do so, but I consider his potential disappearance to be of sufficient seriousness to tell you that in that will he left everything to his daughter, apart from a few small bequests to various charities.'

'Thank you for that, I appreciate your help. Did Mr Berry happen to tell you any details about his travel plans? When he was leaving or where from? Did he mention if he was going by himself, for instance? And you presumably mentioned these travel plans to his daughter when she contacted you?'

'Well, no, I can't say that I did specifically. That probably sounds stupid but as I said we were distinctly at cross-purposes. Her main concern seemed to be about the sale of the house for such a low price, and we were somehow side-tracked into that aspect of it.

'It genuinely didn't occur to me that she didn't know about the cruise. She was asking me about whether or not he'd bought another property which I knew of and if I had the address so she could contact him.

'The reason he wanted such a quick sale – and I must point out here that that was against my advice because I thought he was underselling the property by some margin – was because he was booked to leave on a cruise two weeks after the completion date he was proposing. It made it very tight, but of course at the price he was looking for, he could be sure of a cash buyer and a quick sale.

'I don't recall him telling me that that particular cruise was the big round the world one, although he did tell me he planned to do one of those. As for where he left from, I'm not sure if he said but I rather thought, although I might be wrong on this, that perhaps the majority of such cruises leave from Southampton.

'I appreciate I'm not painting myself in a very good light here by not having been more attentive, but I really didn't see or hear anything at all which made me feel concerned for Mr Berry's welfare in any way. Quite the opposite, in fact. He actually got me thinking about what I was going to do after my own retirement.

'And no, he wasn't travelling alone. He was taking his principal carer with him, to assist him with things like carrying luggage on his various trips, he said.

'In fact the young man was with him at the time. He'd driven him, as Mr Berry was less and less keen to drive himself, although he was still quite capable. A pleasant young man, nice manners.'

'And do you happen to know the name of this young man, please?'

'I do indeed. Name of Simon Ropley.'

* * *

Ted and Oscar Smith had been watching the start of Rob's interview with Ian Hardy from another room, over the monitors.

'He's never going to talk,' Smith said. 'His brief will never let him, even if he wanted to. And I doubt he does, because he knows what will happen to him if he does and if the people he's done the work for find out about him. We need to get into his workshop while he's out of the way and see what we can find to charge him with.'

'All of which takes time while we get a warrant, and time is the one thing we don't have. The more time that goes by before we find Evie, the less likely we are to get a positive outcome.'

'Then let me interview him,' Smith told him. 'If he knows anything at all, I guarantee he'll tell me. Even with his brief present.'

There was a warning edge to Ted's voice as he replied.

'We've had this conversation before, DI Smith. We need to find Evie, but not at the expense of losing all chance of a prosecution.'

Smith's half-muttered, 'For fuck's sake,' didn't go unnoticed, but Ted didn't comment. He had more important things on his mind.

Rob O'Connell came in to join them while Hardy talked to his solicitor.

'He doesn't look like a man about to tell us anything, boss, without wanting to sound too negative. Even if he wanted to, I doubt his solicitor will let him. To be honest, I'm not even sure if he knows anything of much use to us. He looks a bit disorientated and vacant sometimes when I speak to him.'

'Find a way, Rob. Somehow. Appeal to his better nature, if he has one. Find out if he has children. Play on any parental instincts he might have, if so. Mention witness protection but don't make any promises. We need him to give us a steer. Anything at all. If all else fails, mention we're getting a warrant to search his premises, which might do the trick.'

His mobile phone interrupted him. He glanced at the screen. The ACC calling him. It gave him an instant sinking feeling.

'Sir?' he responded.

'Have you seen the gutter press today?' Russell Evans asked him, with no preamble.

Ted wasn't liking the sound of this.

'No sir, not yet. We've just brought someone in for questioning.'

'Well go and bloody look, then phone me straight back.'

'I have to go and make a call. Rob, as soon as they're ready to continue in there, you go in and try your best. I'll send Jo down to keep an eye on things so he'll be close if you need him. DI Smith, upstairs, with me. I'll need your report of what happened with Hardy as soon as possible. I won't have time to do my own yet and I have to present back to the top brass.'

Smith looked furious. Ted braced for an outburst. It was the last thing he needed on his plate for now. Then the DI gave a brief nod in acquiescence before setting off for the stairs in front of him.

'Do your best, Rob. Anything you can get out of him which might lead us to Evie. Any problems, ask Jo, if you can't get me.'

Ted sprinted up the stairs, anxious to find out what the papers had said to prompt the call from the ACC. He was filled with dread, knowing how they liked to twist the truth in search of sensation.

He entered a few key words and found several references to the case from the nationals. He first clicked the link of arguably the worst of them. Always lurid and controversial, they currently seemed to be on a major police-bashing campaign.

'COPS BLAME US!'

The main heading jumped out at Ted from the screen as his heart sank into his shoes.

'Inside: Exclusive as parents of snatch victim Baby Evie tell all'.

It was about as bad as it could get. Things which were standard police procedure in the disappearance of anyone were being bandied about as if out of the normal and 'proof' of pre-judgement by the police. Looking at phone contacts and usage, searching the family home. Precisely the things which, had they not been done and if the parents were later found to have been implicated in the disappearance of their own baby, would have seen them hung out to dry for failing on the basics.

Ted sat at his desk for a moment longer, reluctant to make the phone call. He felt like kicking something. Punching the wall. He was in for a bollocking and he knew it. What's more, he felt he deserved it. Four days the little baby had now been missing. Four days, and still nothing to show for it. No wonder the gutter press were blaming him. He was blaming himself.

He looked up at the ceiling, took a deep breath, then made the call.

'Sir.'

'You've read it then?' Russell Evans asked.

He sounded weary now. He'd probably already come in for some flak himself for not jumping on Ted and his team a lot sooner to get a result.

'It's about as bad as it gets, Ted. You don't need me to point that out to you.

'Tell me first of all how they managed to do all this without the liaison officer stopping them, or at least letting you know. And please tell me they've still got an LO with them.'

'Not round the clock, sir, no. Unfortunately. Needed elsewhere and not enough cover to go round.'

It sounded like a feeble excuse. But it was true, and they both knew it. The Fisher family had been lucky to have been allocated a dedicated FLO for as long as they had. Little wonder they were feeling badly let down now she'd been pulled for much of the time and there was still no sign of their baby.

The ACC let out a long sigh.

'Then we're all in the shit, to put it mildly. Deeper than I thought.

'This is not good for any of us, Ted, least of all for you. You know, of course, that Sammy is having to retire. The Chief and I were discussing making you back up to Head of Serious Crime, as you were before. Simplest thing, and the most economical.

'If you can't get a conclusion on this case soon, especially now all our dirty linen is hanging out to dry in the media, that's simply not going to be an option. You risk someone being brought in over your head. Someone you may not get on as well with as you have with Sammy. None of us want that.

'Right, the Chief is in a meeting at the moment. To say he's not best pleased is the understatement of the week. He wants you and Sammy up here end of play to talk damage limitation. Is there any sign of progress at all you can wave at him?'

'We've brought someone in for questioning, sir. We believe him to be the person who supplied the car used to take Evie to wherever she went from the park. The one later found burned out, with a body inside it. We're getting a warrant to search his premises and he's being interviewed now.'

'Good, that's something, at least. We could throw the media the line of "a man is helping police with their enquiries" in time for the evening news slots. We'll talk later.'

Ted barely had time to get in another 'Sir' before the call was ended abruptly.

He was only halfway through kicking yet another waste-paper basket to death when, after the briefest of knocks, Oscar Smith stuck his head round the door without waiting for an invitation.

He took in the scene at a glance and grinned broadly.

'That good, eh, guv? Done the Hardy report, sent it through to you. So now will you let me have a turn at talking to him? My finely honed policing skills tell me that you might be more in need of a break now than ever before.'

'I don't want you doing anything at all which either puts him off talking to us, or jeopardises using anything he might tell us in any future trial.'

Smith snapped him a sharp military salute, then put his right hand over his tie.

'My technique will be exemplary, guv. I promise on the honour of my regiment. *Exemplo ducemus.* By example shall we lead.'

Chapter Eighteen

When Hardy and his solicitor returned to the interview room from where they'd been consulting in private, Hardy looked concerned to see the big bulky shape sitting there waiting for him.

The copper who'd chased after him had looked big, but somehow in the confined space, the figure sitting opposite him looked a lot bulkier. Even seated, the overall impression was of a hefty build.

The former paunch Smith had been sporting was much reduced since he'd decided to take himself in hand to try to regain the fitness levels he'd been required to maintain as a serving Army officer. It wasn't yet quite at the washboard standard he'd kept up for when he had to do the annual fitness test, but it was getting there.

He'd not yet got his sprinting form back either, but the unexpected sight of a looming presence once more at close quarters was clearly troubling to Hardy. He could read the signs well enough. Not someone to be messed with. Hardy's body language emanated fear predominantly but also something else harder to define.

Ted had firmly marked Smith's card before agreeing to let him take over the interview and had taken Rob aside to assure him of Jo's watching presence. He wasn't convinced of how effective Jo would be if Smith got out of hand. On his own admission, Jo was more of a lover than a fighter. Ted hoped it wouldn't come to any form of a showdown. He was gambling on Smith unsettling Hardy more than Rob or Jo would do, in the hopes he might say something – anything – of use to them.

'You remember me from earlier, Ian. Detective Inspector Smith, Metropolitan Police,' Oscar began for the benefit of the solicitor.

He addressed himself to the man directly. He'd dismissed his solicitor at a glance. He'd filed her under 'Wouldn't say no if it was offered and I was desperate,' at which point he'd lost most interest in her.

'Were you the one who can't run more than fifty yards without puffing like an old walrus?' Hardy sneered at him in a show of bravado, now there was a table between them and his solicitor was sitting next to him. 'I remember that.'

The solicitor intervened at that point with a question.

'May I ask, for clarification, why a Met officer is questioning my client about some incident alleged to have occurred in Greater Manchester?'

'I'm here to collaborate on an ongoing case as there have been ones with identical features in my area. In fact it was someone from my manor who gave me your details, Ian. They were shown the work done to falsify the plates, the VIN and other identifying features on a car which came to the attention of the police up here. One which had been used to snatch a little baby from her mother and which was then found burned out, with a body in it. A murder victim.'

Hardy tried to brazen it out again.

'That's bollocks, that is. No one can tell whose work it is on a stolen motor that's had its plates changed.'

'And you'd know that, because, of course, that's your trade,' Smith told him.

Hardy put on a look of studious indignation. Smith had seen it all before.

'Not for years, though. I stopped doing that ages ago, after the last time I got nicked for it. You can't prove it was me, anyway. Like I said, no one can tell who's done work like that.'

'Are you absolutely sure of that, Ian? Sure enough to stake your freedom on it? Because in the big city, we have our sources. Reliable ones. Ones happy to testify for us. Giving their expert opinion in court when it's necessary. And one of them – the best in the country in the motor trade, as it happens – is right on my patch. And right in my pocket.'

Hardy was starting to shift nervously in his seat now. Clearly what Smith was saying to him rang a bell with him somewhere, although so far it didn't mean a lot to Rob, nor to Jo, watching and listening over the monitors from another room.

'You've probably heard of him, Ian,' Smith told him, his tone now pleasant and jovial. He might simply have been putting one friend in touch with another. 'They call him Rain Man. That's because he's a genius. No one knows their trade more than he does.'

Something he said had hit home with Hardy and was making him extremely nervous. His insides were audibly gurgling away at an alarming rate and Smith made a face at a sudden pungent aroma.

'Bloody hell, Ian, do let us know if you need to use the khazi, mate. Preferably in plenty of time.'

'Perhaps you'd like to keep this interview on a professional basis, inspector. Especially as it's still pre any sort of charge. Perhaps we should take a short comfort break now, for my client?'

'Ian? What do you say? Do you need the lav?' Smith asked him, in a tone which suggested he wasn't expecting the man to say yes.

Hardy wriggled about even more in his seat but shook his head.

'Perhaps you'd like to come to the point, inspector?' the solicitor suggested. 'I think my client is being very patient. You clearly have nothing on which to charge him, or you would have done so by now.'

'Yet,' Smith looked and spoke directly to the man, who was growing increasingly uncomfortable, ignoring his solicitor. 'We're not charging you yet, Ian, but we've applied for a search warrant for your premises and believe me, whatever you have in there that you wouldn't want us to find, we will find it.

'From your reaction, I have a strong suspicion that you know all about Rain Man. That you know about his reputation, at least, and you know, as a consequence, that he is a reliable expert witness. If he says the work on the car was done by you, then it was. No matter how much you deny it. He'll say that in court, too and I can tell you from first-hand experience, juries believe him. Ninety-nine point nine per cent of the time.

'Now, dodgy plates is one thing. If we push for a prosecution on that, you might be lucky and get away with another fine and a rap on the knuckles. But anything linked to baby-snatching and murder ...'

No one present could fail to notice the aroma in the room increasing in intensity. Hardy's nervousness was clearly manifesting itself in a seriously upset digestive system.

'I really think now would be a good time for a short comfort break to regroup, inspector, so that I can advise my client again in light of your disclosures. I'll make sure he doesn't abscond.'

Oscar Smith may behave like a total caveman a lot of the time. But he'd had the training as an officer and a gentleman in the armed forces. He opened the door to the corridor then stood aside to allow the solicitor to go out first.

She paused a brief instant as she drew level with him and said, half under her breath, 'Thank you for allowing the welcome break. I was nearly passing out.'

Smith wasn't sure what to make of the smile she gave him. He'd never been flirted with over a fart before, but there was a first time for everything. For now, he, Rob and Jo needed to go and report to the guv'nor on where they were up to. Oscar really wanted to be the one to get Hardy to talk, to find the link which would lead them to the kidnappers and hopefully even find the kid and bring it back alive. He was determined to show this shower up here that whatever the reputation of the Met, coppers like him could still get the results, and take them all the way to a successful trial.

Ted heard them come into the main office and came out of his own to hear their update. He didn't want Rob or Jo spotting the mangled remains of his waste-paper basket. Bad enough that Smith, of all people, had seen him lose control like that.

As soon as he saw Smith enter the room, Steve half rose from his seat, a print out in his hand. He looked first, as always, towards his own boss, although it was clearly Smith he wanted to talk to.

'Sir, sorry to interrupt, but it's the face, sir. The one DI Smith thought he recognised.'

Even though Ted had proved he could outrun him, Smith could move quickly when he needed to. He was across the office in a couple of strides, hand out for the paperwork Steve was clutching.

'Not thought. I know I recognised him. What have you got, and where's he from?'

He all but snatched the paper from Steve's hands, making him recoil slightly, although he stood his ground.

'South Manchester, sir. A known broker for stolen vehicles made anonymous, but as slippery as soap. A middle man, between the fixers and anyone who needs an untraceable motor. The most recent case against him collapsed because some of the witnesses had a sudden change of heart.

'He's thought to be involved in all sorts of other stuff, usually as the middle man again, but he's very good at covering his tracks.'

Smith was studying the crime record photograph of the man, slapping the paper with the back of one hand.

'That's him. That's the bloke I've seen. I've seen him since I've been up here. Not down south. I don't recognise him in a London context at all and I certainly would if he was anywhere on my manor. Those are the eyes from the second composite. We lost time with the first one because it wasn't accurate enough.

'Alec King,' Smith read aloud from the paper he was looking at. 'Nice bit of previous for all the sorts of things you might imagine, although nothing as serious as being involved in baby snatching.

'Guv, can I show this to Hardy now, to see what his reaction is? I know this is meant to be the phony photographer but I'd say there's an outside chance he could be involved in more than that, and his record bears that out.

'He's not the same bloke as our scouts, like the doting

godfather. But if he's spotting the kiddies, it's likely he has the trust of whoever's behind this because he probably knows, or has a good inkling, what they want them for, and is still happy to go ahead.

'He could even be the man who collected the car from Hardy, and delivered it to the snatchers, if he already has their confidence that he'll keep his mouth shut. He could quite possibly have been the driver for the pick-up. too. Maybe involved in the murder by arson. Whatever, he still might be an important link in the chain. More than we have already. So we need to lift him. Soon. Before he gets any inkling we might be on to him, or he hears on the grapevine that we've got Hardy. And someone is bound to spot us turning over Hardy's workshop, so word will get out.

'We need to find him and bring him in as soon as possible. And we need to let each of them know we have the other one. We've taken a break now because Hardy was literally on the point of shitting himself when he heard we had an expert witness who could point the finger squarely at him for supplying the false plates. Waving this at him, if he does know this bloke, might just tip him over the edge and loosen his tongue.'

'Will he talk, d'you think? Whatever you do, don't offer him false promises we can't then come through on. There needs to be no coercion, no deception.'

'He might already be halfway out of the window in the khazi and ready to leg it off up the road. He's clearly running scared. He knows whoever's behind this has already killed anyone who might risk identifying them, unless they're trusted parts of the team. He's clearly pond life, on their scale. They'd sacrifice him easily enough. He'll know that, so he's going to want some form of protection before he'll say anything at all. And even then he might not.

'One thing I can tell you, though, is he's a shite liar. Literally. Even if his body language doesn't give him away, his guts do. Surely it's worth a shot?'

Ted glanced at his watch. He was going to have to leave shortly for the meeting at Central Park with Sammy. A breakthrough was what he badly needed to wave at the top brass, but only if it was solid enough. This was potentially the most solid to date. And it might give them two people 'helping police with their enquiries' which might buy him more time, if they were seriously thinking of side-lining him from taking over once more as Head of Serious Crime. He made a decision.

'Tell Hardy we've had some positive ID from a composite. Another person of interest. Don't show it to him yet, or mention the context, but make sure he knows we're following a strong lead and any information about it is valuable to us. Tell him we're asking everyone we talk to if they recognise the person, which is true enough. If he gives you a name, or even anything at all which could lead to him, phone me straight away. I have to go to HQ now, and I could really do with something positive to report.'

'So who do you want on which, guv? Who stays on Hardy and who goes and hauls in Alec King?'

Ted's mobile signalled an incoming SMS. He glanced at it briefly. Sammy Sampson, asking where he was and reminding him they needed to leave for Central Park soon or they were going to be late.

He badly wanted to stay. Not just because he wasn't looking forward to a potentially bumpy ride at HQ. That went with his rank and position. But he would have preferred to be in a position to keep an eye on DI Smith. The closer they got to a real suspect, the more delicate things became. The greater the risk of something going catastrophically wrong at the eleventh hour. Not just losing them the arrests they wanted to make but potentially putting baby Evie's life in serious danger. Always assuming that she was, by some miracle, still alive.

In normal circumstances, he wouldn't hesitate to hand over to Jo, knowing he was leaving everything in safe hands. The current wild card came in the form of a truculent Met officer by the name of Smith.

He made a quick decision and hoped he wouldn't live to regret it.

'You stay with Hardy and see what you can get out of him. Refer to Jo before you promise him anything. And please stay within the guidelines. We can't afford to have this all blow up in our faces just when we may be getting somewhere.

'Get Rob to sort a warrant then he can go and bring Alec King in as soon as possible, and get his place thoroughly searched for anything of use. He can interview him, too.

'Don't tell either of them that the other is here, and try not to let them catch a glimpse of each other, either. That could work against us in the future.

'I'm going to be pretty much do not disturb while I'm at HQ but if there's genuinely anything of any interest, or there is any sign of a breakthrough at all, phone me straight away.'

In both his Military and Metropolitan Police careers, Oscar Smith had many times found himself standing, often to attention, in front of one senior officer or another, having to explain himself. He prided himself on his ability to think on his feet, the only reason he had emerged with no serious blots on his copy book. He strongly suspected it was a rare occurrence for Darling, from what he'd seen and heard of him. Hard to imagine a more by the book sort of copper. Not how Oscar operated but, despite himself, he was coming round to feeling some respect for the short, quiet man who clearly got good results, doing things his way.

Ted collected Sammy from her office and the two of them headed out in search of Ted's service vehicle. He was noticing more and more how stiffly she moved, and how despite her self-control, she seemed to be wincing more often. He knew how gutted she was to be forced into early retirement, but it was clear that she was in too much pain too often to carry on for much longer.

'All ready for our appointment in the lion's den?' Sammy asked him as they reached the car and Ted unlocked it.

'I really wish you hadn't put it quite like that,' Ted told her with feeling, as he slid into the driver's seat.

Chapter Nineteen

Bob Norris, owner of the big Great Dane, had been rather left dangling since his confession to tipping off the phony photographer about where and when to find baby Evie. It was a gamble, but a safe enough one. He was clearly not going anywhere. Not with the financial problems he had.

The file with all the details he had given in his voluntary statement had been forwarded to the Crown Prosecution Service for advice about charging him, but was still pending. Ted's personal view was that it would be deemed to be not in the public interest to bring a prosecution. Even though the man had admitted what he'd done, so would almost certainly plead guilty, it seemed unlikely in the extreme that he could have foreseen the consequences of his actions.

With Rob, who'd been speaking to Norris so far, tied up on bringing in Alec King for questioning, DS Mike Hallam decided to go round for an update with the man. However culpable he was, he still had the right to be kept in the picture about his likely fate. He'd also not yet been shown the updated artist's impression of the man he'd seen as the so-called photographer. With the change to the eyes suggested by DI Smith, it really was a remarkable likeness to Alec King, compared against his record. Norris couldn't now be shown any photos of King in isolation, so as not to influence any future identification he might be asked to make. But he could be asked which of the two composites was the more like the man he had seen.

Once they'd brought Alec King in, they'd be likely, at some point, to get any potential witnesses to look at a collection of photos or videos which included him. Norris would be asked to participate, as would the baby's mother herself and her friend, Denise Doyle, mother of the toddler whose seemingly genuine fall had provided the distraction the snatcher needed to disappear with Evie.

Mike doubted whether either of the two women would have noticed the phony photographer, even if they had seen him at any point. He certainly wouldn't have done anything to draw attention to himself, including having the camera on show. If he was as smart as he seemed to be, he wouldn't have gone anywhere near either of them on the same day he spoke to Norris. Or to both Mr and Mrs Norris, if Rob was right about the man lying to protect his wife from being implicated.

So far, they'd not had much luck with identifying the body in the car, or finding anyone other than Mrs Wood, the cat owner, who had seen the woman hurrying out of the park, wearing the bulky coat. There'd been fewer calls in response to the picture they'd released of her, based on Mrs Wood's description, and none so far had led them anywhere.

Professor Nelson was working with experts on a reconstruction of the head and face of the body in the car in the hopes that might then bring forward more witnesses, when that likeness was released to the media. Looking at a 3D head always resulted in more calls than a flat composite image. But such things always took time. The one commodity they didn't have much of.

Mike Hallam got his first look at Bob Norris when he opened the door in response to the ring on the doorbell. Mike had been half-expecting the big hound to come bounding to greet him, but there was no sign of it and the house was silent.

He was shocked, too, at the sight of Norris. He'd seen the effects of feelings of guilt on people before now, as they wrestled with their consciences over what to tell the police. Norris was grey in the face, unshaven. He looked as if he had neither slept nor eaten anything since he'd been in to the station to confess only two days ago. The house had an unnatural stillness about it, as well as the pervading quiet. Not only no sign of the big dog, but none of Norris's wife, either. From what Rob had reported back about them, Mike couldn't believe she'd taken the big beast out for a walk by herself.

Mike held up his card as he asked, 'Mr Norris? Detective Sergeant Hallam. Can I have a word, please?'

The man's face fell instantly. He looked stricken.

'Have you come to arrest me? Oh no, this is going to destroy the wife. Today, of all days. We're just back from the vet's. We had to have our Sidney put down.'

The man's voice broke as he said it. Mike felt uncomfortable. He wasn't much of an animal lover. As a father, he felt a certain hostility towards the man because his actions, albeit unintentionally, had led to baby Evie being snatched, and he couldn't begin to imagine what her parents were going through. But he'd also seen Rob's interview notes, so he knew the big dog, like all of its predecessors, had been a surrogate child to the couple who had lost their only one.

He replied in as gentle a tone as he could manage, 'I'm not here to arrest you, Mr Norris. I need to check a few details with you about the person you saw in the park. The photographer.'

Norris made a derisive noise.

'As I thought he was. Stupid, stupid old fool. This is all my fault. Is there still no word of that poor little baby?'

'Not yet, Mr Norris, although we are currently interviewing two persons of interest. So would it be all right if we had a chat? Perhaps with both of you, if your wife is feeling up to it.'

'She's very upset. We both are. But of course we'll do our best to help. She doesn't know anything about the man, though. That was all my fault. It was me who took the money from him, without questioning.'

He was quick to reiterate what he'd told Rob. Looking at him as he said it, Mike didn't believe him any more than Rob had done.

Norris led the way into the front room. His wife was lying on the sofa, looking even worse than he did. Her face was puffy and blotched from crying, tears clearly not yet done with her as they started again at the sight of Mike following her husband into the room. She shot bolt upright to a sitting position, some sixth sense telling her that this was another police visit, her expression showing she feared the worst from this one.

'Love, this is Detective Halliwell,' her husband told her.

Wrong on both counts, Mike thought to himself, but he didn't bother to correct the man. The pair of them were clearly distraught about their pet. He thought he'd better say something by way of expressing condolences. He wasn't at all sure what the appropriate wording was for a pet, especially when he was here in connection with something far more serious, but he did his best to empathise and to sound sincere.

'Sorry to hear about your dog, Mrs Norris.'

'Is there any news about that poor little baby? Her parents must be frantic by now.'

'We're following up all leads and are currently talking to two people of interest,' Mike fed them the glib official line. 'That's partly why I'm here. Mr Norris, we've made a slight change to the composite you helped to construct of the man you saw in the park, based on what another witness told us. The man you believed to be a photographer.

'If I show you the two pictures side by side, could you tell me, please, which one looks most like the man you described to us.'

Mike didn't know if the house was sparsely furnished because of the size of dog they'd had, or because of their financial circumstances, but there was nothing like a coffee table to hand. No surface anywhere he could put the pictures on, so he held them up, side by side.

Mrs Norris spoke first, before her husband could stop her.

'The one in your left hand. That's him.'

'You weren't there, dear, remember …'

She waved a dismissive hand towards him.

'Oh, it's well past time for us to be honest, Bob. Part of the blame for all this is on us.'

She looked earnestly toward Mike Hallam, tears now flowing freely down her face.

'That's the man who spoke to us in the park. The other one's close but the eyes aren't right. And I was there. It never for a moment occurred to either of us that our actions would have the result they did. We were desperate for money. To help Sidney. Our dog.

'The vet kept telling us "we could try these new pills. They're a bit expensive, but they can work miracles". We just wanted to help Sidney. He was our baby. But we were stupid. And naive.

'Now I'm prepared to face the consequences, and to do anything possible to put things right. That's definitely the man. It's quite accurate, and I'll say so anywhere you need me to. In court or whatever it takes.

'That's the man with the camera who was asking us about pretty babies.'

* * *

Virgil had had no idea how popular cruise holidays were. If he'd considered it at all, he'd rather imagined they were a thing of the past. The glory days, when people seemed to have more money to spare for lavish trips and would board ship with a collection of large leather cabin trunks. Like something out of an Agatha Christie.

Even the eye-wateringly expensive round-the-world luxury ones still seemed always to be booked up well in advance, and there were more of them than he'd anticipated. Not that he knew for certain that's where John Berry had gone, with or without his carer, Simon Ropley. But it was as good a starting point as any, from what the solicitor had told him.

He was even more surprised to find that there were still some travel agents operating from premises in and around town. Not something he'd ever looked into, as his holidays with his wife and small daughter were usually spent visiting family members in various places. The type of commercial budget holidays they could afford didn't appeal to either of them.

He'd rather thought most people would do things like

holiday bookings independently, online, these days. He decided on the personal approach and went out in person, finding one agency where a helpful young woman called Sasha was more than happy to assist him, especially as there seemed to be something of a lull in activity in the shop.

'I'm on a needle in a haystack mission,' Virgil told her as he showed her his ID. 'I'm trying to find an older man who's been reported missing by his family, but there's a possibility he's actually gone off on a cruise with a friend. Possibly even a round the world cruise. So somehow I need a way to check names of passengers on board various cruise ships which might have left at around the right time. And I don't even know where to start looking. Oh, and this needs to be kept confidential, please, if you can even help me at all.'

She gave him an encouraging look as she said, 'Well, the good news is that more than ninety per cent of all cruise passengers embark at Southampton, so that's as good a place to start as any.

'Do you have any idea whether or not this person would have booked independently online or through an agency? It would be a very long shot but I could perhaps start by checking our client list to see if the person you're looking for has booked something through us. I'm presuming the person has local connections.'

'Yes, and can you do that? Is it not confidential?'

'I'd just need to make a quick phone call to my boss to check, but I think it will be fine in the circumstances. After all, if someone is worried about him and he may possibly be missing, I'm sure they'd be reassured if we can find out that he's fine and enjoying the trip of a lifetime on a cruise liner.

'Of course in one of those terrible crime things on telly, he would have booked from here and I'd have sold him the ticket, but I've not sold a round the world one for a while. Just give me a minute and I'll get authorisation to help with your enquiries.'

It didn't take her long to make her phone call and from the possible time-frame which Virgil gave her, she was able to produce for him a list of potential cruises John Berry might have gone on, with detailed instructions of which companies to contact and how to go about obtaining passenger lists. It was going to be a bigger task than Virgil had envisaged, but at least he felt he was making some progress. She was also able to confirm that John Berry's name didn't appear anywhere on their client database. Nor did that of Simon Ropley.

Still quite a few ifs to overcome, but if John Berry had left on a cruise from Southampton, travelling under his own name, he should show up on a passenger list somewhere and would hopefully turn out to be sunning himself on the first class deck of a liner, either out at sea or moored in an exotic port.

The other possibility was darker. That was if the John Berry booked onto one of the ships turned out to be a young man in his twenties, travelling alone.

* * *

'Make it right with the parents, Ted, whatever you do. The last thing we need from the media is a very public show of conflict between us and them. Go round there today, before you even think of knocking off, and smooth things over,' Ted's chief constable, Jon Woodrow, told him at the end of their meeting.

Ted had given him as much of an update as he could,

painfully aware that it didn't actually amount to much. Hopefully it would be enough to convince him he could go off to his squash tournament, knowing they were doing all they could and there was at least the glimmer of some hope and progress.

No hope of Ted doing anything except for work over the weekend, the way things were shaping up. He'd need to make that right with Trev. Again.

The worst part, as far as Ted was concerned, was that since the exclusive article had appeared in the scandal sheet, the parents' home was under constant media siege. Which meant that Ted going there would involve cameras and microphones being shoved in his face while he was pounded with endless questions.

It was enough to put him in another waste-paper basket murdering mood, had he not already killed one today.

He dropped Sammy off back at the station first. It wasn't fair to put her through the ordeal as well. He was SIO. The responsibility was solely his.

He took a brief moment to fire off yet another apologetic text to Trev, explaining he'd be late and not to wait to eat. He didn't dare mention in a text message his likely absence for the weekend, unless they had a miraculous breakthrough. That would be safest done in person.

Ted tried to keep his expression neutral as he ducked his head and ran the gauntlet of the waiting media. It didn't improve his mood to see that police officers had had to be stationed close to the house to keep them back. Total waste of resources, but something the worried parents clearly hadn't considered when they'd agreed to talk to the papers. Ted didn't say anything to any of the press pack, not even a 'no comment'.

The Fishers looked surprised to see him there in person. An initial ray of hope in both their faces quickly turned to one of anguish, wondering what would have brought the Senior Investigating Officer to their house himself, rather than him sending one of the team.

'There's nothing new, I'm afraid. And I'm sorry that you both clearly feel let down by my handling of the case. I apologise for that, and I've come in person so I can update you on everything, to avoid any misunderstanding. I want to stress that you can always contact me, in person, directly, any time you want to. I'm sorry if I hadn't made that clear enough before.'

He sat down with them and spent time replying as honestly as he could to all of their questions. He left the house feeling that at least they were now more reassured of his sincerity and the diligence of his team, if nothing else.

He was pleasantly surprised, when he got back to the nick, long after most of the team had left, to find Oscar Smith in the old DI's office, now usually occupied by Mike Hallam, typing up reports.

He looked up as the boss walked in, took in at a glance how frazzled he looked, and suggested, 'Pub?'

Ted shook his head.

'Not this time.'

'Wife at home waiting for you?' Smith asked him.

'No wife, no,' Ted told him, without going into details. He instinctively felt that he'd prefer not to share his domestic circumstances with the man.

'I suppose having seven judgemental cats is even worse when you're late home, again,' Smith told him.

'Before I can even think of heading home, I need a full update of where we're up to with Ian Hardy, and especially with Alec King.

'I'll put the kettle on. You fill me in.'

Chapter Twenty

'We've offered our hospitality for the night to both Ian Hardy and Alec King, owing to their inability to explain to our satisfaction some of the contents of their respective premises. Although I pity the poor sod who gets to clean the lav in Hardy's cell. His guts are worse than ever since we issued our invitation. I did ask the custody sergeant to make sure he has plenty of bog roll and soap. He seems a bit out of it a lot of the time, like he doesn't know where he is or why, but it's been explained to him.

'Oh, and the two of them may possibly have accidentally clocked one another whilst being transferred to their respective interview rooms, although you said not to let them. My fault, guv. Purely unintentional, as per your orders,' Smith informed Ted, somewhat glibly.

That news bothered Ted. He didn't want the risk of any case against any suspect to be compromised by allegations of improper procedure regarding identification. It was good to know, though, that Hardy's basic needs had been catered for. It wouldn't be the first time some clever lawyer had tried that angle, resulting in someone almost certainly guilty having been allowed out on bail, only to disappear completely off the radar.

'How did they react?' he asked.

'King is a pro, for sure. He totally blanked Hardy, so I can't tell you whether or not he recognised him. Hardy's reaction was strange. He doesn't have a poker face, and his guts always let him down anyway. But he didn't react at all to King. Almost as if he genuinely had never seen him before. But like I said, he seems to be in a bit of a daze some of the time.

'Searches of both premises are still ongoing. Hardy is stupid enough to have made himself a note of the false plate numbers he put on the car we found, so that's going to take some explaining, if he denies having done it. So on the basis of that, I've had the team trawling CCTV from around his place to see if there's any chance we might find a trace of the vehicle, either going there on its old plates, or being driven away on the new ones. And that might possibly, in turn, give us a glimpse of whoever was driving it. Hopefully Alec King, and recognisably him.'

Ted finished brewing up and put the mugs down on the desk, taking a seat opposite Smith, who took a pull at his coffee, still barely below boiling point, and made an appreciative noise.

'That's not bad. You remembered.'

Then he looked at the contents of Ted's mug and pulled a face.

'But what the hell is that? It looks like a urine sample provided by someone with a serious medical problem.'

Ted laughed, in spite of the pressures of the day. Or probably because of them. It was good to have some sort of release from all the tensions.

'Green tea. Good for balancing the chakras, or so I was told.'

Smith still looked dubious as he went on, 'If you say so. Anyway, one of the more interesting, and rather surprising, finds at King's place was a hard copy list of telephone numbers. Hand-written, too. It seems not everyone keeps them exclusively on their mobiles as that way they know how easy it is to lose them, or for them to fall into the wrong hands.

'One of my other party tricks, as well as never forgetting a face, is recognising numbers. I can't always instantly recall whose they might be, but I do know ones I've seen before. There were some on his list that I've definitely come across, so I've got my team working on those.

'I'd say we're in with a sporting chance of getting somewhere, at last, through King. My gut feeling is that Hardy is too far down the pecking order to tell us anything, even if he could do without shitting himself. Literally. But if we can hang onto King and lean on him a bit ...'

'Anything he tells us under duress is of no use to us in court,' Ted reminded him.

'But at least we might get the kiddy back,' Smith countered. 'So far yours is the only case with any chance of that happening. With no sign anywhere of any of the others, alive or brown bread, it's a racing certainty they're already long gone, overseas probably, and will never be found.

'King's on a rest period now, at the request of his lawyer who claimed he was showing signs of undue stress. Total bollocks, of course, but I agreed to it to show we were being reasonable. So what if I grab something quickly at the pub then come back in later on to have another go at him?'

Ted was already shaking his head before Smith had finished speaking.

'No one is speaking to him without a solicitor present, if that's what he wants, and there is to be no form of undue pressure put on him at all. If his solicitor has gone home, you'd have to wait until they got back here before you speak to him again.'

'So meantime we all end up looking like total pillocks if the sprog is smuggled out of the country while we sit here, thumb in bum and mind in neutral.'

He was sounding frustrated to the point of anger now, and Ted didn't entirely blame him. He'd just come from promising the baby's parents the police were doing everything they could to bring Evie home, but in a sense the Met officer was right. Ted was walking the line so carefully they were facing the real risk that his caution could dash any hopes of a positive outcome.

Ted made a decision.

'Find out when his solicitor can get back, and Hardy's, too, as soon as reasonably possible, and let me know the time. Finish what you're doing here, then go and get something to eat in The Grapes. I'll come and join you shortly, if there's time. We can probably use the back room again so we can talk tactics while we eat.'

Ted not only wanted some desk time to catch up on everything, he wanted to phone Trev and at least tell him in person now that his weekend looked like being non-existent, as regards them spending any time together.

'I half-expected it so I've arranged to go riding with Willow tomorrow. She's leaving Rupert to babysit then she and I can have a proper gossip. I can bitch about life with a copper and she can tell me how hard it can be when two super models share living space.

'I'll also find some time to phone my sister to have a long talk with her, to see if I can find out what's going on in her life this time.'

'Is it still sexual identity issues? Why don't you go down and see her?' Ted suggested. 'A bit of bonding with her big brother might be just what she needs, and at least she knows you'll support her however she identifies. It sounds as if she's in need of someone to talk to and you know she looks up to you. What time are you riding with Willow?'

'Late morning. You know neither of us gets up early on days off. But I suppose I could do that. It might be nice, for both of us. What about the cats, though, if you're working all weekend?'

'I promise I won't let them starve. I'll need to go home at some point, no matter how chaotic it gets. Go. We'll be fine. Stay somewhere nice, take Eirian out to eat somewhere you'll both like. I'll put some money on your card. It can be my treat, for yet another ruined weekend, and it really does sound as if she could do with some big brotherly advice and support. If Sir Gethin is worried enough to be discussing it with you, you'd perhaps do best to go and at least find out what's troubling her.'

* * *

One thing in Smith's favour, as Ted was finding out, was that all his report-writing and other paperwork was meticulously done. Whitewashed, no doubt, of anything which could potentially come back to bite him, or scupper a case, but well presented.

Prompt, too. He'd already written up everything that had happened whilst Ted was out of the office. And he was right. Looking at his reports, it seemed that Hardy, the most likely to talk to them, would have the least to say of any use whereas Alec King, possibly the phony photographer, seemed on the surface to be the one unlikely to say anything much.

Ted took the time for a quick overview of everything else which had been reported over the day. He was quick to pick up on Mike's report of his visit to the Norris's address and Mrs Norris's firm identification of the altered image of Alec King. She would make a compelling witness. Anyone prepared to implicate themselves in anything, especially something as sordid as, albeit unwittingly, facilitating the snatching of baby Evie, would have no trouble convincing a jury of the sincerity of their testimony.

King was clearly the person they needed to lean on hardest, and first, to have any hope of locating wherever the baby was being kept, if she was both still alive and still in the country.

Once he'd finished his catch-up, he walked round to The Grapes and found Smith already in the back room, getting stuck into a plate of hotpot, and with the phone to his ear.

'He doesn't like the salmon one with carrots in it. I told you that, and no, it doesn't help if you pick the carrots out. You have to give him the one without any,' he was saying into his phone as Ted approached.

Ted hesitated, not wanting to interrupt on a private conversation, but Smith waved him to his seat and gave an exaggerated eye roll and a distinctive hand gesture to indicate his opinion of whoever he was talking to.

Ted had bought himself a Gunner at the bar, Dave promising to bring his food through to him as soon as it was ready. Ted had opted for the steak and kidney pie. It could be a long night ahead and he felt in need of fortification for whatever was still to come.

He sat down as Smith was finishing his phone call.

'Bloody cattery,' the DI grumbled as he rang off. 'Especially coming hard on the heels of another earbashing from my grandmother. I told them when I booked him in that Clive won't eat carrots with his salmon. Clearly they thought they knew best and I was a neurotic cat owner. I've had the little sod long enough to know what he likes. What do you call your seven?'

Smith looked at him in surprise as Ted recited his cats' names.

'I wouldn't have had you down as a Queen fan.'

'What, then, if not them?' Ted asked him, intrigued in spite of himself.

Smith was studying him as he might someone he was about to interview, trying to read beyond the expressionless face to the person within.

'Classical music, perhaps? Something staid? Or perhaps even some trad jazz?'

Ted laughed at that, despite the seriousness of their case.

'Classical? I'm just a miner's lad from the Lancashire coalfields. Anyway, where are we up to with our suspects? What about King's solicitor? How soon can we interview him?'

Smith checked his watch for timings. Ted wasn't surprised that he wore one, nor that it was an impressive timepiece with all sorts of dials for different functions.

'Half an hour for King. Hardy has to wait for his, who's currently tied up on something else, so we've time to eat and talk strategy. Meanwhile I've sent the list of phone numbers through to Tony, my DS, and he's checking them against any on our radar. He knows it's urgent, so there's an outside chance we might have something to link King to our cases before we talk to him.

'This could quite possibly be it, Ted. We might finally be getting somewhere.'

'There's more, too. I read Mike Hallam's report before I came over here. The man who spoke to the phony photographer, who produced the first likeness of him. Mike showed him the altered one you suggested. His wife was there. He'd denied she was involved, but she's now admitted she was in the park that day, and she picked the second composite as being the more accurate. Straight away, with no hesitation. That's going to make compelling testimony in the circumstances.'

They were interrupted at that point by Dave, bringing in Ted's food.

'Here you go, Ted. Enjoy. Can I bring you gents anything else?'

'Another lager for me,' Smith told him.

Ted noticed the lack of a please. He wondered if that was an Army thing, to do with rank. It wasn't his own style, at all, but he wasn't about to comment though he did look quizzically at Smith. He didn't want to have to remind him in front of Dave about the no drinking on duty rule.

Smith's response was to smile and pivot his empty bottle round before Dave removed it.

'Alcohol free, guv, as Dave is my witness. On duty and raring to go.'

* * *

Ted immediately recognised the solicitor with Alec King. He knew he was good at his job, with an above average record for successful defence. He would certainly not come cheap, which might of itself hinted that King was an important link in the chain of a much bigger organisation.

Ted wanted to keep a watching brief. To see at close

quarters how Smith conducted himself, and only to intervene if he thought he could contribute something useful which had been overlooked by the Met officer. If the solicitor thought it unusual to find both a DI and a DCI interviewing his client, he didn't show it.

Smith was so far going by the book. He was more ordered and methodical in his questioning than Ted had feared he might be, and was certainly a details man. He was quick to pounce on the slightest ambiguity and pick it over again and again until it was straightened out.

King was mostly staying enigmatically silent in response, apart from the occasional 'no comment' or a brief factual reply. Both he and his solicitor appeared to have something of a smug complacency about them. As if they were holding cards which would beat any other hand, and they alone knew about them.

'We have two reliable eye witnesses who will testify that they saw you in the park shortly before the baby disappeared, and that you gave them money to tell you where you could find pretty babies to photograph for a supposed catalogue job.

'In addition, we have someone who can testify that you are the person who collected a car with altered number plates and other ID. A car which we can show to have been the vehicle which was used to transport the baby away from her mother. One which was later found destroyed by arson, with a body inside it.'

This time King's smile was a definite sneer of triumph. The look of someone who definitely knew more than the two officers did.

'Well, good luck with that.'

Ted called for a break, leaving King to talk to his

solicitor. There was definitely a subtext to all of this of which they were not aware, and Ted didn't like that. They were going nowhere as long as they knew less about the suspects they were trying to question than they needed to.

He and Smith went in search of Hardy and found him safely installed in another interview room waiting, together with his solicitor. It was the same one as before, which might suggest someone familiar with his history.

He looked up as the two men entered the room, his expression worried. Almost immediately, as they sat down, they were assailed by the noxious odour of a digestive system under stress.

'Right, Ian, you remember us from earlier on. DI Smith, and DCI Darling. We'd now like to ask you some more questions because we believe you could be a material eye witness to a serious crime.'

The worried expression changed to one of blank incomprehension as Hardy looked from one officer to the other with no sign of recognition.

The solicitor who earlier had smiled at Smith in what he'd taken for a flirty manner was now beaming with evident satisfaction.

'Oh dear, Inspector Smith, I see you haven't had time yet to do all of your homework on my client. It's no secret. It's in his records, and has come up before when he's been prosecuted.

'He suffers from prosopagnosia – face recognition blindness. Genuinely. It's all in his notes. He is medically incapable of recognising faces or retaining any memory of them. I have to introduce myself to him anew every time we meet and I've always represented him. It's one of the reasons he gets so stressed finding himself in police hands. Even if he wanted to, he cannot possibly help you with the identification of any suspect you may have.'

Chapter Twenty-one

The officer from Bolton, DC Whittaker, was the only one still in the main office when Ted led the way through to his own, DI Smith not far behind him. It didn't take many of Whittaker's detective skills to pick up on the atmosphere between the two men. The boss looked on the point of exploding.

Chris Whittaker was surprised. From what he'd seen and heard of DCI Darling so far, he was one of the most polite, quiet and calm Serious Crime senior officers in the force. Something must have gone badly wrong. But Chris had news of additional witnesses, a possible breakthrough in the case, so he didn't want to sit on it, even at the risk of getting his head bitten off.

'Sir, do you have a minute? Only I've found a couple more witnesses to camera man.'

Ted had been on the point of saying no to his question, but news of the prospect of two new witnesses to replace the one snatched from under their noses was exactly what they needed right now.

'Reliable ones?'

Smith wasn't sure if that was a sly dig at him for his omission but decided it was a fair enough question. He was busy mentally kicking himself up the arse for not picking up on something so critical. He'd speed read the file, admittedly, and it might have been mentioned only in passing, but he should still have picked it up. Rodriguez had glanced at the file early but Smith was supposed to do the detailed read-through.

Worse, he'd even commented to the DCI how bewildered Hardy had seemed at times, without checking his file carefully to see if there was a reason for that. He'd make sure to red flag the file with the crucial information so no one else made the same error in future. Assuming the DCI was not planning on putting him on the first south-bound train which stopped in Stockport. And he wouldn't blame him at all if he did.

'I would say so, sir. They were walking in a different park to the one where the snatch was made, a couple of weeks ago, when the man approached them. He was carrying a camera and asked them if they'd seen any children or babies in the park as he needed pictures for a clothing catalogue. He mentioned a finders' fee for them. They were already suspicious about him and that was the final straw for them. They thought the whole thing sounded dodgy so they gave him the brush-off.'

'And they haven't come forward before now? Two weeks ago? They must surely have seen on the news or in the papers about the baby's disappearance.'

'They travel a lot for work, sir. They're both cabin crew for an airline. Sharp and observant, which I suppose they need to be in that job. They share a flat here in town and they're only just back from their latest trips. That seems genuine enough. Their luggage was still in the hallway.

'They didn't report it at the time as it didn't seem all that significant, even though they didn't believe his spin, because they were about to leave. But when they arrived home and saw the appeals on the news about the missing baby, they got in touch and I went round.'

'Right, good work. Liaise with DS Hallam. He's arranging for Mr and Mrs Norris to come in tomorrow and view various images to see if they can pick out King. We've got his mugshot on his record, though not for anything like this. See if your two witnesses are available to do the same at any time. With luck, if they're just back, they may have some leave tomorrow, although I imagine they might need to catch up on sleep first.

'Ask him, too, about getting voice clips, including King, of course, of some phrase or another he may have used consistently.'

'I think probably "I'm looking for subjects to photograph" might do it, sir. I'll get it sorted.'

'This is promising. If any of the four of them, hopefully all of them, pick him out, that's the valid reason we need to continue questioning him and checking all his contacts. And knowing we were doing that might make him a bit more willing to cooperate with us. Hopefully to the point of telling us where Evie is now. Thank you, DC Whittaker.'

He continued heading to his office, Smith following him, slightly surprised by the praise and the thanks. His team would definitely think he'd gone soft if he started that malarkey.

Ted went and sat down at his desk. Smith hovered for a moment, uncertain what was expected of him. Protocol dictated that he should remain standing until the senior officer told him otherwise, but he was having difficulty getting the measure of DCI Darling and his expectations.

Ted looked up at him for a moment before instructing him to sit down, then asked, 'So how did you miss it? How did you overlook something that critical from his record and notes?'

'Honest answer, guv? I haven't a clue. Shouldn't have happened. Believe it or not it's not like me. And if one of my team had done it I'd have kicked their arse halfway round the office and back. I made us look like right pillocks in there and I apologise for that.'

'It's done now. Just please be more careful in future. And flag the file, please, so it never happens again, to anyone.'

'So what's the plan going forward?' Smith asked him, trying, but failing, to see himself dealing with anything as serious as his slip-up in such a laid-back manner. But somehow the way Ted had handled it made him feel all the more guilty for having made the error in the first place. Perhaps that was the intention.

'Use some more of our initial twenty-four hours custody to let them sweat it out while we go and get some rest. Back here early doors tomorrow, and we'll question them again, then see what happens with our witnesses and the photos. Can I give you a lift back to your digs?'

'You're all right, thanks, guv. If we're knocking off, I'll go and try some more of the drinkable schnapps at The Grapes. Sorry again for the cock-up.'

* * *

'You made it home then?' Trev's sleepy voice from the sofa showed he'd once again dozed off, buried under cats, watching some foreign film, in black and white, which he probably already knew off by heart. 'Have you eaten?'

Ted perched on the arm of the sofa, the only free space. Even his number one fan, little Adam, was lazily curled up amongst the others, showing no sign of stirring.

'I had a steak and kidney pie in The Grapes earlier. I wouldn't say no to pudding, if there's anything on offer. Don't get up, though, you look too comfy. Just point me in the right direction and I'll help myself.'

Trev slowly curled himself up into a sitting position, carefully rearranging cats so he could swing his feet to the floor without touching any of them.

'What sort of a husband would I be if I didn't make you something when you do manage to get home finally? Especially as I'm going off for a couple of days, too. You will promise to look after the boys and girls properly while I'm away, though, won't you? I know what you get like on a difficult case. You barely remember to eat yourself. How's it going, anyway? Are you any nearer to finding that poor baby?'

He gave Ted a quick hug before leading the way through to the kitchen where the table was laid for one.

'I'm going in early as we've got a couple of people in custody, one of whom at least might possibly give us a lead.'

Ted had pulled off his tie the minute he'd got in the car to drive home, and had left it in the pocket of his jacket in the hall. He undid his shirt cuffs and rolled his sleeves back as Trev took a bowl from the fridge, flashing his chef's torch over the top of the contents before putting it down in front of him.

'I made *crème brûlée*. Something sweet that wouldn't spoil waiting for you if you were very late. There's plenty of cheese, too, if you need to fill up. Either first, if you want to do it the French way, or after, if you still have room.'

'How are you getting on with the famous Oscar?'

'He dropped a total bollock today. Completely missed something vital on someone's file which made us look very stupid. I was surprised, as his work's been good up to now. But he had his eye right off the ball for that one.'

He'd managed a couple of mouthfuls of his dessert between sentences and added, 'This is seriously good. Thank you. Hits the right spot.'

'Oooh, did you shout at him and kick things?' Trev asked him teasingly.

'He's bigger than me.'

Trev laughed at that.

'As if that's ever stopped you. Well, I hope you get the breakthrough you need this weekend. Promise to let me know, if you can manage to, and I'll keep my fingers crossed for the poor parents and for little Evie.'

* * *

Now he knew the situation with Ian Hardy, Ted was even more careful than usual to ensure their suspect understood exactly what was happening when they resumed questioning him the following morning.

'Mr Hardy, I'm DCI Darling, this is DI Smith. We're the two officers who arrested you yesterday on suspicion of supplying a vehicle with falsified ID.'

'I remember getting nicked. I didn't know it was you two,' Hardy told him, then said, his tone defensive, 'I'm not thick, you know. I just can't recognise faces.'

'I wasn't suggesting that for a moment, Mr Hardy, so I'm sorry if it sounded as if I was. That was not my intention. It's simply my duty to ensure that you understand all parts of the procedure. Your solicitor, of course, is here to ensure that, but please don't hesitate to ask if ever you need clarification of anything at all.

'We're still conducting a search of your workshop, but I can tell you now that based on what we've found to date, we will be proceeding to charging you with offences connected to supplying forged vehicle registration plates. Further charges may yet be brought.

'We know you already have a record for similar offences so I'm sure your solicitor will explain to you that, should you plead guilty, or be found guilty at trial, when it comes to sentencing, there are things which can be presented in mitigation. These would include you showing genuine remorse, admissions made to us in interview, or showing yourself ready to cooperate fully with the authorities.

'In other words, anything you do or say which is helpful to us may result in you receiving a lighter sentence, although that is not guaranteed.'

Hardy's insides were starting up again at the stress of his situation. Now Ted knew what the problem was, he was blaming himself as much for not noticing something was off kilter as he held Smith responsible for not having read the file thoroughly enough to pick up on what the problem was.

Hardy's legal representative was clearly used to dealing with Hardy, quick to step in with a tactful explanation.

'The chief inspector is right, Ian. As your solicitor, I can advise you that if you co-operate as fully as you can, it could well help in reducing any sentence passed on you by the courts.'

'I can't recognise faces, so I can't ID anyone,' Hardy told them, then added, on a note of defiance, 'even if I wanted to.'

Oscar Smith, sitting to the right of Ted, was like an awakening volcano. The first low rumblings before an eruption. He'd so far said nothing but his entire body language was latent menace. A calm before the storm. Ted hadn't had time to do any in-depth research into prosopagnosia so didn't know if it would also prevent Hardy from reading the signs. The last thing they needed now was any escalation of the situation.

He deliberately moved one foot under the table and delivered a warning tap against the side of Smith's ankle to remind him to behave. He hoped it would be enough.

'Any help you can give us at all would be good, Mr Hardy. I'll personally make sure the court hears of it. A name, for a start. That of the person who collected the car for which you supplied the false identification. You must know, I'm sure, if you watch or listen to the news, that this is in connection with the kidnap of a very young child. Just three months old.'

Hardy hesitated as the room was assailed by yet more noxious gas.

'I don't know his name. Like I don't know the names of who ordered the job and paid for it. Some bloke phoned the workshop, ordered the work, then someone came to pay me, cash in hand, when it was ready. They just said a bloke would come and pick the motor up. They called him The King, and said that was all I needed to know about him.

* * *

'Virgil? Inspector Turner here. You're on the John Berry Misper case, aren't you? Are you in the building?

'I am, sir, just ringing round cruise liners seeing if I can find him on a ship somewhere.'

'No need for that,' Kevin Turner told him. 'He came into the station a short while ago to report his daughter missing.'

225

Virgil hesitated then asked, 'This isn't a wind-up is it, sir?'

Kevin Turner laughed.

'Sounds like it ought to be, doesn't it? But no, straight up. He came in to say he's just back from a cruise but he can't get hold of his daughter anywhere and he's worried something might have happened to her. We've had him put in the vulnerable witness room for now, as it's the most comfortable place, and given him a babysitter, although he wasn't alone. He has a very polite and attentive young man with him.'

'Let me guess. By the name of Simon Ropley?'

'That's the one. So can I leave it to you? Only I need the babysitter back for an incident that's going to take every officer I can spare and there are barely enough to go round as it is. As per bloody usual.'

Virgil grabbed his phone and pocket book and raced off down the stairs. Of all the possible outcomes to this case he'd been anticipating, this scenario had been nowhere on the radar. He wondered if he should call John Berry's daughter, Alison, straight away, but decided he'd do better first to listen to whatever the man had to say for himself. If indeed it really was John Berry.

When he went into the witness room he saw an older man he instantly recognised from the photos his daughter had showed him, pacing up and down looking anxious. The much younger man with him, looking less worried, was making drinks for them both from what was provided.

'I've got this now, thanks,' he told his uniformed colleague.

She grinned at him as she said, 'Shame. This was a much more appealing prospect than yet another punch-up in town.'

'Mr Berry? I'm DC Tibbs. Would you like to take a seat, sir, and tell me what it is that you've come in to report. Have your drink, though. You look as if you need something.'

'I'm so worried about my daughter. I did something uncharacteristic. A once in a lifetime thing. I sold the house and I went off on a cruise round the world with my friend and helper here, Simon. I wanted to surprise her so I didn't say anything until we were on the ship, when I took a photo of us leaving harbour to send to her. But my hands are a bit clumsy these days. Arthritis in the joints. I managed to drop my phone overboard into the sea.

'Luckily, Simon has kindly been letting me use his, or rather using it for me, so I didn't do the same with his. I remembered my daughter's number, of course, so I kept sending her messages and photos almost every day, but I've never had a reply.'

He paused to take a drink from the cup Simon Ropley had put in front of him before he continued.

'I wasn't too worried at first because as far as I knew, she was still in Africa and we often have problems trying to communicate when she's in an area with a poor signal. But we got back yesterday and I've been constantly trying her number with no response and she should be back at base by now. So I thought I'd better come in to the police station and ask for your advice about how I can find out if she's all right.'

'Mr Berry, your daughter is fine, apart from being worried sick about where you are and if you're all right. She came in here three days ago to report you as a missing person. I was assigned to the case and I've been trying to find you.'

The man was frowning now.

'I don't understand. She's in England? So why hasn't she replied to me?'

'Sir, can you please tell me the phone number you've been using to try to contact her?' Virgil asked him, opening the contacts on his own phone.

John Berry recited it confidently, without hesitation, as Virgil followed the numbers he had saved.

'Sir, the last two digits of your daughter's mobile number are five nine – not nine five.'

Chapter Twenty-two

Virgil was quietly seething as he made his way back upstairs, having asked John Berry and Simon Ropley to wait for him in the witness room. He was glad things had been resolved but angry at the time he'd spent looking into it all when he could have been helping with the baby Evie case.

He appreciated how worried both daughter and father had been, because of a misunderstanding, as it turned out. But he felt he could have been more useful on the kidnap case. Uniform would no doubt have handled the Berry situation in exactly the same way as he had, with the same result.

He'd phone Alison Berry to come into the station to collect her father, leave them to sort things out between them, write up his report, then get back to Serious Crime. First he'd need to check with DI Jo Rodriguez, who was the senior officer currently on duty and available, if he was happy with that.

He found him in the main office. The inspector's office door was closed but Virgil could see through the window and the open Venetian blind that DI Smith was in there, on the phone.

Jo listened carefully to everything Virgil had to say then asked, 'And you've checked the phone yourself, have you? Simon Ropley's? Would he have any reason to recognise the daughter's number? Because isn't that pivotal here? If he didn't know it and for some reason he didn't want her to know what was going on, would he really have sent all those messages, and did he actually do so? If he did know her number and realised John Berry had given him the wrong one, then he'd only send them, knowing they would never arrive, if he had some sort of hidden agenda, surely?

'Inspector Turner passed this to Serious Crime because he clearly thought there was more to it than appeared on the surface to be the case. Not simply a question of someone going off somewhere and forgetting to tell anyone. He's an experienced officer, with good instincts.

'Before we heave a sigh of relief and write it up as over, you need to check that phone, Virgil. After all, if Simon Ropley is some sort of a conman bleeding an older man dry of his money, he could quite well have the effrontery to come with him to the police station and happily explain away the lack of contact.

'What do we know about Ropley? Really know about him? Have you done a thorough background check?'

'The agency he was with checked him out before taking him on and said he came up clean.'

Virgil realised as he said it that he was starting to sound on the defensive.

'Virgil, this isn't like you. Their check isn't likely to have been as thorough as anything we would do, and you know how clever any type of conman is at hiding their background. Please tell me you have a copy of theirs, at least, and it's on file pending follow-up?'

Virgil's silence said it all. Jo sighed. He was even more laid back than the boss. He actively disliked having to play the senior officer and come down hard on anyone, which is why all of the team used his first name, at his request. But this was sloppy work from someone who should know better, so he couldn't let it go.

'Look, the baby Evie case is having an effect on all of us. Especially those of us with children of our own, and all the more so for those with young daughters. But this Berry case could still turn out to be something serious. Yes, we know John Berry is safe, at least, but where's all his money from the house sale gone? Have you checked? Is it sitting in some offshore account in the name of Simon Ropley, for instance?

'Come on, Virgil, this is all basic stuff. I shouldn't have to be telling anyone of your experience all of this. Whatever you do, finish it off properly before the boss sees the file. You could be allowing a clever and ruthless crook to walk away free, still in the company of the vulnerable person he might be bleeding dry.'

It was so unusual to get such a pep talk from Jo that Virgil replied with a brisk, 'Sir,' which was a first.

'Promise me you'll buck up,' Jo told him, but in a lighter tone.

* * *

'Right guv, of those phone numbers you sent through, there's one in particular which you certainly would have known by sight,' DS Tony Taylor, from the Met, was telling his boss, DI Oscar Smith, over the phone.

'Frenchie Williams. Mr Fix-it for the Martin brothers.'

'Bloody Frenchie! Of course, I should have remembered it was that little weasel's number. So have you hauled him in and applied the thumbscrews? If he's in contact with our bloke King up here, then this whole thing is bigger and nastier than any of us imagined so far. The stuff those boys get involved with, I dread to think what's happened to the kiddies.'

'Working on it now, guv. Sean and Craig have gone out to find him and lift him. Dai's sorting out for us to get access to his phone history to see if we can trace who he's been in contact with up there, or anywhere else which could be relevant. It would be a miracle if this turned out to be something we could finally lift the Martins for, at the same time, if we manage to follow the trail to its end in both directions.'

'Nice one, Tony, cheers.'

Oscar was about to end the call when Tony asked him, as hesitantly as before, 'Are you sure everything's all right with you, guv?'

'Of course everything's bloody well all right. Why do you keep asking me that?'

'You sound … different, guv, that's all. Should we set up a code, like a safe word? In case one time you really are trying to let me know something isn't right?'

'Tony, for fuck's sake, we work together. We're not having sex, and certainly not kinky sex. Everything's fine. Get on with the bloody job in hand.'

Smith jabbed the call to an end, angry with himself. He'd so nearly thanked his DS, for the first time in living memory, for simply doing the job he was paid to do. No wonder Taylor thought he was being held at gunpoint and trying to signal that he was in danger.

DC Dai Evans was the only other person in the office in the capital city with DS Taylor. He'd caught one side of the conversation and asked him, 'Something wrong with the gaffer, sarge?'

Tony Taylor was still looking at the screen of the mobile in his hand, as if that might somehow give him a clue.

'I don't know, Dai. It was like I was talking to someone else. He almost praised me and thanked me for doing my job.'

'Bloody hell fire!'

* * *

Armed with the latest information from London, Oscar Smith went in search of Ted to pass it all on and to discuss their next interview with Alec King. Smith particularly wanted to know at what point to tell King of the phone number they'd traced. His reaction to that news would be interesting.

Ted asked for a quick run-down on the Martin brothers whom Smith had mentioned, to assess the weight of the new information.

'Think modern day Kray Twins, guv. Anything bad going on, they're probably behind it. Drugs, extortion, human trafficking, especially of prostitutes, and they're not too fussy about age, which is worrying in our context.'

'Anything known with regards to child trafficking?'

'Not as far as I'm aware, but that's not to say they're not at it. There's three of them and in fact it's two brothers and a cousin, although everyone calls them brothers, and they've lived in each other's pockets since forever. John, Louis and François.'

'François?'

'That's the cousin. His mother was French. Disappeared off the planet. The story was she didn't like England so she went back to France, but we've always suspected they might have killed or trafficked her. The phrase about selling your own mother might have been invented for those charmers.'

'So is there a link there to the fact that the phone number belongs to someone called Frenchie?'

'Well spotted. He's another very distant cousin from the French side of the family. His real name is Eugène, but he never, ever uses that. Hence being known to everyone as Frenchie.'

'If Alec King, the phony photographer and car deliverer, was in contact with Frenchie Williams, how likely is it, do you think, that he knows the trail goes back to the Martins?'

Smith shook his head.

'Not even remotely, I'd say. The role of Frenchie, and the many, many others like him on their payroll, is to see that nothing can be traced back to the bosses. They're very well paid to keep schtum. If they do go down, they know their affairs and their families will be well looked after and they'll come out to a nice little bonus for following the rules.'

Ted leaned back in his seat to process what he'd just been told.

'We're clearly going to get nothing more of any real use from Ian Hardy, so we're going to have to remand him soon. Even if he wanted to help us, he can't, and if he tried to, we couldn't regard his testimony as safe. Him mentioning The King isn't much to go on, but it's a tenuous link, at least. We could drip feed that to King and see what reaction it provokes, at least.

'But there's no point in us even talking to King until we hear whether or not the four witnesses picked out his picture, which should be happening soon. The minute we get those results, we can try again with him, because that's going to be powerful testimony which might well shake things up a bit. That and voice ID, if we can get that, as the photographer spoke to all four of them.

'If Hardy's solicitor has any sense she won't push for bail for him. She must guess he'll be in danger if word gets out he's even been brought in. And he'll be at a huge disadvantage because he won't be able to recognise anyone coming after him. He presumably only ran when he saw us coming because of some sixth sense which told him we were coppers.'

Smith chuckled at that.

'It's all right, guv, you can say it, I won't be offended. Because a big ugly bastard like me, built like a brick shithouse but wearing a suit and tie, is bound to be the filth – or something else equally as bad news.'

Ted responded with a quote from an older political TV drama series he'd watched on DVD with Trev.

'"You might very well think that; I couldn't possibly comment".'

Then he stood up from his desk as he said, 'Right, let's go and see if Mike Hallam has had any success with his eye witnesses.'

* * *

They met a triumphantly grinning Mike Hallam sprinting up the stairs in search of the boss, so they regrouped in Ted's office. If even two of the witnesses had come through, they could finally be heading somewhere.

Mike could contain himself no longer.

'Four out of four, boss. They all picked out King's mugshot as the phony photographer, with very little hesitation. The cabin crew women were both thorough and methodical and worked in pretty much the same way. Both picked out King early on, but then looked very carefully at all the others before confirming.

'Same with Mrs Norris. Straight for King but also looked at all the others. Mr Norris-like-the-Heaton, as he still keeps saying, was a bit more hesitant, but in a way I felt sorry for him. He's still beating himself up over his actions. I did tell him it was likely someone like King would have found someone else to fall for his yarn, if not him, but he's beside himself.'

'And we're getting statements from each of them confirming the IDs they've made?' Ted checked.

'I've had Jezza and Maurice doing that. I've put Maurice with Mr Norris. We know he's a softy about babies, but he's basically a kind and caring man so he won't do anything to make Mr Norris feel worse than he already does. I'm sorting out voice tapes, too, although that might take longer.'

'Good work, Mike. Meanwhile we've got a solid link now between Alec King and what sounds like a delightful gang in London.'

'So are you saying that's potentially not good news in terms of getting little Evie back safely?' Mike asked.

'It means we've got it all to play for now with King,' Ted told him.

He left Mike to sort out a remand in custody of Ian Hardy while he and Smith went down to see what, if anything, they could get out of King which might advance them.

They'd discussed their interview strategy so Ted began, outlining the simple facts.

'So in summary, we have four eye witnesses prepared to testify in court that you are the person who approached them in a park, asking where they could find babies and small children to photograph, and offering to pay them a finders' fee for their help.'

Alec King looked calm and unconcerned.

'I've got one of those faces. People always think they've seen me before. I'm not a photographer, not even an amateur one, so whoever they saw it wasn't me. If you tell me when these supposed sightings are meant to have happened, I can probably tell you where I was at the time. Oh, and I don't even have the sort of camera for that work, just my phone.'

The team had anticipated that the camera used by the phony photographer would have been long gone or well hidden. One reason they'd applied for search warrants with as wide a remit as possible. Ted left that one dangling, to come back to at a later stage.

'You also seem to be the old-fashioned type who keeps a hard copy of important telephone numbers.'

The man's eyes narrowed briefly at that. He'd clearly thought he'd been clever in where he'd put the list, but it hadn't taken long for experienced officers searching his premises to find it. He tried bluffing his way out of that one.

'Nobody does that these days. Only an idiot. If you've found some numbers, you can't prove I wrote them down.'

'That's true, in the short-term, without expert analysis of the handwriting,' Ted conceded. 'But as we are also checking your phone records, you would need to give us a suitable explanation should any of those numbers have appeared there, either as incoming or outgoing calls.'

King's expensive solicitor, who hadn't said anything up to this point, spoke up.

'If you really have discovered a one hundred per cent effective means of stopping all unwanted phone calls, chief inspector, I hope you will share it with me at some point.'

'But then I presume you don't make outgoing calls to nuisance numbers, sir. So if we were to find both incoming and outgoing calls from Mr King's phone to any of the numbers on the list, that might take some explaining.'

Ted distinctly heard Smith make a low noise of amusement in his throat, before taking over the questioning at the pre-arranged point.

'Does the name Frenchie Williams mean anything at all to you, Mr King?'

Smith couldn't ever remember being as polite to a suspect. But he wasn't playing on home turf so was trying to follow northern rules, even though they were alien to him.

The distinct flicker of King's eyes told the true story, at the same time as his voice was denying all knowledge.

Smith was about to continue when, after a hesitant knock at the door of the interview room, DC Steve Ellis put his head round the opening and addressed his boss.

'Sir, have you got a minute, please?'

Ted tried not to get his hopes up too soon, but he knew there was no way Steve would disturb an interview unless he had something important. He followed him out into the corridor.

'Sorry to disturb you, sir, but I've got some street camera footage. I had to do a fair bit of enhancement, but I think it might be clear enough now. I've brought the original, too, in case the solicitor says it's been doctored. Not doctored, sir, just enlarged and made brighter.'

It was never quick, getting anything from Steve, but always worth waiting for.

After the explanations, Steve handed the boss several photos of a car waiting at traffic lights. In one of the blow-ups, Ted could read the number plate of the car and knew from memory that it was the false plate from the vehicle later found burned out with the body inside.

He pulled up the next image. If that wasn't Alec King sitting in the driver's seat, then he must have a twin or a body double somewhere.

Chapter Twenty-three

Oscar Smith made a mental note never to play poker with Ted Darling, if he was even into that sort of thing. He'd been hoping to pick up a clue from his body language as to whether the news the young DC had just imparted was the lever they needed to get anything useful out of King.

Smith was good at reading people. It was in part what made him such a good copper. He could always spot the weakest link to lean on, often succeeding in bringing down the entire chain. From DCI Darling he picked up the sum total of nothing at all.

He clearly had something new as he'd returned to the interview room armed with papers, but he held them in such a way that their contents were hidden. He then put them face down on the table. It seemed that both Smith and King would have to wait until the DCI was ready to reveal whatever it was they showed. King was looking just as intrigued by the latest development. His solicitor continued to look as if he would far rather be doing something else. Anything else.

Ted waited for Smith to finish the line of questioning he had started then, slowly and deliberately, he turned over each image and fanned them out across the table. All bar two.

'Mr King, I'm showing you some CCTV captures of a car on stop at traffic lights. It's of interest to us because it's taken close to the scene of a serious crime which we're investigating,' Ted began in his usual quiet tone.

'First of all, Mr King, do you recognise the car in this shot? You can read the number plate in the enlargement.'

King barely glanced at the image the DCI was indicating. Instead his eyes kept flicking to the enlargement which showed the person behind the steering wheel. Ted noticed and pointed to the car, bringing King's attention back towards it.

'The car, Mr King.'

'It's a Ford Focus.'

He looked up at Ted as he said it and asked, 'Have I won a prize?'

He was trying to look and sound unconcerned but was fooling no one.

The solicitor spoke at this point. He had something of a lazy drawl to his voice, always managing to sound profoundly bored by the whole proceedings.

'I presume you are heading somewhere relevant with this line of questioning, chief inspector? Because I believe that Ford is the most common make of car in England and the Focus is, I think, one of the most popular models.'

Ted was surprised he knew those statistics, but careful not to show it. He didn't have the man down as anything of a petrol head. He was right in what he said, though. Perhaps it was a line of defence he'd already used in court for another case.

'And what about this enlargement showing the driver of this vehicle, Mr King? Is that someone you recognise?'

The solicitor pulled the image towards himself before his client could move, gave it a scornful glance, then pushed it back to where it came from.

'Oh, come on. Surely you can do better than this? CCTV footage is notoriously unreliable and never looks much like anyone. And that's clearly been blown up, so possibly enhanced in various ways, therefore unlikely to be admissible. You must have something more to compel my client's continued presence here, surely.'

Smith cut in at that point. A distraction from the other flank.

'What d'you do for a job, Alec?'

'I help businesses with stuff. Things they might need which I can source for them. Pretty much anything, really. All legit.'

'Cars, for instance?'

King shook his head.

'I'm not a car dealer, no. Things like good refurb computers, office equipment, that sort of stuff. I help a bit with recruitment, too. If someone from out of town needs workers, I can recruit and vet for them. It's all on the books, for the taxman.'

'D'you have a nickname you're known by?' Smith asked.

'Don't most people?' the solicitor asked sardonically. 'I would guess you probably have one or two of your own, inspector.'

Smith ignored him as he went on, 'The King, for instance?'

He could tell immediately that it struck a chord with King, although the man was quick to brush it off with a glib reply.

'Oh, well, sometimes people say I'm the king of computers, when I sort out a software problem for them, one they've been struggling with. It's not my speciality, but I can fix some stuff that others might not be able to.'

Ted took over next, following more or less the rough lines of interview they'd discussed before starting.

'What can you tell me about the list of hand-written phone numbers which was found on your premises, Mr King?'

'Nothing.'

The reply was instant and somewhat glib.

'Nothing?' Ted queried, slowly turning over the next sheet of paper.

King blinked rapidly, twice. It was obvious he recognised the list of telephone numbers which had been photocopied and was now confronting him from the table.

'This was found during a search of your premises, Mr King. Hidden, but not very effectively. Have you ever seen it before?'

King looked to his solicitor who told him, 'You don't have to answer anything at this stage if you don't want to.'

'That's perfectly true, of course, although it would help us enormously if you did, Mr King. Somewhere, a very small baby's life might be in serious danger.'

'I don't know anything about a baby in danger.'

'The problem with that statement, Mr King,' Ted went on, as formally polite as ever, 'is this CCTV capture. You see, we contend that the person driving the car in the capture is you. And we have evidence to show that the missing baby was at some point in close contact with the passenger you can also see here in the photo. A person who subsequently died in that same car when it was deliberately set on fire.'

King was shaking his head in denial.

'Not me. Could be anyone in that picture. It's got a timeline. I can check my diary and tell you where I was at the time. Not driving a Ford Focus, for sure.'

Smith was clearly getting bored with not having more of a role in the interview. There was currently too much of the softly, softly approach for his taste, and he wasn't used to it.

'The false plates and the rest of the ID work done on this car was the work of a man who told us it had been collected by a man known as The King. That's a bit of a coincidence, wouldn't you say?' Smith asked.

King's snort was derisive.

'Could be anyone, that. King of computers, me, yes I'll give you that. But cars aren't my thing.'

Smith decided to do a bit of a fishing exercise, on the off-chance. He'd expected the DCI to have reined him in by now but he was sitting quietly, which encouraged Smith to go on. Especially as the solicitor was being so quiet Smith thought he might possibly have nodded off.

'We'll be showing this other witness the photos too, of course, to see if he recognises either the car or the driver.'

'He can't recognise anyone, him.'

The solicitor found his voice an instant too late. The jaws of the steel trap had already clanged shut around his client before he had chance to say a word.

Smith said nothing, waiting for the realisation of what he'd just said hit King to the full. The solicitor looked angry. With himself, with his client, or with the interviewing officers? Hard to judge. Smith knew he was smirking, watching the reactions, but he couldn't help himself. He'd played a blinder and he knew it. He was entitled to feel smug.

'Don't say another word, Mr King.'

The solicitor's advice could definitely be filed under too little, too late.

By tacit silent agreement, both Smith and Ted now sat and waited to see how far into a hole King was going to dig himself, unless his solicitor shook himself and remembered why he was there. Inevitably, he was likely to go 'no comment' on them, unless they could find a way of pointing out to him how much trouble he was potentially in, and that the only way he was going to see light at the end of the tunnel was by cooperating with them.

The tension was high. Both officers realised that this was probably the closest they'd come to a trail to the missing baby. The wrong word by either of them now was a potential death sentence to her. Always supposing she was not already dead, or out of the country long since.

Smith's eyes were focused on King. Ted took the opportunity to observe the solicitor. The situation had got away from him quickly and he was now on the brink of a precipice. The degree of discomfort he was showing told Ted all he needed to know. This wasn't a solicitor worried for his client because of a moment's lapse on his own part. This was a man afraid for his own skin if, or more likely now, when, things blew up in his face.

Ted imagined he was being paid over the odds to make sure King did not join up the dots for the police to lead them to whoever was behind the whole thing. The wrong word or action now could sweep away any advantage they currently held. More vitally, it would signal the end of any hope of bringing baby Evie back home safely.

He didn't yet know Smith well enough to know if he could trust him to stay silent as long as necessary, so once again he made the point with a sideways kick to his ankle, more forceful than the last one.

Ted was like one of his own cats, stalking prey. He could wait any length of time, still and silent, for the perfect moment to pounce. Only when he judged the moment was right did he speak again.

'Who can't recognise anyone, Mr King? And how do you know that?'

'I meant no one could recognise me connected to that car because I've never seen it before. Never been in it.'

'And yet you said, and I quote, "He can't recognise anyone, him." I'll happily replay the recording for you, should you wish to hear for yourself. We did tell you your interview was being recorded.'

Ted stayed calm and quiet, his tone always reasonable. Smith admitted to himself that he'd have been halfway over the table by now, wanting to throttle the suspect.

'Say nothing,' the solicitor repeated, his tone more urgent now.

'Does the name Frenchie Williams mean anything to you, Mr King?'

Ted's voice was conversational. He might almost have been asking him if he'd seen a particular recently released film. His eyes missed nothing. They told him instantly that King was not the only person in the room who recognised the name.

'I would like to take a break now to consult further with my client,' the solicitor said. 'In the meantime, my advice to him remains to say nothing at all.'

Ted didn't so much as look at him. His eyes were locked onto those of King. He was on the brink of something. A breakthrough, at last. He could feel it. He couldn't refuse the solicitor's request. But King could.

Ted put everything he had into his next delivery. Everything was riding on it. The wrong word or tone from him now and King was going to clam up completely. Probably their last chance of finding out what had happened to little Evie would disappear forever, as would she.

'Mr King, I can't make you any promises, or offer you any deals. It would be wrong of me to even suggest that. So I'm appealing to your better nature. Stop this, now. Tell us where Evie is, before she pays the ultimate price.'

Smith was fascinated. He felt himself wanting to confess to something, anything, in response to that impassioned plea. Even the solicitor was silent, although that could simply have been that he knew he was on a hiding to nothing.

Ted played his final trump card. He turned over the last piece of paper still face down on the table. A smiling baby Evie, gurgling up from her big pram, looking trustingly towards the camera.

It was also a wild card. Someone who could knowingly spot and possibly transport snatched babies for a London gang wasn't likely to have many feelings, nor a soft spot. Ted's only bargaining point was to set out the difference it could make to charges and future sentencing for King if he offered up information which led to the safe recovery of Evie, rather than leaving her to her fate.

'Remember, too, that we now have four reliable eye witnesses who have identified you facially, and will also be asked to identify your voice.

'It's up to you, Mr King.'

The solicitor made to speak again but Ted held up a hand to him, waiting for King's words. A small, insignificant gesture, but somehow the man decided to hold his peace and wait.

King's eyes were everywhere round the room. Looking for an escape route. Figuratively, if not literally. He sensed his back was against the wall, now, more than ever. Whatever help might come his way, he seemed to know it would not now be from his solicitor, who was starting to look as uncomfortable as his client.

Another warning foot movement under the table from Ted to Smith. The wrong word or gesture at this critical point risked everything.

Finally, King let out a pent-up sigh.

'I didn't kill anyone. I didn't know the car was going to be torched, nor that the woman would be killed. I was told my role would be to collect the car with the false plates from a bloke in Chorlton. They said that would be easy. He's got summat wrong with him which means he can't recognise faces so there was nothing to worry about there.

'I was told right from the start that nothing would happen to the baby. I wouldn't have got involved otherwise. They were being taken to order for wealthy childless people abroad, to be adopted by them, so they'd have a good new life and be loved and taken care of. Not just up here but other places, too. I was only doing the one.'

Smith was on the point of saying something but another sharp kick to his ankle stopped him in the nick of time. Ted wanted nothing at all to halt King in his flow just as they were hopefully getting somewhere.

'I'd done a bit of stuff for Frenchie before so I knew it would be well paid and they covered their own tracks so well that I'd be protected under the same umbrella. I don't know the people behind him, the big chiefs, but I know enough to know they have plenty of the right sort of people in their pockets down there in London, so I guessed it would be the same up here. Cops, lawyers, some judges, too. Good money, good protection, and the kiddies wouldn't be harmed, so why not?'

The solicitor had turned a greenish shade of white at his words. The lid was coming off the can of worms. Now King had started, he showed no signs of wanting to stop.

'I went scouting for likely babies. It was easier than I could have imagined. Some old bloke with a big dog told me pretty much everything I needed to know, so I gave him a few quid for his trouble.

'After that, all I had to do was go and pick up the car from the bloke in Chorlton, who couldn't ever identify me, store it in a lock-up, then be ready, as soon as I got a phone call, to go and pick a woman up from one of the parks I'd checked out and drive her to an address I'd be given. I didn't have any info in advance and I had to be ready to drop everything and go whenever they said so. But I was being bloody well paid for it.'

'And that's what happened?' Ted prompted him. 'You got the phone call and you took the woman there? The one we now believe to be the baby's kidnapper, probably with the child hidden inside her coat.'

'The woman I picked up did have a thick coat on, but she wasn't from round here. Not English at all, so I thought maybe she just wasn't used to the climate. I didn't see or hear no baby, though, I swear.'

'And where did you take her? Where was the handover? At a house?'

Ted was trying to keep his voice neutral. He could sense Smith, beside him, full of the same sudden hope and anticipation as Ted was himself. Were they finally going to get Evie's current whereabouts?

'Not a house, no. It was like a lay-by out in the country a bit. But there must have been a house or something not far away because two blokes turned up on foot, took the car with the woman still in it and drove off. They came walking to the meeting point and there was no sign of any other vehicle.

They took the Ford to go off in so I had to walk back to civilisation and get a bus home.'

'So you could take us to exactly where the handover took place?' Ted asked him. 'Or show us on a map?'

'I could,' King replied, his expression turning sly. 'But that would depend on what protection you could offer me in exchange for my help.'

Chapter Twenty-four

'And before we reach that stage, certainly before I allow my client to say anything further at all, I insist on time alone with him to consult,' the solicitor was trying to sound more assertive now. 'You're out of order continuing to ignore my request, chief inspector, and you know it.'

Had there been a waste-paper basket in the room, it would have met a violent end. Ted was struggling to contain himself. He felt they were so close to the breakthrough they desperately needed. But now was not the time to start bending all the rules of interview, and in doing so, to blow any chance of a successful prosecution. Certainly not in front of DI Smith.

'Mr King? Think very carefully. For yourself. Don't simply accept what your solicitor tells you. You have the chance to potentially save a baby's life …'

'I must insist,' the solicitor began.

Ted stood up abruptly.

'I'll leave an officer outside the door. Let them know when you're both ready to continue and we'll come back. And yes, of course, all recording equipment will be turned off so you can consult confidentially.'

Ted swept out of the room, stopped the first uniformed officer he found, and asked them, politely enough, to find someone to wait at the interview room door and to leave it open at all times. He didn't want either King or the solicitor trying to make a run for it. He was starting to think that was as likely for either of them.

Once that was sorted, Ted sprinted for the stairs, Smith lumbering in his wake and grumbling audibly.

'Slow down, guv, I think you might have knackered my ankle.'

Ted headed first to find Jo Rodriguez. Jo looked up hopefully as the boss, with Smith in his wake, walked into his office.

'Anything yet?'

'Getting frustratingly close but we've hit a brick wall,' Ted told him. 'King is running scared, now he knows we can connect him to Frenchie Williams. I don't know if he actually knows the Martin brothers are behind it all, or what that signifies, or even who they are. But he certainly knows he's in it up to his neck and if anyone gets wind of him even risking talking to us, he's in serious trouble.'

Ted was pulling out chairs for Oscar and himself. Joe stood up and headed for his coffee machine.

'No tea in here boss, certainly not green, but I can go and find some, unless you'll have coffee?'

'Make it as weak as weasel water and drown it in milk and that will do, Jo, thanks. Meanwhile I have another fairly urgent job for you to put someone on. King's solicitor, Andrew Lewis. I get the feeling he's dodgy. Even King says the people at the top have police, lawyers and some judges in their pockets in various places, and I'd bet my pension on his solicitor being one of them.'

When he mentioned the man's name, Jo's eyebrows went up.

'Well, that would explain why he always seems to have the very latest and best model of car. I'd assumed there might be money on his wife's side. The things he drives are beyond a normal humble solicitor's reach, I would have thought.'

'I want to know everything about him. Literally everything. I don't care how you manage it but get us reasonable cause to search his premises, to start with. Any he has, including work and home. At the moment, I can't stop him being present while we talk to King and I really want to do that. I think King could be on the point of telling us where Evie might be, or at least getting close to doing so, but he's not going to do that with his solicitor there. Especially if Lewis is in the pay of the people pulling the strings, because he might well know or suspect that.

'I can't stop Lewis being there – unless and until we find something which would potentially implicate him in the wider case. I'd settle for an outstanding parking fine for now, because then I could. His own professional ethics should, so that would keep him nicely out of the way.

'The Martin brothers might, of course, immediately replace him with someone else, at their expense, if they judge King to be a risk to their identity. I'm betting they know he hasn't had contact with anyone who could lead to them directly, so they may simply order him to be dropped and he'd have to rely on a duty legal aid solicitor who might not have the same incentive to see him cleared.'

'So what's the plan now, guv?' Smith asked him. 'Only, stating the obvious, how do we know the dodgy solicitor isn't on the phone right now to someone within the gang to get the baby shifted asap, by whatever means needed? Or worse.'

'We don't,' Ted conceded, 'but that's why I asked the PC to leave the door open. He knows what I meant. He'll be a visible presence that should deter the solicitor from phoning anyone. They can talk between themselves quietly enough without being overheard. But as soon as a mobile phone makes an appearance, the officer will become a visible deterrent. Best we can do for now.

'Meanwhile, DI Smith, can you talk to your team. Mention the solicitor's name. See if they can find out from anyone if the name rings any bells. I assume they're talking to Frenchie Williams, for a start, as part of your enquiries. We need some connections from here to anyone down south and it sounds as if Frenchie is the likely link. I imagine they'll be working round the clock on this one?'

'My lot sleep when I tell them to and not before,' Smith told him. 'I'll put Dai on it. He's a lazy bastard, always glad of a desk job, but he's thorough enough. He knows he'll have me to answer to if he misses anything.'

Ted could well believe it, but he might as well take advantage of his methods.

'I don't have to spell it out for either of you, but if we have to start looking for wherever the baby is being held, it would be far better to get that part done today if we possibly can, rather than tomorrow. No matter how careful we are, depending on the premises, it could look suspicious if there's suddenly a lot of activity around the place on a Sunday, if it's a residential area. Anything out of the ordinary would stand out a mile and reduce our chances of getting in there. They're bound to be keeping a sharp lookout. They're clearly not amateurs.

'Our main priority has to remain Evie's safety, above all else, whatever we do. Favourite would be if we can at least get a steer from King as to where to start looking today. As soon as possible. I'll check with Sammy what she's happy with me offering him as any kind of a deal to start talking. If all of this really is gang related, King will know his life is in danger on the inside as much as let out on bail.

'If we could find anything at all solid to implicate the solicitor, we could at least object to his continued involvement. Conflict of interest, if nothing else. Anything he can find, and the faster the better. We might possibly be in with a chance – a slim one – of getting Evie back safely and home to her parents.'

*　*　*

Ted was keeping half an eye on the time. Not simply because he wanted to find wherever the child snatchers might be holed up, with plenty of daylight left to plan how they were going to proceed. He was also acutely aware that he had sole custody of the feline family and that was a serious responsibility.

He knew that Trev would have left them with plenty of fresh food and water before setting off for the West Country to visit his sister. They'd survive for at least twenty-four hours if they had to. And as an emergency measure, the next door neighbour kept a spare key. He could always phone her to go in in a case of genuine need. But the cats were their family. His and Trev's. And he would feel as bad about abandoning them as any of the parents on the team would feel about missing time with their children.

He phoned Sammy with an update. If and when – and it was still a big if – they found where Evie might be being held, she would have to sign off on the whole operation, so she needed to be kept in the picture at all times.

'I wish I could say promise him whatever it takes, Ted, but you know I can't,' she told him. 'Tell him we can and will ensure his safety, as far as possible, if he cooperates, and that we will inform the courts of his valuable assistance. Dress it up as best you can, but you know it doesn't boil down to a lot.

'If you find the baby, and I hope to god that you do, and soon, what do you need in terms of extra officers if it comes to a raid to get her out?'

'Firearms,' Ted told her decidedly. 'As a precaution, at least. If all of this really is related to a London gang DI Smith says are the modern equivalent of the Krays, I don't want any risk to anyone. Certainly not the baby, and preferably not to any officer, nor any civilian who might perhaps get in the way.

'After all, we don't know if Evie has been handed over to foster parents, although the intelligence and my gut feeling is that she'll be destined for overseas and simply hasn't been shipped out yet because in a sense, we got lucky with the burning car and what it told us early on.'

'You can have an armed unit but this time I don't want an angry Firearms commander bellowing down the phone that you've been re-enacting scenes from The Karate Kid and putting yourself and his officers in danger.'

Ted was glad they weren't on visual. He couldn't contain a grin as he recalled the incident. He'd only got away with it because it resulted in the arrest of someone they'd been after for some time who had looked on the point of slipping between their fingers at the last minute.

'Noted,' he told her.

'Whatever it takes, apart from risking yourself, though, Ted. Seriously. We need to get that poor mother her baby back. Keep me posted, any time, day or night.

'And if you do pull it off, let's have a big piss-up for the whole team to celebrate. I'll be in the chair and it can double as my leaving do. Just promise me you won't let anyone make any soppy speeches.'

There was no mistaking the catch in her voice as she said it. Sammy loved her job. She was good at it. She'd fought her way up to a senior rank in a difficult field and she was beyond gutted that it was her own body letting her down which was costing her the job and forcing her into early retirement. She still had no idea what she was meant to do with herself when the day came.

Ted had left his office door open, so he saw Jo and Smith approaching. Jo in particular looked pleased with himself.

'I have to get back to our interviewee now, but I'll keep you posted all along,' Ted promised her, hastily ending the call.

'Jo, you look as if you have good news.'

'Early days, boss, but something unexpected. On a whim, and after saying a few prayers, I phoned Sal Ahmed, in Fraud. It occurred to me that if anyone anywhere might be looking into King's solicitor with the taste in expensive motors, it could well be that team.

'It was a long shot, but well worth it. Sal was surprised by my call, to say the least. They've had a covert op keeping an eye on Mr Andrew Lewis on suspicion of various fraudulent activities, not least of which is tax evasion. And as we know, the powers that be clamp down hard on tax dodges from individuals, even if a blind eye often gets turned to big corporations.

'Long story is that Sal is on his way down with the ink still wet on a warrant to search Lewis's office premises to start with, with the possibility of extending it to his home if necessary. He's coming in an area car on blues so he could well be here within half an hour. So will that be enough of a distraction to take him away from Mr King?'

'Jo, you know religion isn't my thing, but can you light a candle or something on my behalf for whichever of your saints has fixed this for us? This could be exactly the breakthrough we need, if we can talk to King with his solicitor safely out of the way, legitimately so. We'll offer him the chance to wait for a replacement but, with any luck, this might rattle him. If he thinks the net is closing on the people he's been working for, he might start talking, hoping to bargain his way to a lesser charge with his cooperation. Because he doesn't need to know at this stage that it's Fraud after his solicitor, rather than Serious Crime.'

'So are we going to go down and give the pair of them a hint of what's coming?' Smith asked.

'I think we should leave them in blissful ignorance until Sal, DS Ahmed, gets here. It will be a nice surprise for both of them. In the meantime, you'd better update your own team on our development here because it could have relevance to how they're handling their end of the case. After all, it was the taxman who finally brought down Al Capone, so let's keep our fingers crossed.'

* * *

Ted received word that King and his solicitor were ready to start again shortly before Sal Ahmed arrived at the station. He sent a message back to say he would be down shortly and to leave the lookout in place. He'd been in touch by phone with Sal, who said there was more traffic than he'd hoped but with the use of blues and twos as necessary, they wouldn't be all that far behind their ETA.

Sal Ahmed came straight upstairs when he arrived, to a warm welcome from those of his former colleagues who were in the office, then he went to find the boss. Ted was in his own office, the door open, talking strategy with Jo Rodriguez and another person Sal didn't recognise.

Ted stood up to greet him when he came in.

'Sal. Nice to see you again. This is DI Smith, from the Met, liaising with us as there's crossover on cases. We really need Andrew Lewis out of the way, legitimately, so we can have a proper in-depth interview with our suspect, Alec King.'

Smith did no more than lift his chin in Sal's direction. His action didn't escape Ted's attention. He certainly lived up to his bad reputation at any opportunity. He seemed to show as little respect for people of colour as he did for female officers. Sal blanked him and responded to Ted.

'Yes, Jo filled me in, and I'll be delighted to take him off your hands. He's a slippery customer, and no mistake. We don't have a warrant for him – yet – as that will depend on what we uncover on a search of his office premises, for which we do have one. But we can certainly get him out of your hair for now. Best of all, he should have no inkling we're this close to him, so he shouldn't have had the chance to dispose of anything which might be useful to any of us.

'It goes without saying that anything we come across which could possibly link in to your case or DI Smith's, I'll feed back straight away.'

Sal would have dearly loved to ignore the Met officer in the same way he'd been pretty much ignored by him, but he had too much respect for his old boss to do so. He knew he'd still get his chain jerked if he did, even though he was no longer on Ted's team. He hoped and suspected the same would happen with DI Smith, although not with anyone else in the office.

Ted stood up and led the way to the door.

'So, shall we go and show Mr Andrew Lewis that his worst nightmares have all come true at the same time? And if that doesn't loosen King's tongue for him, nothing will.'

Chapter Twenty-five

Alec King and his solicitor Andrew Lewis both looked curious to see a third officer enter the interview room with the DCI and DI. As discussed between them beforehand, Sal Ahmed spoke first.

'I'm Detective Sergeant Ahmed, Greater Manchester Police, from Fraud Investigation. It's actually you I've come to see, Mr Lewis, not your client. I know it's a bit unorthodox, but I have been trying to see you in your office and getting fobbed off, so when I heard you were here, I took the opportunity of knowing where to find you.'

'Well, as you can see, sergeant,' Lewis's tone was decidedly testy, 'I am with a client who is being interviewed by your colleagues. So you will have to make an appointment with my secretary for another time.'

'I'm afraid that's not an option, sir.'

Sal's tone remained polite, but there was no mistaking the meaning of what he said.

Smith was watching, puzzled. All this politeness and 'sir' stuff. He or any of his team would have simply marched in, stuck the warrant under the brief's nose, grabbed him, shoved him in the area car, and away with him.

Waste of time, he considered it. What's more, even if they found where the sprog had been taken, they were never going to get it back with procedure so much by the book. Not before it was old enough to start nursery school at least, if it was still alive, with all this pussyfooting around. He'd have to make his feelings known to Darling at some point.

Sal was showing the solicitor the warrant. The man looked on the point of exploding. It had obviously come as a huge shock. Whichever direction he might have been anticipating trouble to come from, clearly it wasn't from police fraud investigators.

'I can't leave my client. He is entitled to legal representation …'

Ted cut in at this point, also way too polite for Smith's taste.

'We'll arrange an alternative, Mr Lewis, if that's what your client requests. You have my word. We always go by the book on procedure here, you can rest assured of that.'

Which is why you're still pissing about five days after the kid went missing, Smith was thinking to himself. *When was anyone going to start doing some real coppering, of the sort he and his team would do? They were never going to get anywhere with all this please, thank you, follow the rules crap.*

'Sir? If you'd like to come with us, please. We'll be taking you in a police vehicle so as to ensure there is no contact between you and anyone in your office until you arrive. We'll keep it all as low key as possible, though. Others from my team will be joining us there but won't go in until we arrive. And I'll see to it that you're brought back here to recover your own vehicle as soon as we're finished, although I can't promise how long our searches will take. This way, sir.'

'Say nothing, Mr King. Nothing at all,' Lewis flung over his shoulder to his client, as Sal escorted him, politely but firmly, out of the room and shut the door behind them.

Ted switched the recordings back on before he sat down opposite Alec King, who was now looking more than a little worried. Smith sat down next to Ted. This was starting to look more promising. He'd thought the DCI would abandon the interview until another brief was found. He carefully moved his feet as far as possible out of range under the table. He knew he'd have trouble staying schtum and he didn't fancy another clout right on the bone if he said something Darling didn't like. The DCI was surprisingly accurate with his footwork.

'First of all, Mr King, let me remind you that you are still under caution, so you don't have to say anything at all if you don't want to. Although it would help us enormously if you would voluntarily answer a few questions. You can, of course, get another solicitor before doing so. Either one you choose yourself, or a duty one. Do you have someone else in mind?'

'I don't know anyone.'

'How did you find Mr Lewis? I don't believe he's on the list as a legal aid solicitor, but perhaps I'm wrong.'

He said it in such a conversational tone that it seemed an innocent question. Smith had to concede that the DCI was good at luring suspects into saying more than they probably should. He wondered if he was a fly fisherman. Certainly he must practise something requiring infinite patience. Smith could see that his methods might well be effective, but with the clock firmly against them, it was like waiting for a tortoise to run the last leg of a relay race. He probably wouldn't drop the baton, but his time was going to be crap.

'He said I shouldn't say anything to you,' King told him, looking worried.

'That is your right, of course. But you do need to tell me,

please, whether you want me to arrange another solicitor for you, to replace Mr Lewis. Because we do need to continue questioning you. We have the grounds to do that.'

King sat in stubborn silence. In his mind, Smith reached across the desk to shake him by the throat until his teeth rattled. They were going to be here forever at this rate.

'That's your right, of course, Mr King. Remember, though, that you've already admitted, on tape, to having transported the kidnapper from the park to a handover location. We have forensic evidence, and a timeline, which shows the woman almost certainly had the baby with her at that point. Which makes you an accessory to whatever has happened to the little girl, and to the woman who snatched her. A person we know to have been unlawfully killed.'

King opened his mouth to speak, but Ted hadn't finished his piece yet.

'You can say you weren't aware she had the baby with her when she got into the car with you. Some members of a jury might well believe you. I wouldn't personally be optimistic that that view would be widely shared.

'A new solicitor would almost certainly advise you to continue to say nothing. That is still your right. All I can say to you at this point is that I would strongly recommend that you cooperate with us now to help return little Evie to her parents who are, of course, frantic with worry. That would be very powerful mitigation to put in front of a court.

'Up to you.'

Ted's short leg somehow managed to stretch far enough to deliver another warning knock to Smith's ankle. More cat and mouse stuff. Ted's speciality. He could sit quietly and wait, for as long as it took. Smith's bull in a china shop approach could destroy all the rapport he was slowly building up, as well as any chance at all of getting the vital information they needed.

King was weighing up his chances. He was no fool. He knew they weren't good. And now he knew his dodgy brief was also under investigation, he was starting to realise to what extent the net was tightening around the whole operation. Which meant that he had become the sprat the police were clearly hoping to use to catch a shoal of mackerel.

'I didn't see where they took her,' he said finally. 'They drove off with the woman and I set off walking, back the way I'd come. I didn't want to know. Situations like that, knowledge is dangerous.'

Smith was bored of sitting round like a stuffed toy. Five minutes alone with King and he'd have him begging to talk. He first swivelled himself in his seat so could stick his feet out to the side, well out of range.

'They clearly know you, though. The people behind all of this. Know all about you. Enough to know you weren't going to run straight to the first copper you found and tell them everything. The woman ends up dead in a burned out car but you're left to walk back to the nearest bus stop rather than being found in a ditch with a bullet to the back of the head. What's that all about, then?'

King was instantly on his guard, eyeing the bigger bloke suspiciously. If they were playing good cop, bad cop with him, there was no doubt in his mind who was the baddy.

'People know of me. They know I can be trusted to do stuff without asking questions.'

Ted picked up immediately on the lead Smith had fed him.

'You didn't even stop to ask yourself what they wanted

with very small children when they first approached you? Babies? Specifically, I think you said to the man with the dog, pretty ones? Did it not even enter your mind that there were other possible uses for such stolen children, not just the happy ever after adoption scenario you seemed to have settled for? Very disturbing ones?'

King hesitated for a moment, looking confused, before finding his stride once more.

'Well, I don't imagine anyone would pay money to adopt a minger, would they?'

Encouraged by having got one question in without injury, Smith fired off another.

'And you weren't even curious? Once they were safely driving off and you knew you were being allowed to go home, didn't you at least turn round to see where they were heading? Or even to check that one of them hadn't doubled back to follow you? Pretty sure I would have done.'

King hesitated. He'd said far more than he knew he should have, but the only way he could see now of digging himself out of the pit was probably to start cooperating, and hope to hell the kid could still be found alive.

'I can tell you where I handed the car over,' King eventually said, still with some reluctance, then mentioned a road.

Smith already had his phone out, jabbing letters in, instinctively sensing he might be faster at such things than the DCI. Besides, it was obvious that King was more at ease talking to him than to Smith.

'And you saw where the car went from there?' Ted asked him, still quietly spoken, patient.

King was looking all round the room for help or inspiration, neither of which was forthcoming. He said after a pause, 'I looked back, yes, once they'd moved off and were driving away,' then clammed up again.

It was probably as well the DCI was doing the questioning. Smith knew he'd probably have physically attacked the man by this point. Ted simply prompted calmly, 'And?'

'They drove up a hill, going away from me, bearing left. They were almost out of sight then they turned left so they were running like parallel to the road where I was walking and glancing back at them. I didn't stand still and stare. That would have been a bit obvious if anyone was watching me.'

'How far away did they drive?' Ted prompted.

King considered before replying.

'Inside half a mile, maybe.'

'And then?'

'They took a right, then I lost sight of them. It was out in the middle of nowhere, though. Not many houses around. No idea where they went after that.'

Smith, who'd been plotting the course on his phone app as King was speaking, gave Ted a loaded look. There was more than a hint of triumph about it. Clearly the information was worth more than it seemed on the surface.

'Thank you, Mr King, you've been very helpful. We'll take a break now. I'll arrange some refreshments for you, should you wish. You're not free to leave at this stage, however.'

'What about my safety?' King as him. 'Witness protection, or something.'

Ted had already stood up. He turned back to look at him.

'You're in a police station, Mr King. Under constant watch. You can't really get more protection than that.'

* * *

Ted did his usual sprint up the stairs, Smith trailing not far behind and no sign of grumbling this time. They were both on a bit of a high, feeling that they were as close as they'd yet been to finding out where Evie might be being held.

Ted headed first for Jo's office where he found him checking every piece of information which had come in, in search of the elusive key which might unlock doors to somewhere.

'Let's have a catch-up with everyone available asap, Jo, please. Better be downstairs where there's more room. We'll need some officers from Uniform. Who's duty inspector today?'

'Roly. I'll let him know. And does this mean you've got somewhere, boss?'

Smith answered for him.

'King's given us a last seen fix on the car he delivered. If where he says he last saw it is accurate, that road ends in a something of a cul-de-sac, from the looks of it, which is handy. It's why I need some local knowledge as it means nothing to me. We need to look at it on a bigger screen.'

He moved over to Jo's desk, phone in hand, while Jo found the relevant app on his computer. They'd at least be able to partially assess the terrain on screen to help with planning their next move.

'That's nearer to my patch than yours, boss, but still your side of the line,' Jo told him, entering information in the app and pulling up the image.

'As we might expect, for an operation which has shown itself to be slick, it's not going to be easy to get anywhere near them without them seeing us coming a mile off.'

He leaned closer to the screen, looking at detail, as Smith suggested, 'Drone?'

'Tactically tricky,' Ted told him. 'Low enough to capture much of any real use and it risks being spotted. I don't want anything at all to tip them off that we're getting close. If baby Evie is alive and in one of those houses along that road, the risk to her life is too great if we show our hand too soon.

'Favourite tactic would be to check the place out discreetly but thoroughly, then go in maybe before dark tonight, if we can set it all up in time. Probably at first light tomorrow morning is more realistic to set up, with least risk of casualties, but we'll see. If we go in the dark they're going to see any light at all approaching, even if we turn car lights off.

'And it will take time to set up. I want a Firearms unit, for a start. Whoever the local lot are, with gangland connections they're bound to have firepower.'

Smith let out a loud and scornful snort.

'Firearms? Bunch of bloody cowboys! Kiddy stands no chance if she gets caught in the crossfire when that lot get let loose.'

Jo put his head closer to the screen to hide his broad grin, despite the seriousness of the situation.

Ted didn't so much as raise his voice as he replied.

'I'm an ex-SFO, DI Smith. There will be Firearms. The risk of going in without their cover is unacceptably high.

'Right, Jo, make the briefing for fifteen minutes from now, so we can get everything and everyone together. Let's get any and all intel we can find on the potential site. I'll talk to Firearms myself, but before any of us go in, we need to know an awful lot more about where we're going, and that will need eyes on the ground to spot potential pitfalls.

'If there's a footpath anywhere nearby, I could go myself. Check out all the rights of way, Jo, or get someone to do it, please. I've got all the gear and I don't look anything like someone to be concerned about. Plus I know what Firearms will want to know about the raid. I could take my own car, too, in case the suspects have eyes out all round the place. No one would ever take that for a police vehicle.

'I know time is short, Jo, but see if Roly can find us someone who knows that area well. DI Smith, can you put Steve onto checking the electoral role for the area, cross referenced to any names on criminal records anywhere. We need to know who we might be up against. And we somehow need to find a way to keep a watching brief on the area from a safe distance in case they get wind of anything and try to move the baby.

'We're getting close. Let's not blow the whole thing now by rushing in half-cocked with no proper idea of who we're dealing with.'

Chapter Twenty-six

'You're psychic, Mr Policeman. I have literally just turned off the motorway for a drink and a pee stop,' Trev told Ted when he answered the phone call. 'How's it going? Are you still at work?'

'I've just come home to change into walking gear so I can go and do a bit of a recce on a place of interest. I'm checking on the boys and girls at the same time and topping their crunchies up because I'm not sure what time I'll knock off tonight.'

His words immediately put Trev on alert.

'What sort of a recce? Is it going to be dangerous? Is this to do with the little baby? Promise me you're not going to be taking any risks, Ted.'

'No risks. I just have to go for a country walk to check out the lie of the land. I'm bringing Firearms in later so I'll be hiding behind them if anything kicks off.'

'Just see that you do. I don't want anything happening to you and I know what you're like. How are you getting on with Oscar?'

Ted chuckled down the phone.

'Speaking of kicking, I had to give him a few sharp reminders under the desk during an interview that it's me who calls the shots and he doesn't speak without my permission.'

Trev laughed out loud at that.

'I'd have bought tickets to witness that. Promise me you'll take good care, though. Might it be all over bar the shouting by the time I get home tomorrow? And will I get to meet the famous Oscar, at some point?'

'I'd like to think we'll get a result by tomorrow but I don't want to tempt fate or count my chickens. As for Oscar, I'd say it was highly unlikely you'll get to meet him, and it could well be a disaster if you did. He's already shown himself to be the original misogynist, racist caveman. Much as I hate to judge, I'd say there's a good chance he's homophobic too, so I can't believe it would be a comfortable encounter. I have to confess to not having told him I'm married to a man.

'Ride carefully, have a good time with Eirian, and I'll see you at some point tomorrow.'

He couldn't resist touching the nearest wooden object for luck as he said it. Then he laced up his light walking shoes, swung his day sack onto his shoulder and left the house.

* * *

Ted had his earpiece in and was periodically talking on his phone to Jo Rodriguez as he did his walk round the area to look at possible approaches and what cover was available. Dressed as he was, he definitely looked more like a serious walker than a police officer. He even had a local Ordnance Survey map tucked through the belt of his walking trousers. It didn't quite include the area he was interested in, but he always found a paper map to be a good prop. Something to take attention away from his face and where he might be looking if anyone saw him.

Jo was busy fixing up a full briefing for all involved,

including someone from Firearms, for later in the day. No final plans could be made until the vital intelligence had been collected from every possible source.

An operation on this scale, with so much riding on it, would need signing off by someone senior to Ted, so Sammy Sampson would be attending probably her last major briefing in her role as Head of Serious Crime. Undoubtedly the Ice Queen would also appear at some point, too.

Ted's weren't the only feet on the ground in the area. Jezza Vine and Rob O'Connell had been entrusted with Sammy's Italian greyhound, Luka, and were walking along a country lane separated from the back of the target houses by fields. Seemingly a young couple out on a drive, stopping to allow their dog to relieve itself. In reality, two observant officers looking at what the access and, more importantly, the cover were like from the rear of the properties. That would be the favoured route for at least some of the firearms team to move in, under cover of semi-darkness.

In the office, Virgil was helping Steve to find out who the occupants of the houses they were interested in were. The last thing they needed to happen was for a house where the occupants had nothing to do with any child snatch to be raided by armed officers, setting off panic all round and losing any element of surprise.

If that happened, and if the baby was being held in one of the adjacent properties, it would almost certainly signal her death sentence. Always supposing she was still there, alive and well.

DC Steve Ellis lifted his head from his computer screen and looked across the office towards Jo Rodriguez. He was the only one on the team uncomfortable with calling him by his first name.

'Sir, I have a bit of a coincidence here that's worth mentioning.

'Let's hear it, Steve. Anything.'

'Virgil and I are checking the house occupants. I know we pretty much all thought the last house on a dead end road would be unlikely as it would be too easy to block off any escape route in the event of a raid.'

As usual, Steve was literally going all round the houses. Jo waited patiently, knowing that whatever he had to report would be worth the wait.

'One with property on either side would be harder for us to approach without raising the alarm. We haven't yet got full details of all of the occupants …'

Virgil decided to finish off for him at this point, sensing some of the others were getting more than a little impatient.

'The second property from the top end, as you turn off the access road, is a rental. Recently let, to a couple. They've been there just over a month. Their surname is Williams. Like Frenchie. And his name is Georges. French spelling, with an S. She's Beverley.'

'It is the third most common surname in England and Wales, though, sir, so it really could be just a coincidence,' Steve put in, a stickler always for accuracy and every relevant detail.

'Well, we all know how much the boss hates a coincidence, but we can't afford to ignore that one. Can we get a background check on them? If they're renting they'll probably have had to supply references, so where do they take us?' Jo asked him.

'Already on it,' Virgil assured him. 'I've been in contact with the letting agency. They're digging out the files and getting back to me. And I have stressed how urgent it is.'

With the DCI out of the way, Smith waded in to start throwing his weight around a bit, testing the water. He had a feeling Rodriguez wasn't going to stand up to him too much if it came to it.

'We're wasting time here getting hung up on a name. Pissing about setting up an op with no real knowledge of whether or not the kiddy is even there.'

'That's why the boss, Rob and Jezza are out there now, doing a recce,' Jo told him patiently.

'On a possibly empty house,' Smith bit back. 'We need to get round there, kick doors in if necessary. Search every property.'

'But only when we're sure we're not putting any lives in danger,' Jo told him. 'Especially not the baby's.'

'Then we need a distraction,' Smith responded swiftly. 'We need whoever's behind all this to think we're nowhere near them. Get their eyes and their attention focused somewhere else entirely while we go in.'

'What are you suggesting?' Jo was interested, almost in spite of himself.

'A press release. Soon as. Put out a statement that we're following up on a lead. We're searching a property somewhere as far away from where we're actually going to be looking as possible. Somewhere at the opposite end of your manor from where we will be searching, wherever that would be.'

'Bury? Rochdale?' Jo speculated. 'The boss would have to sign off, of course, and it would need clearance higher up. I'll put it to him.'

Smith rolled his eyes to the ceiling.

'Halle-bloody-lujah! Do that. Then we might have a chance of finding her before she starts her A Levels.'

* * *

'Are you seriously telling me there are people who do this sort of thing for fun?' Jezza Vine asked Rob O'Connell.

She'd just jogged another few dozen yards, towards a field gate, holding her hand, with the little greyhound's lead in it, up high as she'd seen people from the dog showing fraternity doing on the rare times she'd caught a glimpse of any of Crufts dog show on the television. Each time she was directly in front of the gate, she'd made an attempt to get Luka to stand like a show dog, although she had no clue if she was doing it right.

'That's perfect, darling,' Rob told her, loud enough to be overheard by anyone nearby. 'He looks like a real champion. Perfect for his social media presence.'

Jezza couldn't contain a snort of mirth at her colleague, throwing himself into the role so effectively. She was the one with the acting skills, but Rob was giving it a good go. Luka obviously realised he was in the hands of complete novices, but he was biddable enough to cooperate.

Although the dog was in the frame on Rob's phone – just – he was more concerned with filming as much of the rear of the houses they were interested in as he could, without it looking suspicious. He periodically zoomed in to the maximum to show access to the back of the properties as best he could. There was little in the way of any cover for those approaching, but he panned enough to show the edges of the field where at least there were hedges, rather than just fencing, against which shapes could blend.

It was pasture, though there was currently no livestock grazing there, which was another positive. No matter how quietly officers went in that way, they could potentially cause panic with any animals in there. A stampeding flock of bleating sheep or of bellowing cattle was not what they needed for a covert raid.

'Have you got enough now? I don't mind the jogging but I'm not sure if the little chap is actually enjoying himself or just humouring us. And I wouldn't want to be the one to hand the Super's dog back to her with something broken or at least damaged in some way. He's cute but he looks so fragile. Mind you, he's done this sort of thing before so he's an old hand at it.'

'I think I'm sorted now. Do we carry on a bit further up this hill, d'you think?'

Jezza shook her head.

'Best not. We might run into the boss coming from the other direction. Even if we ignore one another it might be more people than would normally be out walking round a backwater like this on a Saturday. We don't want to blow it now.'

* * *

Ted was talking to Jo again. He'd now reached the stile which led from the footpath he'd walked up to the road with the target houses on it. He paused to perch on the stile and unfold his map so he could just about see over the top of it. But to any onlookers, he would hopefully seem like nothing more than a weekend walker, deciding which route to take.

'That's a good idea of Oscar's. It's one that's well worth a shot. Can you set it up with whichever of the Supers you can get in contact with, please? You'll need to make sure that whichever division we mention has at least a couple of units available to have as a visible presence to add weight to the cover story.'

'We've also now got the 3D reconstruction head image for the body in the car. Perhaps we could release that at the same time? Make it seem there's a connection? As if we're acting on a tip-off from a possible ID on the body in the car.'

'Good idea. If we can get something out for the evening news, a breaking newsflash, if nothing else, it might even distract whoever has the baby while we go in. Any update on the property occupants?'

'Last house, at the end, seems the least likely. Apart from the fact of getting easily caught in a trap there, it's a single occupant, elderly man, disabled, motorised wheelchair user, who has carers going in four times a day because he's high dependency. Not the ideal person to be looking after a small baby. And if one suddenly turned up there, one of the carers would be sure to ask questions.

'Current favourite seems to be the second one down from the top end. A couple. Recent rental. And Steve is setting great store by the fact that their name is Williams, as in Frenchie, but he qualifies it by saying how common a surname it is, so it could be entirely coincidental. The man's first name is the French spelling of George, though, with an S, which might be significant.'

Ted flipped the map down and carefully made a show of refolding it to display a different section. While his hands worked, his eyes were scanning the house Jo mentioned as he said into the mouthpiece, 'Well, that one certainly has the security lights and cameras. More than any other. I'll take a walk past there on my way back to the car and I'll see you shortly.

'Any word from Rob and Jezza?'

'Jezza said they've run the paws off the Super's little dog so they're dropping it off and heading in. Rob's apparently got some useful footage of the rear of the properties.

'I'll sort the press release and see you shortly.'

'Make sure to pass my thanks to Oscar for his idea, please. Anything like that seems to floor him completely, but perhaps some of the culture will rub off on him, if we keep it up.'

* * *

As Ted had expected, Debra Caldwell attended the operational briefing later on, as well as Sammy Sampson. It had in fact been the Ice Queen whom Jo had got hold of to authorise the short press release about the fictitious raid taking place well away from the one which would actually be happening just as dusk was falling.

The Tactical Firearms Commander, in charge overall of the raid on the house, was attending the briefing. He knew Ted of old, and the two of them got on well. He couldn't resist a friendly dig at him to start with. He also wanted to establish the chain of command from the start for such a delicate operation. He'd also summed up the visiting Met officer at a glance and decided he might potentially be a boundary pusher if not kept firmly on a lead.

'A friendly reminder for everyone before we begin, that I, as TFC, have the final say on everything from start to finish of this op. It's a delicate one. We're all hoping to find the baby safe and well and to extract her in one piece. The best way to do that is for everyone, of all ranks, to stick to the plan and follow orders. Are we all clear on that?'

Only when he'd seen suitable assent from every officer

present did he hand over to Ted to give all available details so far based, on the recce and online research.

'The house considered to be the most likely target does have the most security lights and cameras of all of them. Seemingly a disproportionate number of them, too.'

'Unless they really are the latest state of the art technology, our blockers will disable those effectively enough for us,' the TFC told him. 'So the occupants shouldn't get any advance warning that way, at least.'

'Not wanting to sound flippant, boss,' Jezza Vine began, 'but how will you know for sure it's the right baby, assuming you find one at all? Not something I'm experienced in but I'm trying to imagine a scenario where someone triumphantly delivers a baby to the Fishers only for them to say it's not Evie and they've never seen her before.'

'Very good point, Jezza,' Ted told her. 'Even if we send a photo from the scene, assuming we do find a baby there, a baby girl, it could be catastrophic if it isn't Evie. Any suggestions, anyone, please?'

'Trust me, guv,' Oscar Smith told him. 'I said I could do faces and I proved it with Alec King. I've never tried it out with babies but there's no reason why it shouldn't work. If we find a baby inside, there's a fair chance I'll be able to tell whether or not it's Evie Fisher.'

Chapter Twenty-seven

'Is it all right now? Settling down and stopped whingeing?' the man asked as his wife came back into the room from upstairs.

'She's not an it. She's about the best one so far. The quietest, for sure. She just needed changing, then she went off back to sleep.'

'For fuck's sake don't start getting broody and attached to it. You know you can't keep any of them. We have the same thing every time. Think of the money instead, not the brat. And you know they're going to good homes where they'll be looked after.'

'We're a bit like those – what do they call them? – puppy walkers – who take guide dog puppies and so on to get them started in life. What we're doing is charitable.'

He laughed at his own humour, but his wife was still grumbling.

'I hope we can at least go somewhere else for the next one. I hate it here. All this countryside and no shops. And the weather's crap too, most of the time. I'd rather be back in London.'

'You know it was hotting up far too much down there. Time for a change. And it's only temporary. The cops were getting a bit too close. But we'll be back there, one day soon. We might even have made enough to retire. We could go and live somewhere warmer. With lots of shops. You'd like that.

Spain, or the Canaries or somewhere.'

The man had just taken a swig from the beer bottle he was holding when he nearly choked on the contents. He was looking at the television screen which was showing a local news bulletin with a 'breaking news' flash across the bottom of the screen.

'Bloody hell! Look at those dozy bastards. Wherever they're raiding a house for the missing sprog, it's nowhere near here. Look at that shot! That's right in the middle of a town somewhere. Fucking idiots, the lot of them. Couldn't find their own arses in a thunderstorm. I wonder what set them off on that wild goose chase?'

Then he sat bolt upright, staring at the screen as the camera shot changed to a revolving 3D image of a woman's head.

His wife's hand flew up to her face as she said, 'That's her who came here with the baby when they dropped it off. I'm sure it is.'

'Don't be daft, woman, they all look the same, these foreign types. You can't tell them apart. Besides, there'd have been nothing left of her to make an image like that ...'

They were both silenced at the exact same moment by a monumental crash, which shook the house to its foundation. In an instant, before either of them could react, there were loud shouts of, 'Armed police! Stand still!' and figures in dark uniforms seemed to be swarming everywhere.

The man made an attempt to recover himself, one hand scrabbling down behind the sofa cushions and emerging with a handgun which immediately fell from his trembling fingers as he found himself looking at the business end of a Heckler & Koch, the officer behind it bellowing at him to get down on the floor with his hands on his head.

It was all over in seconds, with both the couple immobilised and handcuffed. Ted and Smith were right behind the Authorized Firearms Officers, Ted himself arresting the couple on suspicion of abducting baby Evie. He then had them taken out of the house and into the van which arrived as soon as the driver got word, to be driven to the station and processed.

There was a female officer from Uniform present who went upstairs as instructed in the direction of the sounds of a loudly crying baby which had followed all the noise and disruption.

The PC came back down the stairs carrying the baby, who was by now demonstrating considerable lung power.

'Is it Evie?' Ted asked her anxiously.

'I think so, sir, but it's hard to tell with her face all screwed up like that. At least it seems as if she's fairly healthy,' PC Julie Holt replied. 'But we can't really send a picture to the parents to check her identity with her looking as distressed as this.'

She was carefully rocking the baby in her arms in an effort to soothe her, but so far without success.

Oscar Smith stepped forward and held out his hands.

'Give her to me,' he told her.

She hesitated, looking to Ted for instruction. She didn't know this Met officer, other than via station gossip, and he didn't look remotely reassuring. Ted didn't know enough about him to know if he would be any better than PC Holt with the clearly distressed child. But anything was worth trying in the circumstances so he nodded assent.

Little Evie looked tiny against Smith's broad chest, held in arms that looked strong enough to do serious damage to the worst villain.

To Ted's surprise, Smith moved her gently from side to side as he started to sing, in a decent baritone voice.

'*Guten Abend, gute Nacht,*
mit Rosen bedacht.'

Brahms' Lullaby, the words sung in German.

The effect was astonishing. The baby stopped crying before the end of the first verse. By halfway through the second, she was almost asleep.

Smith grinned at Ted, clearly pleased with himself, as he said, 'I think now would be a good time to take a picture to send to her parents, don't you, guv?'

Ted got his phone out, took the photo, then called Carrie Fisher on visual.

'Mrs Fisher? DCI Darling. I have someone to show you. Can you please confirm if this is baby Evie?'

Seconds after he sent it, he heard a shriek down the phone, so loud he couldn't tell whether it was joy or despair.

It was Dave Fisher's face which appeared on screen next, his wife's buried against his chest as she sobbed. Ted held his breath until the man spoke, so emotional it took him a couple of attempts.

'Yes! Yes! That's our Evie. Our little girl. Thank you. Thank you for getting her back for us.'

'She's on her way home to you very shortly. I'd like to arrange for a doctor to check her out thoroughly but she appears to be unharmed and well looked after. I won't come in person today; there are still a lot of loose ends to be tied up here. But I will try and call round tomorrow some time or perhaps on Monday.

'Oh, and can I ask you, please, not to say anything to the press at this time. We'll need to carefully control any and all information given out so as not to prejudice the enquiry and risk compromising a conviction.'

Dave Fisher was still thanking him effusively as Ted ended the call. He'd need to oversee a few things before he could think of going anywhere. The property would have to be secured and preserved as a crime scene. But at least for now, there was a happy ending for the Fisher family with their baby safely on her way back home to them, seemingly none the worse for her separation from her mother. Although Ted couldn't begin to imagine the torment her disappearance had put both her parents through.

Ted and Oscar walked up to the car they had travelled in, to head back to the station, once Ted was satisfied that everything was in hand at the house. He would need to arrange for a press release to go out as soon as possible with news of the successful outcome, for one thing. The media had been all over them like a rash whilst the baby was missing but he doubted they'd get much coverage for the successful outcome, against all the odds, and certainly little credit.

'That was a neat trick with the baby,' he told Smith. 'Where did you learn that?'

'Works on my cat Clive every time, when he's being a little sod. But if you breathe a word of that to anyone else in the station or especially to my own team, I shall have to kill you.'

'Are you threatening a senior officer, DI Smith?' Ted asked him, although his tone was light.

'Just a friendly word of advice, guv,' Smith told him as they reached the car. Then, as they opened the doors to get in, he asked hopefully, 'Pub?'

'I wish,' Ted told him. 'Too much to do first, but as we both need to eat at some point, then as soon as we can decently knock off, pub. Why not?'

* * *

The mood was jubilant for the end of operation debriefing. Ted had phoned both Debra Caldwell and Sammy Samson to give them the good news, whilst he was driving back to the station. He wasn't surprised to see the Ice Queen turn up in person for the meeting, where she began by saying a few words. Never her speciality. But she at least managed to sound warm and sincere as she praised the work which had gone into the op by all concerned, resulting in such a good outcome.

Once they'd finished, Ted took a few moments to discuss with her the press release, and its timing, to announce the successful outcome. She surprised him by saying, 'I'll do the piece to camera for that one. I imagine you have too much to do, and it need only be brief.

'By the way, I wanted to ask you about some sort of a leaving do for Superintendent Sampson. She'll be pleased to be going out on a high note with this successful outcome. Do you have any ideas of the sort of thing she would like, and also what would be a suitable leaving gift for her?'

Jezza Vine was nearby, getting her things together ready to go home. She spoke up.

'Ma'am, I'm sorry to interrupt and I wasn't meaning to eavesdrop, but I have a gift in mind for Superintendent Sampson which I think might be the perfect thing. If you'll trust me with it?'

'You haven't let us down so far Jezza, thank you,' Ted told her, then turned back to the Ice Queen to continue, 'I know Sammy doesn't want a big fuss, and she's already said she'd be happy with a quiet evening with the team at The Grapes, so I was going to sort that with Dave. I was planning on eating there later, if I get finished here in time.'

He looked round the room to see where Smith was before continuing. He saw him talking to Jo Rodriguez, so he asked the Ice Queen, 'Do you think I should include DI Smith, ma'am? I know he's not really a part of the team, but he's away from home, on his own. I thought it might seem a bit churlish to exclude him. He was actually surprisingly helpful on the raid, especially with little Evie. He does have a civilised side, even if he clearly doesn't show it very often.'

Superintendent Caldwell also looked across the room as if seeking some sign that Ted was right in his summary of him. Jezza finished packing up her things, then excused herself, announcing mysteriously that she was going to see if the leaving present she had in mind was going to be feasible.

Eventually, the Ice Queen replied, 'Invite him, by all means. I shall look forward to seeing that side of his nature. Oh, and between us for now, please, but I happen to know that Superintendent Sampson is not returning to work. She is using up leave to take her to her official medical discharge date. So she won't be back in any official capacity. Which means that you may well be asked once more to act up as Head of Serious Crime. You've had a good result on this one, so you will no doubt once again be the candidate of choice, but that's unofficial at present, and I shall deny ever having said it, if challenged.'

It was the closest she ever came to any sort of humour so Ted chuckled politely. He wasn't bothered either way. Head or Deputy, his role was unlikely to change, nor was his salary.

He headed for his office to get everything written up before he could even think of knocking off. He was impressed to see Smith going into Jo's office, presumably to do the same thing. If they were both swift, they'd still have time to walk round to The Grapes for a drink and a bite to eat before stop-tap.

In the meantime the couple they'd arrested at the scene would be processed, separated and kept in police custody. Ted fully intended to eat something before he began any questioning. His stomach was reminding him that he'd been a bit light on feeding it.

Smith came to find him after he'd done his own report writing. Ted was just finishing off and had been on the point of suggesting they take a break to eat.

'I'd like a go at talking to these two for our enquiries down south, guv. I know I'm on your turf up here but their accents are definitely London, not Manchester, so there's a possibility at least that they know something about our side of things.

'It's not likely, but there's always an outside chance we could still track down at least one of the kids from our cases, if they've not left the country yet, for some reason. It's less time critical for you, now you've got Evie back.'

'That's fair enough, as long as you fully understand that within this station, things are done correctly, following the procedure. I won't tolerate any heavy-handed tactics,' Ted warned him.

'These two are from London, guv,' Smith protested. 'Hard as nails, I guarantee it, even without seeing their records, because you can bet they will both be known to the police. None of your soft-soaping, please and thank you crap is going to have any effect on either of them.'

Smith was looming ominously over Ted's desk, his voice getting louder with his frustration.

'When in Rome, DI Smith,' Ted told him mildly. 'You can question them, of course. I agree, we would be negligent not to even consider the possibility that not all of the children will have been taken out of the country. You can sit in with me when I do initial interviews, but you either follow our rules or I will remove you. Up to you.'

It could have been an empty threat. A metaphor. But something about the way the pocket-sized DCI sat there calmly, hazel eyes, which seemed now to flash with a hint of emerald, warned Smith's finely tuned senses that this was not bluff. He made himself a mental note to find out more about the man before he pushed his luck too far. The DCI certainly didn't look remotely intimidated by Smith's greater height and bulk.

This was clearly not the moment to push things any further. Smith realised that if he did, he'd be unlikely to get to talk to the couple at all until the DCI and his team had wrung out of them every bit of information they could get. First rule of engagement – pick your battles. He backed down.

'Fair enough, guv. You're the boss.'

'Wise choice, DI Smith. So, for now, pub?'

'Pub, guv.'

Chapter Twenty-eight

First thing Sunday morning and already DI Oscar Smith was in an argumentative mood. Once again he'd refused Ted's offer of a lift to his digs the evening before, staying on at the pub. Although he was correctly dressed and cleanly shaven, he looked as rough as the proverbial rear end of a badger and his eyes were bloodshot. A definite case of the morning after the night before.

There was only a skeleton presence in the office. Now baby Evie was home safe, there were endless reports to be sorted, but Ted was more than happy for team members to catch a bit of time with their own families after such an intense case.

Officers like Chris Whittaker, who'd been drafted in from other areas, were all in, making their reports, then they could return to their own stations. Ted made a point of thanking each of them in person. In his Specialist Firearms Officer days, he'd often been called in to work with other teams and always remembered how much he'd appreciated at least a word of acknowledgement from someone senior.

As soon as he'd done the rounds and gone back to his own office, Smith followed him, looking truculent.

'Guv, now you've got the kiddy back in your case, like I said, I need to have a crack at all four suspects, to see what I can get out of them to move our enquiries forward down south. I led you to King through face recognition, so now I need quid pro quo to get ours moving again. They've been stalled too long.'

Ted was shaking his head before Smith had finished speaking. For the moment he left him standing there, looming over his desk. He wasn't trying to make a point. It was simply that he didn't want the conversation to linger. He had too much to do and Smith needed to hoist in the fundamental principle. Ted's nick, Ted's rules.

'You're not going anywhere near Ian Hardy, for one,' Ted told him firmly. 'Pointless. We know he can't ID faces, and it's more probability than guess that he has no direct link to your Martin brothers or anyone else in London. Any attempt at hard questioning of him and his defence team would be able to get most of his testimony disallowed because of his difficulties and the stress he would have been under.

'As for the others, you are welcome to sit in on those three interviews. But you won't be taking the lead, you will be being observed, and I will personally stop you and remove you if you cross any lines.'

'I need a shot at the Williams's though, definitely,' Smith insisted. 'They're the strongest link to our manor …'

They were interrupted by Ted's mobile phone ringing. He checked the screen. The number meant nothing to him. As ever, an inevitable policeman's reaction to an unknown caller – it must be bad news. Trev had had an accident on the bike, or on a horse, and the call was to tell him he was lying seriously injured in the back of an ambulance somewhere. Or worse.

'Thank you, DI Smith, we'll talk later. Now I need to take this call,' Ted told him firmly.

The Met officer managed to make almost as much noise shutting Ted's office door as the enforcer breaking open the door to the Williams's house the evening before had done. It clearly wasn't over between them.

As he normally did, with an unknown caller, Ted answered with a guarded, 'DCI Darling.'

'A DCI now? You've done all right for yourself, for a short skinny runt from the Lancashire coalfields.'

The voice, with a soft Scottish accent, repeating Ted's own frequently quoted words back to him, was familiar to his ear but he struggled, for a moment, to put it into context. The caller picked up on his hesitation and laughed.

'We last shared a basha during what felt like a monsoon, high up on the Brecon Beacons, as I recall. On one of Mr Green's famous yomps. But I'm only a humble DS still, so why would you remember me?'

'Jock McClintock!' Ted said in triumph. 'This is a surprise. To what do I owe the honour?'

'You'll excuse me if I don't call you sir. Only, when you've wild camped with someone, listening to each other's farts all night, formality doesn't come easily.'

'Fair enough. And out of interest, how did you get this number?'

'Come on, Ted, you remember Mr Green's Rule Number One – if I tell you …'

'You'll have to kill me,' Ted finished for him, both men laughing at the memory. Then Ted went on, 'You're still serving, then?'

'Still serving, still doing the funny stuff, and that's as much as you need to know. But I know enough to know that you carelessly let a suspect slip away recently. That's not like you, and this was a particularly nasty scrote. A serial rapist. Last heard of somewhere in Qatar and not traceable anywhere from there.'

'Not just the serial rapes, although they were bad enough,' Ted told him. 'We were after him for a suspected murder but he gave us the slip in Leeds and flew out of Manchester heading east. Disembarked in Qatar and disappeared off the radar ever since. There's an Interpol Red Notice out on him, as I'm guessing you're aware.'

'Hold that thought of your homicide, Ted. I'm here to tell you that it gives you the winning hand, the royal flush, in the inevitable international game of poker which is taking place right now.

'Your charming Joel Hammond is currently cooling his heels in a German prison cell. He started up some of his filthy tricks on a visit to Germany, where he was arrested. He then made the very foolish mistake of thumping a police officer. Silly man. Instant remand in custody and he's likely to stay there a lot longer than he thinks, with precious little he can do about it.'

'So does that mean we can get him extradited here, with the Red Notice?'

McClintock chuckled down the phone.

'Ah, Ted, such innocence for a DCI. You'd be lucky to get consulted and allowed any input at all, never mind having first dibs in having him shipped to you. You might well see your pension before you get your hands on him. In normal circumstances.

'But I'm calling you as a fairy godfather. There's a multijurisdictional meeting on Tuesday, in Germany. Chances of you getting a place round that table without friends on the inside are lower than absolute zero. But I have a seat in that meeting and I can, as the saying goes, bring a plus one.

'Now, I'm not promising you will get him ahead of all the other countries who want him. But at least you'd be there in person to put your case, and there is no way on god's earth you'd get that chance without a friend on the inside. Like me.'

'Where is the meeting?'

'Oh, come on, Ted, surely you know that all information on this is on a need-to-know basis. In fact the less you know, the better, as I'm going way out on a limb even trying to get you in there. All you need to know is you'd fly to Frankfurt and I'll be there to meet you. You'd need to get an early morning flight, as they're the only non-stop ones from Manchester, I think, but you'd need to check.

'The meeting will run all day, until probably late evening or even the next day, so I'd drive you straight back to wherever you're staying as soon as it finishes. There's a few hotels within easy walking distance of the airport, if the closer ones are full, for some reason. Easy for someone who's done Mr Green's training hikes. You can stay at one of those for the night and catch an early morning flight back.

'It's up to you entirely, Ted, but I can tell you honestly – this is your one and only chance to get into that meeting to have your say. And I'm doing it because, rightly or wrongly, I've a feeling you'd do the same for me in similar circumstances. So what d'you say?'

What Ted's inner voice was saying to him was that when something seemed too good to be true, it usually was. He hadn't seen McClintock for years. He could check easily enough if he was still a serving officer, as he claimed. Unless he worked under such deep cover that anything about him was classified. But even if still serving, he could easily be a corrupt copper, setting Ted up to be the fall guy for something he didn't even want to think about.

His optimistic inner voice was thinking how perfect the

timing was, with the kidnap case neatly wound up, leaving him free to go.

If McClintock was totally on the level, he wouldn't remotely expect Ted to be able to make the decision himself, on the spot. He'd know it would need clearance higher up.

Ted would definitely need to run this past the Ice Queen before he could give his answer. And there was another phone call he wanted to make before taking any action.

He kept his tone light as he replied. No big deal, just the usual mountain of paperwork and red tape to sanction anything like this. McClintock would be expecting that.

'I'll have to run it past my Super before I can give you an answer, Jock. You'll have expected that, no doubt. I'll try to call you back within the hour, though. Is that okay?'

McClintock had clearly anticipated that answer and seemed to accept it. That lent more credibility to it all, as far as Ted was concerned.

'Fair enough, Ted. I'll wait for your call.'

Then he went on, 'Tell me, what happened to old Green? I heard about his supposed drowning off the coast of South Africa and didn't believe a word of it. We both know he was part dolphin and could out-swim anyone he ever met. Didn't he compete internationally? Diving, or something? Have you heard any more of him after that?'

'You know the answer to that already, Jock. If he is still alive somewhere and I tell you, he'll kill both of us,' he said it with a laugh but both men knew Green would not hesitate to remove anyone who could potentially compromise his cover. 'I'll call you back as quickly as I can.'

As soon as he ended the call with McClintock, he pulled up a saved number and called it. Not to the Ice Queen, but to someone else. As ever, the call went straight to voicemail.

His message was brief.

'Ted here. Jock McClintock. Should I trust him?'

He didn't expect a swift answer. He knew he might not get one at all. He thought he'd at least wait the time it would take him to make himself a brew and start to drink it before giving up and doing something else.

He was just adding the milk to his mug when the phone rang.

'If you even have to ask me that, then you don't trust him and you should go with your instincts.'

Green's voice, as testy as ever. No greeting, certainly no niceties. The minimum number of words to convey his message. Always. And no pause to allow Ted any input.

'And Gayboy, the next time you forget I am officially retired, I'll come down there and give you a reminder.'

Then he was gone.

Now Ted faced a dilemma. As he'd said to McClintock, this meeting, out of the country and especially unofficial as it all was, was definitely something he should run past a senior officer to sign off on, even if it was all done under the radar. If he didn't and the whole thing went drastically wrong, potentially causing an international incident, he could kiss goodbye to taking over again as Head of Serious Crime, and would be lucky to cling on by his fingernails as Deputy. It could potentially even signal curtains for his whole career. Not to mention leaving a dent in his self-confidence if his usually reliable instincts let him down on this one.

He'd have had no problem running everything past Sammy Sampson. She was sufficiently informal that he could have sat down with her, gone through the whole thing, especially the need for secrecy, and he was sure she would have given him the nod. Not to mention signing off on his travel expenses, and watching his back for him if things should go badly wrong.

It would certainly have been the same with her predecessor, Ted's old Big Boss, Jim Baker. He'd have growled, grumbled, made a fuss, but would eventually have given him the nod without drama, Ted was sure.

But now he would have to run it by the Ice Queen. The most formal and by-the-book senior officer he'd ever served under. He knew instinctively that she wouldn't like it. Not one bit. And she'd like even less that he couldn't really tell her a great deal about, since he knew very little himself until he got out to Germany and met up with Jock McClintock.

The one beam of light at the end of a very long tunnel was that she did, at least, know Mr Green, and therefore the type of officers selected for his courses. Like Ted, she'd also started her career in Firearms and had done some of his shooting courses, although never the type of training the likes of Ted or Jock McClintock had done. And at least he knew she would listen to him.

She did. In a silence so complete Ted wondered if she was still there. He found her hard to read in the flesh. At the end of a telephone, and not on visual, she was impossible to.

'Let me get this right, chief inspector,' she began, as formal as ever. 'You are asking me to give the nod for you to go off on a completely unofficial jaunt abroad. Without even specifying which country, to a meeting with mysterious forces, where you have absolutely no legal authority or jurisdiction.

'You're asking me to accept that this is in the best interests of a case which you refuse to name, although it seems obvious to me which one it might be. And that, at some undisclosed point in the future, this may or may not result in the extradition and subsequent possible conviction of someone, which would close cases not only for us, but for some other forces as well.

'Does that just about sum things up, or have I missed out any vital information which you haven't given me to begin with?'

Ted was starting to feel like all kinds of an idiot. He'd been clutching at straws. So desperate to get some sort of conclusion on their last big case, the serial rapist turned murderer, that he'd made himself look like a complete pillock asking the Ice Queen, of all people, to turn a blind eye to something so far off the books it didn't even register on her usual scale of ethics.

He nearly fell off his chair in surprise when, after an extended pause, she finally spoke.

'Well, chief inspector, we absolutely did not have this conversation. Not even a part of it. However, hypothetically speaking, were we ever to have had any such debate on ethics, in circumstances like these, I would have been inclined to say that the potential risks were outweighed by the prospect, no matter how slim, of justice for several victims who have so far been let down by the system.

'The same philosophy applies to covering your travel costs, and presumably accommodation. If all goes according to plan, I'm happy to sign off on those retrospectively on your safe and triumphant return.'

Ted was so stunned by her words he struggled to reply, finally managing to at least mumble a 'Thank you, ma'am.'

'Oh, don't thank me, chief inspector. Let me make myself clear beyond all doubt. If at any point the wheels come off all of this, we categorically never had this conversation, and you're on your own.'

Chapter Twenty-nine

The first thing Ted needed to do before he could even think of making the trip to Germany was to ensure there was someone to keep DI Smith firmly in check during his absence. Not an easy task for anyone.

He even briefly considered sending him back to London, if only for a two-day break, on the excuse that he hadn't had any time off since he'd joined them. He quickly dismissed that idea, knowing Smith would see straight through it for what it was and would probably disregard the suggestion, the minute Ted's back was turned.

He couldn't rely on the Ice Queen, either, to hold the fort and rein in Smith while he was away. That would involve her letting it be known she was aware of his absence and she'd made her feelings clear on that point.

The only other solution he could come up with was to ask Jo Rodriguez to step up for the day he was away. He knew Jo would be in later on, after his usual Sunday morning mass, probably intending to finish his paperwork so he could go back to Ashton the following day, Monday.

While he waited for Jo's arrival, Ted thought he might as well at least try to remind Smith of his role, and of the rules he was expected to follow. He wasn't intending to tell him anything about the reason for his day's absence, not even his destination, except in the broadest terms.

He called him back into his office, determined to keep

things on a civilised and professional basis if he could.

'Sorry about the interruption, but I needed to take that call. It means I'm going to be out of the office all day on Tuesday, back, hopefully, by midday or thereabouts on Wednesday.'

'Going somewhere nice, guv?' Smith asked.

Whether it was ironic or a genuine attempt at polite conversation was never easy to tell from him.

'Probably not,' Ted told him. 'It's a multi-disciplinary meeting about an open case we have an interest in, but that's genuinely about as much as I know until I get there.'

Smith's eyes narrowed at that. Coming from the military side of policing, he'd be reading between the lines and joining up the dots as Ted spoke. He was intelligent enough to know he was not going to get another word about it from the DCI.

'I'll be leaving DI Rodriguez in charge while I'm away, so I hope you'll support him and not make his task any more difficult than it is.'

'Goes without saying, guv,' Smith told him flippantly.

'Our main priority for today needs to be to sort out a remand in custody, for Alec King certainly and possibly for Ian Hardy. We can't keep them in police custody much longer. Hardy's solicitor will no doubt fight us all the way because of her client's vulnerability, so we might have to concede and go for bail with him.

'What's your gut feeling on him? Risk of absconding? Or even being taken out by some of your friends from down south if they find him?'

Smith seemed mollified at being consulted on something, at least. He settled his weight into the chair Darling indicated to him. This was more like it. At least he was being asked his opinion on things he knew about.

'I honestly can't see the Martin brothers being all that worried about him, guv. They'll know perfectly well he can't ID anyone, and because of that, pretty much anything he says is going to be weak, evidentially. He's a very small cog in the works, not much of a risk to anyone. If they were worried, they'd have had him taken care of long before we got to him, for sure.

'King knows a lot more, though, for certain. Probably more than he's told us already. Yes, he helped us find the kiddy, but he clearly knows more than he's said, and we need that information. I need it more than you do because so far we're lagging way behind in terms of results. That's why I want a proper go at him.'

'If by that you mean Met rules, you can forget about it. We do everything by the book here, and we still get the results. We all know your force has lost too many important cases because of bad procedure. You can ask him questions, of course, but stay within the red lines.'

Ted could see that Smith was still in the mood to argue so he stood up to end the conversation. He'd heard Jo come into the main office and wanted a quick word with him before they went any further.

'Can you ask the custody sergeant to have the two of them put in separate interview rooms and call up their respective solicitors, assuming King has another one. Then to let us know when they're ready. Thank you.'

Smith went off, seemingly happily, to start things rolling. Ted hoped he wasn't taking the risk of him doing or saying anything intimidating to either man. Then he went to talk to Jo.

'Sorry to dump this on you, Jo, but I have to be out of the office all day Tuesday, probably until around midday Wednesday. So I'll need you to stay on here to try to keep a tight rein on Oscar in my absence.'

Jo looked at him with an expression of mock offence.

'Have I done something to upset you, boss? Is this my penance for something? And what precisely am I supposed to do if he kicks off? You know I run away from conflict.'

'I don't know. Pray for him?' Ted suggested with a grin, interrupted by his mobile, once more. He looked at the screen and said, 'This is Sammy, I better take it.'

'You heard I'm not coming back, Ted?' she asked him without preamble. 'No point, and I hate long mawkish goodbyes. Bloody well done, though. You and the whole team. Make sure they know I said so. And when can we have this piss-up? Just promise me you won't let anyone say anything soppy or I can't guarantee I'll hold it together. I really don't want to be leaving, but shit happens. So let's celebrate, and the sooner the better as I've promised myself a holiday, somewhere warm, where the booze is cheap.'

'I have to be out all day on Tuesday. Sworn to secrecy for the moment, but we might possibly get another result on an outstanding case, so what about tomorrow?'

'That sounds good, if you can fix it. And I shall ply you with extra ginger beer to see if I can get it out of you. Seriously, though, Ted, I'm counting on you to make sure there's no mushy stuff.'

* * *

Ian Hardy was with the same efficient solicitor as before. He was showing the effects of a restless night. Police cells were not notorious for their levels of comfort and luxury.

Ted was careful to begin by introducing himself and DI Smith once more before attempting to put any questions to the man.

The solicitor went on the offensive before either Ted or Smith could start questioning.

'You must understand, surely, chief inspector, how very stressful being locked in a police cell, constantly seeing faces he can't recognise, is for my client. He needs certainty, familiarity, for the sake of his mental health, never mind his legal rights.

'So are you going to apply for a remand in prison custody, or would you at least consider remanding him on bail? Mr Hardy is perfectly willing to abide by any reasonable reporting or other restrictions you might impose on him, but keeping him in police custody is detrimental to his well-being.'

Oscar Smith spoke before Ted could. But this was the other Smith. The one who'd been able to calm a distressed baby. His tone was reasonable. Almost kind. Ted listened, surprised, but let him carry on, always ready to jump in should it be necessary.

'Look, Ian, mate, we know you probably didn't do anything much. Some dodgy number plates. You're not likely to go down for that, not even with your previous. But you've got yourself mixed up with some real villains here. Dangerous types. I'm sure you weren't meaning to, but you've unwittingly got yourself involved with much worse. We're talking child kidnap, at the least, and murder. That's why you're still in custody.'

There was no mistaking the anxiety his words were causing for Hardy. The air within the confines of the interview room was rapidly turning into a health hazard.

'I understand about the faces thing. But we need your help. What are you like with voices? Can you recognise people from their voice?'

'Course I can. That's easy.'

'Do you mind if we test that? A little experiment?'

Smith was looking from the DCI to the solicitor and back, willing them both to be on side. He finally had a chance of getting the vital link to his own cases, and he wasn't about to give up on it without a fight.

Neither raised any objection, so he took that as assent and told Hardy, 'I just need you to shut your eyes for a moment, Ian. Nothing dodgy, I promise you. Trust me. Just a little experiment.'

For some reason which even Smith couldn't explain, Hardy did seem to trust him, enough to do as he asked. Smith had no idea if his experiment would work, but he needed to test how good the man's voice recognition really was before he could even think of relying on it for any identification purposes which a court might accept.

He motioned to the DCI to stand, the two of them then changed places and stood behind the chairs. Smith spoke first.

'Which of us is speaking now?'

Hardy spoke without hesitation.

'The heavy bastard. The sprinter with no staying power.'

Without saying anything, Smith signalled with his index fingers for the two of them to change location in the room and for Ted to speak next.

'Which of us is speaking now?'

Ted was careful to use the exact same phrase. Again, the answer was immediate.

'The short one who knows how to run proper.'

'Thank you, Ian, you can open your eyes now.'

'I was right, wasn't I?' he asked, showing confidence for the first time since he'd been brought to the station. Finally able to show skills he did possess, rather than always having to explain his difficulties.

'You did well, Ian. Thanks.'

Again, this was Smith showing an unexpectedly softer side to his nature, and it was working wonders. Ted liked his thinking. He'd effectively built into his assessment the perfect counter to any clever lawyer saying Hardy's testimony couldn't be relied upon because of his face blindness.

'What I'd like to do now, Ian, is to arrange some voice recordings for you to listen to, to see if you can identify the person who phoned you to arrange the work you did on the car. The voice you said told you it would be picked up by someone known as The King. But that will take some time.'

Hardy's solicitor cut in at that point, addressing herself to Ted. She knew how the system worked and who the senior officer was.

'What about bail now for my client, chief inspector?' she asked. 'He's shown himself more than willing to cooperate, and he'd be happy to accept any and all reporting conditions you might choose to impose. I'd go so far as to say he would welcome them as, of course, his cooperation has potentially put him at some risk, so I hope that would be something else which could be brought to the attention of the court when it comes to the question of sentencing.'

Ted was happy enough to agree to that, on the basis of Hardy reporting twice daily to his local police station. Ted would also ask officers from there if they could keep an eye on him, whenever possible. He was a potentially vital witness. They couldn't afford anything to happen to him.

As they walked back up to the main office together, Ted told Smith, 'That was good work, Oscar. Well thought out and properly executed. How are you planning to handle the voice ID?'

'We've got endless interviews with Frenchie Williams where we've tried to pin something on him, so far without success. I'll get Tony to put someone on trawling through it for any little phrase in particular that he likes to use. Something he may well have said to Hardy when he booked him for the work. Then I'll get someone here to record random bodies from within the station saying the same phrase, and see which one, if any, Hardy picks out. Male and female voices, so we can't be seen to show bias towards a particular gender to try to influence him.'

They'd reached Ted's office by now so he put the kettle on and offered Oscar a coffee. Time to regroup before they tackled Alec King. Ted would oppose any suggestion of bail for him, worried he'd either disappear or be taken out of the equation before he could say the wrong thing. It was time to stress to him that because he had admitted to driving the getaway car, later found with an incinerated body inside it, he was effectively a murder suspect and as such, could potentially be held in police custody for much longer than for a minor offence.

They were so close, finally, for both their cases, that they couldn't take the risk of anything at all going wrong at this stage.

'Steve is the one to help you with that. He'll do it for you in no time, as long as you approach him the right way. You've shown you can tread softly, so please do so with

Steve. He has a valid reason not to react well to any hint of a bullying tone.'

'Fair enough, guv. We're so close to the finishing line I can smell it, so I'm not about to do anything to rock the boat at this stage.

'So, pub, when we knock off today?'

'For a swift one, yes, but then I'm off home with a tandoori takeaway.'

'Back home to the pussy cats?' Smith asked conversationally.

Ted nodded, not yet ready to mention Trev and the fact that he would be home that evening after his weekend away.

'I need to talk to Dave at the pub anyway. We're having a bit of a do tomorrow evening, if he can fit us in. Superintendent Sampson is retiring, and we'll want to raise a glass to her and to a good outcome to the baby Evie case. You're invited, of course. You've made a valuable contribution to the case, for one thing.'

Smith looked surprised. Touched, too. He was clearly not used to getting recognition for anything himself, which no doubt explained his failure to express it to others.

'Cheers, guv. I'd like that.'

* * *

Trev leaned back in his chair, rubbing a full stomach and sighing in replete contentment. As feline as any of the seven cats who had surrounded him ever since he got back from the West Country and discarded his motorbike leathers in a heap on the floor of the hallway.

Even young Adam was making a point of fussing more over Trev than Ted for once, to show his displeasure at how little he'd seen of his usual favourite human over the weekend.

'That was really nice, thank you,' Trev said on a long sigh of the sated.

'I'm sorry it was all bought in, but it's been one hell of a weekend. I've hardly been home, which is why Adam isn't talking to me.'

Trev sat up to take his hand across the table as he said, blue eyes sparkling with pride, 'But you did it, Ted. You got the baby back, against all the odds. I am so proud of you.'

'Hold that thought, because I might not be very popular after you hear what's still to come.'

Trev sighed.

'I should have known better. After all these years of living with a copper I should know by now that the force gives with one hand and takes back with two. How many late nights are you going to have to pull this week?'

'It's not that bad, really. I have to be at a leaving do for Sammy tomorrow night, but I can probably slip away not too late from that. It's team only, no partners, though. Sorry.

'But I have to be up at some truly godforsaken hour of Tuesday morning because I have to attend an international police conference that day.'

He paused for a moment, gauging his partner's reaction, before he continued, 'I don't know all the details yet myself until I get there but I have to fly to Frankfurt, where I'll be met by a copper I know through Mr Green's courses. But I should be back mid-morning on Wednesday, flights permitting.'

Now Trev was sitting bolt upright in his chair, looking increasingly concerned.

'I'm not liking the sound of any of this, Ted. Anything to

do with the mysterious Mr Green usually has danger written all over it. Are you sure this is all on the level?'

'Yes, absolutely sure,' Ted told him, with far more confidence than he was actually feeling. 'I checked with Mr Green and he didn't raise any red flags.'

It was a not inconsiderable white lie, but he was trying to convince himself as much as Trev.

'It's going to help solve another major case. And I'll keep in touch by phone whenever I can. I'll be back home on Wednesday evening at the latest, although don't count on me for the dojo. But I'll be here when you get back from there.'

Chapter Thirty

Ted was in early on Monday morning, determined to sort everything he needed to before his day trip to Frankfurt. DI Smith wasn't far behind him once again and headed straight for the office he'd been sharing with Jo Rodriguez to update his own paperwork.

Ted had managed to snatch a few minutes on his way to the takeaway the day before to call in on the Fishers. The sight of the happy and harmonious young couple once more united with the baby they both clearly worshipped was reward enough for Ted, without the endless effusive thanks of the doting father.

Dave Fisher was also still full of remorse for his outburst of anger which had caused their liaison officer to fall and cut her head. He was still facing the possibility of an assault charge because of his actions, but Ted fervently hoped it wouldn't come to that. He was anticipating the file coming back from the CPS as a No Further Action, given the circumstances. Hopefully one which would be judged to be not in the public interest to prosecute. The newspaper headlines didn't bear thinking about otherwise.

Jezza was one of the first of the team to arrive and made straight for the boss's office, pausing in the open door to wait for an invitation to enter. She was carrying a laptop bag with her and took out what looked like a picture frame, turned away from him to start with.

'Boss, this is what I had in mind for the Super's leaving present. I thought I'd show it to you first while there's still time before this evening to get something else, if you don't think she'd appreciate it.'

She couldn't resist a theatrical, 'Ta-da!' as she turned the frame round to face him.

Knowing Jezza's wicked sense of humour, Ted was half expecting something like a cartoon in somewhat dubious taste. Instead he found himself looking at an exquisite line drawing of Sammy's little Italian greyhound, Luka.

The dog was standing proudly, as if in a show ring, his delicate head turned slightly so he appeared to be looking directly back at anyone admiring his image.

'Jezza, that's incredible! Who drew that?'

Jezza was now beaming her pleasure at his seal of approval.

'Tommy did. Or rather, his latest obsession did. I got him some software which converts photos into realistic line drawings. They really do look like sketches, and it's the quietest he's been for ages. He worked on it half the night.

'I had the photos of Luka from the recce on Saturday, of course, so I gave him some to work with, and this was the best of them.'

'It's so incredibly lifelike,' Ted told her, then frowned as he went on, 'But he's not got a collar and lead on. Please tell me you didn't take risks with the Super's dog by taking him off the lead against her orders.'

Sometimes Jezza's tone to the boss was as big sisterly patient as with her difficult younger brother.

'Boss, the app can do all sorts of magic tricks, as well as drawing. It can even make a dog's collar and lead vanish. I never let go of Luka for an instant. You think it's all right, then? Do you think it will do?'

'I think it's perfect. What do we all owe you? We'll do a whip round.'

'Oh, it's just the cost of a replacement frame. This is one I had in and it wasn't expensive. I'll wrap it up properly before I hand it over, don't worry. Can I leave it in here for now, boss? It would be typical if someone put a foot through it before tonight, if it's in the main office.'

The rest of the team were in now. It was rare for any of them to be late for the boss's morning briefings. They'd need a good excuse to satisfy him if they were.

'My news to start with,' Ted told them all. 'I have a meeting to attend tomorrow which might possibly open up new leads for us on something else. I'll be out all day, hopefully back by Wednesday late morning. In my absence, DI Rodriguez is in overall charge.'

Even Ted, who, as he'd told DI Smith, liked to keep things formal at work, seldom used Jo's title and surname. No one did. He was Jo to almost everyone. Ted did it to emphasise who would be senior officer, especially for Smith's benefit, so there would be no jostling for position the minute he boarded the flight he was not looking forward to.

'Firstly, Steve, we need you to collect some voice samples for comparison purposes. Ian Hardy can't do faces, but he can do voices, and DI Smith demonstrated cleverly that we can rely on him for that.

'Next, the priority for all of you, please, today and tomorrow, is to get everything up to date and on file so we get some solid convictions out of this, at least. Jo, I want every available CCTV footage searched for any more shots of King driving that getaway car, or anywhere on foot or public transport. He says he simply handed the car over to two men who drove off in it with the woman who had the baby, but did he?

'If these two men exist, where are they? Where did they go after they dropped the baby off with the Williams? Again, CCTV trawls, please, until we find their trace. And speaking of the Williams, what did initial interviews and processing of them tell us, if anything?'

'Boss, I spoke to Mr Williams,' Virgil began. 'He said very little, mostly no comment. And he wouldn't even say that until we'd let him call his lawyer who, as you can imagine, was a pricey one, no doubt charging him a hefty fee to keep reminding him to say nothing.'

'Exactly the same for me with Mrs Williams, boss,' Gina Shaw told him. 'Nothing, other than confirming her name and address, then she clammed up. And again, a decent calibre of legal representative.'

'Those two are the closest link we have yet to the Martin brothers, via Frenchie Williams, especially with him having a French name,' Smith put in. 'The two who picked the baby up and took the snatcher away to be disposed of will be foot soldiers, nothing more, I would bet. Well paid, but expendable. They'll know as much as they're told, but no more. The Williams are our best bet. I'd like to talk to them …'

'First priority today for you and me is to sort out Ian Hardy and Alec King. We especially need to decide what to do with King. We're running out of time to keep him here in custody based on suspicion of involvement in the murder. And barring anything miraculous showing up on CCTV, I can't see us making that stick against him.'

'Fair enough, guv, but I'd still like to talk to the Williams.

Knowing there's a Met officer up here digging into the case might well rattle them more than anything concrete to date.'

'We'd better go and make a start, in that case. We can take one each for now then compare notes and see where we go next.'

'I'll be right with you. I'll check a few details first with my team, see what, if anything, I can dig up about either of them from on the ground. I'm not surprised she has a clean record and he's got nothing very serious. If they are part of that inner circle, they'll be well protected.'

'Five minutes, then. I'll be in my office.'

Smith ducked into Jo's empty room whilst he was still busy sorting the day's actions. His phone was in his hand and he was already calling up his DS, Tony Taylor.

'Tony, it's me and I'm fine. Listen, and act. I want a Met warrant for Georges and Beverley Williams. Yes, Georges with an S, one of Frenchie's distant cousins, I think. I don't care how you do it. God knows, we've got enough bent JPs down there on side. Get a warrant from one of them, preferably for suspicion of murder.'

'But we've never had much on the Williams clan …' Tony tried to protest but was cut short.

'Tony, this is no time to be a bonehead. It doesn't have to amount to anything. I just want to be able to arrest them and get them shipped down there. And Tony, I want to be able to execute this warrant myself, tomorrow. Certainly before early morning Wednesday. While the cat's away. Clear?'

Tony Taylor sounded far from comfortable with the whole idea, but he knew what that tone meant from Smith. Only one answer would do, so he gave it.

'Clear, guv. I'll get it sorted.'

* * *

It was an intensely frustrating day for Ted. Realistically, he kept telling himself, the sort of instant breakthrough which would wrap up every loose end and tie them in a neat bow before he went away was the stuff of fantasy. Something which could only happen in some of the worst of the crime drama series he was sometimes persuaded by Trev into watching on TV, as he was an avid viewer of all sorts of rubbish.

Ted knew he could trust his own team to work carefully and diligently the following day when he wasn't there. But Oscar Smith was the wild card. There was no telling what he might get up to in the boss's absence. Ted could only hope that Jo would be up to managing the situation if Smith went rogue. At least he had some solid muscle in the shape of Virgil to call to his assistance if necessary.

All he could do for now was try to tie up as many loose ends as he possibly could, then enjoy Sammy's leaving party, which he'd arranged with Dave, at The Grapes. Dave had offered him the upstairs room they normally used at Christmas, but seeing the increasing pain Sammy was in, although she tried to hide it, had made Ted decide against the stairs, and that the smaller room at the back on the ground floor would be better. It was only the team, without partners, so it wouldn't be too crowded in there.

The evening went off better than he could have hoped. Sammy was thrilled with the picture which moved her to tears. To the point that she thumped Ted on the arm and reminded him he was supposed to see that there was nothing mushy.

Dave's wife Susan had put on finger food, as requested.

It was great for Ted to sit and watch the team unwind after such a hard case. There was still a lot to tie up but Evie was home and that was the main thing. With luck, Ian Hardy could identify some voices to move things along, and Alec King had wisely decided that his only chance of escaping implication in the murder case was to be as cooperative as possible. Then to hope he could go to ground afterwards before any of the Martin brothers' people found him.

Ted and Sammy were sitting together companionably watching as the rest of the team started throwing some shapes to the music Dave had put on for them. It was good to see them all relaxing and enjoying themselves.

'Now there's a sight I never thought to see,' Sammy said drily, nodding to where Oscar Smith and Jezza Vine, of all people, were performing a foot-perfect energetic jive routine, in the space the others had cleared for them, while they stood round applauding. 'Misogyny personified, dancing in harmony with our equality champion. I'm surprised young Jezza knows the old stuff like that.'

'Drama training,' Ted told her. 'That's what she did at university before joining us on graduate entry.'

'And she's still a DC? She could go a lot further. Fast track.'

Ted shook his head.

'Doesn't want to. Happy as she is, she tells me, and lucky enough not to need the extra money from promotion.'

'You will stay in touch, won't you, Ted? I know what coppers are like. Occasions like this, they promise each other the world, stay in touch forever, one big happy family to all eternity, and all that shite. Then they never see each other again.'

'I promise. After all, where else can I get the use of a

trusted undercover dog, free of charge?'

Sammy laughed at that. It was the right thing to say, to stop the conversation verging on the mawkish which they had both been striving to avoid. Ted used it as the perfect moment to make a quiet getaway.

'Now if you'll excuse me, and cover for me, I'm going to slip away while everyone is distracted by John Travolta and Olivia Newton-John over there. I have an obscenely early start tomorrow for a long and doubtless fairly boring meeting.'

* * *

Ted was striding toward the exit at Frankfurt after an uneventful flight, apart from the odd bit of light turbulence. His phone was in his hand and he was firing off a text to Trev to let him know he'd landed safely and would try to phone him at the first opportunity.

He only had one small cabin bag with him with his overnight things and a clean shirt, so was making his way out when he heard a voice hail him.

'Ted Darling! How come you still have all that hair when my head looks like a baby's arse?'

He spotted Jock McClintock straight away and saw exactly what he meant. Ted still had all of his thick dirty blonde hair, with barely a strand of grey running through. Jock's head was as polished and shiny as a billiard ball. His figure certainly hadn't gone to seed, though. Ted could tell at a glance he still had the taut form and defined muscles of old. He reckoned the man would still have no trouble on one of Mr Green's training hikes on the Brecon Beacons, same as Ted himself, who always kept in shape. Old habits die hard.

Ted strode across to him. It started out as a warm handshake but became an awkward man hug, with a good deal of genuine affection evident on both sides. As Jock had said, Green's training sessions were as much about bonding as survival.

'Got a car outside. Good that your flight was on time. If I get my foot down, we'll be in good time for this meeting. I'm not going to do anything dramatic like stick a bag over your head or any of that shite, but best if you forget any signs or landmarks and pretend you don't know where we are.'

As soon as they were away from the airport, Jock's foot flat down on the accelerator, weaving in and out of traffic with bare millimetres to spare, Ted was able to tell him, with complete sincerity, 'I won't know, Jock, I'm keeping my eyes closed until we get to wherever we're going, you mad lunatic.'

Their destination was clearly a police headquarters of some sort. Ted's German was non-existent so he didn't even attempt to work out what all the signage said. Such buildings seemed to look similar wherever he'd been, as did the large conference room Jock led him to.

There were more people there than Ted had anticipated, representing several different countries, all seemingly there to make their own claim on Joel Hammond, the serial rapist and, in Ted's case, presumed murderer. Several languages were being spoken, too, with interpreters on hand to translate, as Jock would do when it came time for Ted to say his piece.

That was scheduled for so much later in the day that Ted was beginning to worry that he wasn't going to be heard at all and that he'd made the journey over for nothing. When the meeting broke up for a late working lunch, Jock was quick to reassure him.

'Don't worry, Ted, it's always like this. In fact, this is one of the speediest I've attended. But remember you're the only one with a murder warrant. Make your pitch in English and I'll simultaneously translate. Don't worry, I am fluent, and being a copper myself, I'm not going to leave out the important bits.

'Thing is, though, once we've done that, you'll be free to go as the stuff at the end will be more hush-hush, and I'll need to be here in person for that. Don't worry, though, I'll fight your corner every step of the way, and you have a rock-solid case. There's a very good chance you'll get your man, but these things are never quick. Ever.

'No earthly point you hanging round here waiting for me, though. God knows how long I'll be. Pity, because I was going to suggest dinner together somewhere tonight but that's gone right out of the window. Next time, for sure, though.

'I'll borrow a couple of coppers to see you safely back to your hotel, as soon as we finish the public part of the meeting and carry on in camera. It'll be fine. Oh, and I'll make sure at least one of them speaks some English.

'Sorry about the change of plan. You can never tell how these things will pan out, and you might as well be in your hotel as hanging around here. You can trust these guys. They're coppers.'

McClintock was true to his word, and even found time to slip out of the meeting to escort Ted to the waiting police car and introduce him to the officer who spoke English. Well, as it turned out, although with something of an American accent.

He kept up a running commentary on the journey, telling Ted of anything interesting in the vicinity, whilst his partner drove in silence, with a style which made Jock's efforts look like those of a little old granny.

Ted really wanted to at least send a text to Trev to let him know he'd phone him later, from his hotel. Somehow he hadn't found time to all day, and he was thwarted now by the conversation.

After a while, Ted interrupted the flow to ask the one speaking English to him, 'We are heading for the airport, aren't we? That's where my hotel is. Only I've noticed a few signs for the airport, but we seem to be going off in a different direction altogether.'

The one doing all the talking – Ulrich, he'd told Ted his name was – turned to give him a reassuring smile.

'Well spotted, sir, I can tell you're a policeman. But don't worry. We had a message over the radio just now to say there's been an accident on the approach road and the traffic is very bad, so we're taking the scenic route. You won't have understood it, of course, not speaking German. But going this way means we'll get you there safely much faster than if we'd taken the main roads where the delays are. Nothing to worry about.'

* * *

DI Oscar Smith was heading through the reception area on his way out at the end of the day. He was feeling pleased with himself and was heading round to the pub for a well-deserved drink or three and something to eat. He had to confess to acquiring a taste for the hotpot round there. Especially served with a suet crust and pickled red cabbage on the side.

Tony had played a blinder with the warrant Smith had requested. It was now all in hand. The DCI was later back then he'd said he would be, and he now risked getting back to find the Williams couple on their way down south in Met custody.

Smith could see the bloke behind the front desk was dealing with someone who seemed to be in a bit of a state. Smith knew from station gossip that the man was called Bill, he was a retired police sergeant, decorated for bravery, but now pensioned off due to injury, and reduced to reports of stray dogs and drinking after hours.

Except the young man he was dealing with didn't look like a worried pet owner. He looked like someone in genuine distress, clearly worried about something more serious.

Bill caught site of the visiting Met officer and his look changed to one of relief, which surprised Smith. He wasn't used to anyone looking pleased to see his big bulk and ugly mug.

'DI Smith, sir, perhaps you can help, please. This is DCI Darling's partner, Trevor, and as you can see, he's very worried. He says the boss has disappeared.'

If Smith was surprised at the revelation that the DCI was gay, he let no hint of it show in his face. He tried to sound reassuring as he said, 'He's been at a meeting, hasn't he? Up at HQ?'

Trevor shook his head.

'No, he had to fly to Frankfurt. He sent me a quick text when he landed yesterday morning and said he'd phone later, but he hasn't. Not even another text, and that's not like him. And nothing all day today either. The flight he was due back on landed safely and on schedule this morning, but there's still no word from him, and he's not been back to the house. I checked.'

'Frankfurt?' Smith echoed in surprise, then went on, 'He'll have been stuck in a no phones meeting somewhere, that's all. Believe me, that sort of thing means phones are banned. Then no doubt he's had to go straight up to HQ here when he got back, to report on whatever it was all about. He'll call you when he can, or he'll turn up at home. He could be there now.'

'Something's wrong, though, I know it,' Trev said stubbornly. 'He knows how much I worry about him when he's away. He'd have found a way to get in touch. They must have a loo break, or a stop for refreshments or something. And why didn't he phone me from his hotel last night? He'd have sent me a text at the very least, by now. I can't get any reply from his phone. It seems to be switched off.'

'Well, there you are, been stuck in a meeting with a no phones ban. That's not unusual. Or he's somehow lost his phone and can't remember your number to phone you.'

'Ted knows my number off by heart. He's very considerate. He always keeps in touch.'

Trev was sounding tearful now, making Bill look increasingly uncomfortable. To his own surprise, Smith felt a pang of genuine sympathy for him. It was many many years since he'd known that kind of closeness to any person. But after all, he had been phoning up to check on his cat and his Oma while he was away, and clearly this Trevor loved the DCI more than Smith did his cat.

He reached out strong arms to pull Trevor into a spontaneous hug. At the precise moment two young constables were walking past, eyes out on stalks at the sight of the gesture by the visiting Met officer.

'What are you two staring at?' Smith barked at them. 'You're not paid to gawp. Get on with your job.'

They snapped out a simultaneous, 'Sir,' and scuttled on their way.

In a much softer voice, still holding him, Smith told Trev, 'Don't worry. There'll be a rational explanation for it all. He'll be fine. We'll find him. If he's lost in Frankfurt, I'll go over and bring him back, if necessary. I am half German, after all. But he'll be back some time today, if a bit later than planned. Don't worry. He'll be back.'

TO BE CONTINUED

About the author

L M Krier is the pen-name of former journalist (court reporter) and freelance copywriter, Lesley Tither, who also writes travel memoirs under the name Tottie Limejuice. Lesley also worked as a case tracker for the Crown Prosecution Service. Now retired, she lives in Central France and enjoys walking her dogs and going camping.

Contact details

If you would like to get in touch, please do so at:

https://www.teddarlingcrimeseries.uk/

tottielimejuice@gmail.com

facebook.com/LMKrier

facebook.com/groups/1450797141836111/

twitter.com/tottielimejuice

For a lighter look at Ted and Trev, why not join the fun in the We Love Ted Darling group? on Facebook. FREE 'Ted Darling is billirant' badge for each member.

Acknowledgements

I would just like to thank the people who have helped me bring Ted Darling to life.

Alpha and Beta readers: Jill Pennington, Kate Pill, Karen Corcoran, Bren Kübler, Alan Wood, Paul Kemp, Eileen Payne, Valérie Goutte, Margaret Johnson.

Police consultants – The Three Karens.

Finally a very special thanks to all Ted's loyal friends in the We Love Ted Darling Facebook group. Always so supportive and full of great ideas to be incorporated into the next Ted book. FREE 'Ted Darling is billirant' badge for all members.

Discover the Ted Darling
Crime Series

If you've enjoyed meeting Ted Darling you may like to discover the other books in the series. All books are available as e-books and in paperback format. The First Time Ever is also now available as an audiobook, brilliantly read by Christopher Corcoran. Watch out for audiobook versions of other books in the series, coming soon, as well as further books in the series:

The First Time Ever
Baby's Got Blue Eyes
Two Little Boys
When I'm Old and Grey
Shut Up and Drive
Only the Lonely
Wild Thing
Walk On By
Preacher Man
Cry for the Bad Man
Every Game You Play
Where the Girls Are
Down Down Down
The Cuckoo is a Pretty Bird
Dirty Old Town
The End of the Line
It's Oh So Quiet
A Woman's Heart
No Way to Say Goodbye

The First Time Ever is also available translated into French by Jean Sauvanet, under the title of 'Darling.'

Printed in Great Britain
by Amazon